SITKA

THE BIG, BOLD NOVEL OF JEAN LABARGE—SAILOR, LOVER, ADVENTURER—WHO FOUGHT HIS WAY TO WEALTH AND POWER IN THE MIGHTY STRUGGLE FOR ALASKA . . .

LOUIS L'AMOUR'S BRILLIANT SAGA OF HIGH ADVENTURE! "Those who have watched Louis L'Amour grow tall in stature as a writer might have expected that some day a book like SITKA would roar out of his blazing typewriter!"
—*The Oklahoman*

SITKA

LOUIS L'AMOUR

BANTAM BOOKS · TORONTO · NEW YORK · LONDON

SITKA

*A Bantam Book / published by arrangement with
Hawthorn Books, Inc.*

PRINTING HISTORY

Hawthorn edition published April 1957

Bantam edition / January 1957

2nd printing	.... October 1967	11th printing	.... June 1973
3rd printing	.... October 1967	12th printing	.... October 1973
4th printing	.... January 1968	13th printing	.... July 1974
5th printing	.... April 1970	14th printing	.... May 1975
6th printing	...... August 1970	15th printing	.. December 1975
7th printing	.... May 1971	16th printing	.... June 1976
8th printing	.... October 1971	17th printing	.... June 1977
9th printing	.... March 1972	18th printing	.... June 1978
10th printing	. September 1972	19th printing	.. February 1979
	20th printing	.... March 1980	

ISBN 0-553-13965-7

Published simultaneously in the United States and Canada

*Bantam Books are published by Bantam Books, Inc. Its trade-
mark, consisting of the words "Bantam Books" and the por-
trayal of a bantam, is Registered in U.S. Patent and Trademark
Office and in other countries. Marca Registrada. Bantam
Books, Inc., 666 Fifth Avenue, New York, New York 10019.*

PRINTED IN THE UNITED STATES OF AMERICA

29 28 27 26 25 24 23 22

To Kathy

SITKA

1.

Jean LaBarge stopped beside the trunk of a huge cypress, scanning the woods for Rob Walker. By this time Rob should have reached their meeting place by the Honey Tree, so after only a momentary pause, he started to go on his way. Then he stopped abruptly.

The woods were very still. Somewhere, far-off, a crow cawed into the stillness, but there was no other sound except the faint murmur of wind in the high leaves. The boy felt his heart begin to pound heavily.

In the leaf mold just beyond the cypress was a boot print, its toe pointing southward into the deeper woods.

At fourteen Jean LaBarge knew the track of every man in the small village closest to the swamp, of the farmers who worked the fields nearby, and even the occasional cattle drovers who traveled the road along the swamp's edge. But this was the track of a stranger.

Sunlight filtered through the leaves and dappled the forest with light and shadow. No breeze stirred more than the topmost boughs, for at this place, deep within the Great Swamp, all the wind was shut out, as were the sounds. In this place one found oneself walking with stealth, moving in these lonely, secret woods as one might have moved in the days of the earth's first awakening.

Under the feathered hemlock, beside the stagnant pools, upon the spongy, moss-green earth there was no movement but the flight of some small bird, or a butterfly on wraithlike wings suspended for an instant in a shaft of sunlight. Only the green golden twilight of the forest, only the rustling of a tiny animal among the leaves. This was a place lost, remote, unvisited, and this was home, the only home he had known since his father

1

went to the far lands beyond the Mississippi, and his mother died.

No townsman came to the Great Swamp, nor used the trail through the deserted valley beyond, the trail known as the Shades of Death. Not many years before, during the War of 1812, soldiers had been ambushed here by Indians, and in both earlier and later years men had disappeared from that trail, leaving no evidence to explain their going. The old trail was grass-grown now, forgotten by outsiders, and the village people when passing either did not look at all, or darted hasty, half-frightened glances into the green, cavernlike silence. In the Pennsylvania villages along the nearby Susquehanna they believed the ghosts of dead soldiers marched endlessly here, mourning for homes to which they would never return.

The Great Swamp was a land untouched by plow, as lonely as upon the morning of the world's birth. Here was no columned corridor of mighty trees, no majestic avenue, but a dim, murky, silent place, dark even at noontime, shadowed except in the rare clearings or above the stagnant pools where lilies lay empty-eyed in the stillness, or forested themselves with cattails, or veiled themselves with green scum. A tossed stone into such a pool gave off few ripples, more the sodden gulp of something swallowed in darkness.

One of the soldiers who survived that long-ago march spoke of it as "a horrid, rough, gloomy country." Yet there was life in the swamp, life other than the birds and small animals. Throughout the swamp and in the rugged highlands that backed it there were squirrels, muskrat and mink, but there were deer, wolves, panthers and black bear, also.

Where Mill Creek Road divided the world of people and farms from the jungle of the swamp, it also divided the world of Jean LaBarge, divided the one he visited from the one in which he lived and where he was wholly himself. The swamp had been his first playground, and since then a school as well, and source of a precarious living.

Beside the cypress he waited, listening. The forest is a place of silence yet it has its own small sounds, the sounds a hunter knows. A wind stirring among the

2

branches, the creak of boughs, the drop of an acorn or a pine cone, the movements of small animals . . . these sounds Jean knew and his brain accepted, catalogued and ignored, tuning itself for only the unfamiliar sound, the movement unnatural to the forest.

The man whose track he had seen was large, for the stride was long and the indentation left by his boot was deep, and he was a man not unaccustomed to woodland travel. This much became obvious as Jean followed along the trail the man had left, noting where he stepped and how he moved. Moreover, the man was neither hunting nor wandering at random, but moving directly toward some known objective, and his direction was generally south.

Nobody knew the swamp as Jean did. He had grown up on a small farm at its edge, and before his mother died he had come regularly to the swamp to help her collect the herbs she sold in the village. Now that she was gone he continued to gather herbs and take them to the village to sell to old man Dean.

Jean was a tall fourteen, a slender boy with large dark eyes and a shock of curly, almost black hair. Already his shoulders were broad, although his body was painfully thin. There was more than a hint of the man he would become in the size of his frame and the easy way he moved. Growing up in the forest he had early learned to move as silently as would a fox or panther.

After his mother died his Uncle George had come to work the small farm, but Uncle George was a good-natured, gregarious man who liked people and hated the loneliness of the cabin. Moreover, he disliked work as much as he enjoyed loafing and idle talk. The boy accepted his coming, and when one day Uncle George failed to return from one of his longer absences, he accepted his going.

Left alone in the cabin Jean carried on as always; there was nothing else to do. His uncle had gone but once to the village where Jean sold most of his furs and herbs, and his disappearance caused no comment: there were several villages within easy walking distance of the swamp, and he might be frequenting any one of them. Jean, a lonely, self-sufficient boy, had common sense enough to tell no one that his uncle had deserted him.

3

The boy's coming and going had long since been taken for granted in the towns; and no one ever believed—or very much cared—that he was alone.

Of his father he remembered little except what his mother told him, that he had gone to the western mountains to trap and hunt, and that he would return eventually. To Jean he remained a vague, shadowy figure, bearded and in buckskins, who smoked a pipe and seemed always in a good humor. From time to time Jean heard mention of him in the villages, for he was that most fabulous of persons, a mountain man. And he was what Jean wanted to be.

Jean LeBarge had no friend but Rob Walker. To the village people he was the son of "that gypsy woman" and the way he lived was regarded with suspicion by the mothers of tamer sons who wanted them kept tame, and felt that his might be a dangerous influence.

The other children of the village despised him as a poor boy and the son of a gypsy, and admired him because he lived in the dreaded and fascinating Great Swamp. To the children of the village Mill Creek Road was a boundary they had been warned never to cross. Not even the village men ever hunted in the swamp: game was, after all, plentiful along the fences, and much easier to get than in the depths of the swamp—where a man might easily become lost or disappear in the treacherous sinkholes.

There was no reason for any stranger to be in the Great Swamp, so far from the road. But this was a stranger who seemed to know exactly where he was going. It had been four years since Jean had seen any man's track in the swamp . . . and then it was rumored that one of the Carters had returned to the country from which they had been driven.

To Rob Walker the swamp had been a dismal, frightening place, for he knew that even the older men, including his father, hurried along Mill Creek Road at the approach of darkness, and not without reason. Two years before a man had been severely mauled by a bear he had come upon in the night, and there was a story persistent in the neighborhood that a child had been carried off by a panther.

4

Rob was older than Jean, but shy due to his small size. As other boys of his age grew bigger and stronger he turned more and more to books for companionship, yet his alert mind and imagination were fascinated by a boy several years younger than himself who came and went in the Great Swamp without fear. From time to time he saw Jean LaBarge come to town with his sacks of herbs and finally he began waiting at the store to watch Mister Dean sort them carefully into piles. From listening he learned the piles were of many kinds, but the largest were usually bloodroot, wild ginger, senega snakeroot and sassafras.

The friendship between the boys began with a question. One afternoon old Mister Dean was totaling the amount owed to Jean. Rob watched him as he bent over the figures, peering through his square-cut steel-rimmed glasses, his great shock of iron-gray hair making his head seem much too heavy for his scrawny neck. Catching Jean's eyes, Rob asked, "Where do you get all those?"

Naturally shy, Jean recognized the even greater shyness of the smaller boy. "Over in the swamp," he replied.

"Aren't you afraid?"

Jean considered the question with care. He was, he realized, afraid sometimes. But it was not when he was in the swamp. It was only at night, those nights when he awakened in the silent cabin and knew he was alone. Sometimes then he would lie awake straining his eyes into the darkness to see the fearsome creatures his imagination told him would be lurking there, in the corners of the room or just outside the walls. But he knew he must never speak of that fear because once the well-meaning people of the village knew he was a boy alone they would take him away from the cabin and the swamp and find a home for him, or send him to a workhouse, and he wanted no home but the one he now had.

At least until he had a rifle. Once he had a rifle he would go west and become a mountain man like his father, and perhaps in some trappers' rendezvous in the mountains he might meet him, a big, powerful man who knew Kit Carson and lived among the Indians. But was he afraid of the swamp? "Not very," he said.

"Folks say it's haunted."

"I never saw any haunts. It's wild, though, and a body

better know where he's stepping or he can sink clean out of sight."

"How do you know which plants to pick?"

"My mother taught me." He knew what they said in the village about his mother being a gypsy. "She grew up in a house near a field where gypsies used to camp."

Dean counted out a few coins, peering at Jim over his glasses when he had completed the payment. "I can use more of that sassafras, son, and when berry time comes around I can use all the blackberries and huckleberries you can gather. Don't know where you find 'em. Biggest I ever did see."

Jean remembered those big, juicy berries. They grew in the thickest and most dangerous part of the swamp. Leaves fell there and rotted away in the dampness and upon their moldering remains grew the bushes with the fattest, sweetest berries. He had thought about that a good deal, and the place frightened him, but fascinated him also.

"Yes, sir.

"Ain't seen that uncle of yours," Dean commented, "the one who came here when your ma died."

"He goes to Selinsgrove," Jean told him. "Or to Sunbury."

The question had been more in the nature of a comment, merely making conversation, and Dean turned to greet another customer, adding, "Don't you forget that sassafras."

Jean stood where he was, his fingers on the edge of the counter, soaking up the rich smells of the old store. There was the fragrance of tobacco, licorice, and dry goods, mingled with the smell of new harness leather, and all the aromas of the old-fashioned shop. Rob Walker waited until Jean started for the door.

"That ol' swamp," he said, when they were outside, "I hear it's a mighty gloomy place."

"I like it."

"I'd think you'd be scared, out there alone."

"Nothin' to be scared of . . . not if you know where to walk." Jean dug into his pocket for the rattles clipped from a snake he had killed. "Got to watch for rattlers, though. There's big ones in there."

6

"They say there's a new rattle for every year a snake lives."

"Ain't so," Jean said. "There's a new rattle or button every time he sheds his skin, and they do it two, sometimes three times a year."

"Would you take me sometime?"

"You'd be scared."

"I would not. I've almost gone in alone—lots of times."

"All right. You can come now if you want."

That was how it had begun, nearly three years before their planned meeting at the Honey Tree. United in their loneliness, the boys had discovered they shared a dream, the dream to go west, far across the plains where the buffalo were, far away to the land of the Sioux and the Blackfoot, and there to be mountain men.

Around the village, wherever men gathered to talk, at the livery stable, the mill or the tavern or blacksmith shop, men talked of the mountains and dreamed aloud to each other, those men who often wish and never will, men who, bound to business, job, or family, dream great dreams of the far-off lands and the wonderful adventures they may someday have. And those other men and boys without ties, who will never take the lone trail because they want but they will not do. Perhaps because subconsciously they know that every dream has a price, and the price for the wandering life is hunger, loneliness and danger, the blistering thirst of deserts and the icy crash of waves, the tearing winds and driving sleet far from hearthside and the warm arms of loved ones.

Yet for Jean dreams would never be enough. The swamp became the training ground for that great day when he would be "big" and could go away. Yet in the secret places of his own mind Jean knew he would not wait for the remote time when he was big enough, a man grown. He would wait not longer than it required to save money for a good rifle, not the cumbersome old gun the cabin afforded . . . and the money was almost half saved.

It had been midafternoon when he found the track of the stranger, and Rob would have reached the Honey Tree. If so, he would be waiting there when the stranger arrived, as the man had chosen a route that could not

7

miss the clearing around the tree. Rob would be there and he would see the stranger and be seen by him.

Jean's trap line was long and Rob had agreed to work half of it so they could hurry back to the village to listen to Captain Hutchins, who was in the village for a last visit before going across the Great Plains to the lands on the Pacific. He would be in the tavern that night talking of the fur trade and of his plans. Both boys knew about Captain Hutchins. He had made a fortune manufacturing shoes for the Army, as well as in the shipping business, and he was taking his capital west.

Jean had worked his trap line swiftly, finding little. It was time he moved his traps deeper into the swamp. Maybe he would move them over near the stone house; it had been long since he trapped that area.

Nobody else seemed to know about the house. It was very old, built of stones rolled down from the ridge behind it, and it stood hidden in a grove of hemlock, giant trees that kept the house invisible until one was almost at the door. Yet despite its seeming remoteness, Jean knew there was a place where Mill Creek Road bent within a mile of it. Of late he had not been so sure that he was the only one who knew of the house, although whoever did know of it was not anyone from the country around. Once he had found the ashes of a fire that he was sure had not been there when he visited the house before . . . that had been the morning after they found Aaron Colby's body on Mill Creek Road.

Jean descended into a hollow and crossed the creek on a fallen log, working his way up the slope through a thick stand of trees. When he reached a low hummock of firm ground he followed along its ridge, almost running, scrambling through the brush, hurrying to meet Rob. The Honey Tree was only a little farther on.

Quite suddenly he saw the footprints again. The man had taken the same route Jean had chosen, but when in sight of the Honey Tree he had veered sharply away and leaped back across the tiny stream: Jean could see where his feet had landed after the jump, and where he had slipped in climbing the wet bank.

Looking through the trees from where the stranger had suddenly turned, Jean saw Rob sitting on a deadfall waiting for him.

The tracks were very fresh; the stranger could be only minutes ahead of him. Obviously, the man had seen Rob and turned quickly away. Why should a man be afraid of being seen by a boy?

Jean walked into the clearing. "Hi," he said.

2.

THE HONEY TREE STOOD at the edge of a small clearing, its long-dead limbs stripped and bare in the late afternoon sun. A gigantic cypress, lightning-blasted and hoary with years, it was all of nine feet through and hollow to at least sixty feet of its height. In that vast cavity generations of bees had been storing honey, and to Jean LaBarge it had been a source of excitement and anticipation since the first day of its discovery by him. Not a week passed that he did not attempt to devise a plan for robbing it.

Thousands of bees hummed about the tree, for not one but a dozen swarms used different levels of its hollow. Towering high above the clearing, it must once have been a splendid tree; now it was only a gigantic storehouse. When first Jean took Rob to the swamp, it was to the Honey Tree they had gone, and ever since it had been the focal point of their wanderings and explorations within the swamp.

Shortly after he arrived at the farm, Jean's Uncle George was shown the tree, and immediately plans were made to smoke out the bees and steal their honey. But that was before Uncle George realized that there was no way in which smoke could be made to affect all the bees simultaneously. Long before the smoke reached the bees near the top the wind would dissipate it, and to attempt the robbery would be to die under the stings of thousands of bees. Uncle George grumbled, threatened the bees and went away. He did not return to the Honey Tree and Jean did not mention his tree again, yet the thought of all that stored-up sweetness fascinated the boys.

"You going to smoke them today?" Rob was eager. "I'll bet there's bushels of honey!"

"Bushels?" Jean was scornful of such an estimate. "There's tons!"

He stared up at the tree, awed by the thought. Then he hitched up his too-large pants, remembering suddenly what he had meant to ask. "Did you see him?"

"See who?"

"The man . . . there was a man came this way, just ahead of me. When he saw you he turned off into the swamp."

"Who was it?"

"I'll bet he's gone to the stone house." It was strange he had not thought of it before. The trail the man was making would lead that way, and this might be the man who had left those ashes there. "I don't know who it was," he added.

Rob's eyes were big with excitement. Strangers were few along the Susquehanna in those years and most of them either passed by or occasionally stopped at the tavern for a meal or a drink. There was nothing to keep anyone in the village. And for anyone to leave the safety of Mill Creek Road for the dangers of the swamp was unheard of.

"Maybe he's one of the Carters."

Jean's heart began to pound heavily. The thought had not occurred to him before. The Carters were a band of outlaws known for their robberies, murders and brutality in all the regions near the Susquehanna in the early 1800's. The name was given them because the first of their number had worked as carters hauling goods along the high road. There had been some trouble at Sunbury and one of the cart drivers had killed a man in a most brutal fashion. Three of them had then looted the man's store and fled into the wild country along the West Branch of the Susquehanna. Later, they were believed to have shifted their operations to the Great Swamp.

In time their numbers had increased, although how many there were was never exactly known. A man caught stealing cattle had broken jail and joined them, and shortly after a farmer en route to the Mill had seen six of them gathered together at the bridge. A number of times in the months that followed travelers were beaten and robbed along Mill Creek Road, and two

11

men were found murdered near Penn Creek shortly after they had been seen displaying money from a sale of cattle.

During succeeding years the Carters became notorious in all the country around. One was hanged, and another was shot and killed by an old soldier while attempting to steal a horse. By the time a concerted effort was made to deal with them they were already guilty of a score of murders. Two of them belonged to a family of evil character named Ring. It was said in the villages along the river that the Rings were all a little insane, but whatever else they were, they were also vindictive and dangerous men. It was believed the Carters had spies in the towns who warned them of impending trouble and let them know when prosperous travelers were on the road. The few attempts to capture them failed because the Carters knew the swamp and the villagers did not. Then after some fifteen years of terror the Carters suddenly vanished and for a long time travelers were safe again.

During those fifteen years the Carters had won a reputation as evil if not as widespread as those other murderers who haunted the Natchez Trace, far to the south. The stories of their crimes made exciting listening, and every lad along the river knew tales of the Carters and their bloody doings.

"What will we do?" Rob asked anxiously.

"Let's go look."

Rob was frightened but he was even more curious, and moreover, was afraid to admit his fear. With Jean in the lead, the two boys started at once into the woods.

The afternoon was already late and in the forest it was noticeably darker. The direction taken by the stranger would take him nowhere but to the stone house or one of the several trails leading away from it. That stone house, Jean now realized, must have been one of the hide-outs of the Carters. If this stranger knew the swamp and knew of the house he could only be a Carter. There was no other alternative that made sense.

Rob was apprehensive. Not accustomed to shouldering responsibility for his actions, nor to being in the swamp this late, he was worried. He knew that if his parents ever learned what he was doing he would never hear the last of it, yet quite as much as Jean he wanted to know who the stranger was and where he was going.

"Maybe we should get somebody to come with us," Rob suggested.

"Nobody believes there's any Carters left hereabouts. They'd just laugh at us."

This, Rob knew, was exactly what would happen. Everybody was sure the Carters were gone for good, and it was unlikely that anybody would go into the swamp to investigate a rumor started by two boys.

The forest grew thicker and darker. Twice Rob fell, and once off to their right, something fell into a stagnant pool with a dull *plop* and both boys jumped. It was cooler now . . . the trees began to take on weird shapes and landmarks lost their identity as night made all things anonymous.

Some small creature sprang from the trail ahead of them and darted off through the woods. Probably a rabbit. They came down to a creek bank, the water gleaming a dull lead color in the vague remaining light. They crossed another log and entered a narrow opening in the forest wall. About them the darkness made tiny warning sounds, and they listened, aware of a strangeness they had not known before. It gave them an eerie feeling as if some great dark thing lurked in the shadows ahead, peering out at them, waiting for them to draw nearer, watching for the moment to spring. A loon called, far off beside some lost pool, and the lonely sound made their flesh crawl.

"Shouldn't we go back?" Rob whispered.

They should . . . Jean knew they should. He had no business spying on this stranger, and less business bringing Rob Walker into it, yet he could not turn back now. "You can if you want to; I want to see what he does."

It was not bravado that drove Jean on so much as an innate sense of self-preservation. The swamp provided him with a home and a livelihood. The presence of an intruder could only mean trouble for him.

If the Carters had returned he would no longer be able to move freely along his trap lines, and the source of his income would certainly be curtailed and might disappear. Young though he was, the idea frightened

13

him, for the swamp was all the home he had ever known. He found nothing to attract him in the life of the village boys. Lonely though he was, often wistful with longing for the mother he had lost and the father he had scarcely known, he nonetheless loved the woods and would not have abandoned his free, easy life for anything.

The boys pushed on for some minutes; then Rob stopped again. "Jean. Please, I think we should go back," he insisted in a hushed tone. "We should tell somebody."

"We've nothing to tell. Anyway, Dan'l Boone wouldn't go back, nor even Simon Girty."

It was an argument for which Rob had no answer. But sometimes he doubted that he would make another Boone. It was one thing to play at such things, but when the swamp grew dark Rob was no longer positive he wanted a life of adventure. Jean, on the other hand, seemed as much at home here as any young wolf or deer. He belonged to the forest and the forest belonged to him.

Both boys had listened for hours to talk of Mohawk, Huron and Iroquois, of Simon Girty and Dan Boone, stories of hunting, Indian fighting and travel. They heard tales of the mountain men, and of the far lands of Mr. Jefferson's Louisiana Purchase, lands yet known to few. Many of the stories had originated with Jean's own father, who like most mountain men loved to yarn away the hours when he found himself among the wide-eyed citizens of settled communities.

The stone house huddled against the wall of the ridge that hemmed the swamp at that place, hiding itself in the deepest shadows under the ancient hemlocks. The boys crawled under a bush where no grown man could have gone and stopped just behind a huge hemlock, only a few yards away from the house.

Jean tried to remember what it was like close along the wall. He did not want to step on anything that would cause even a whisper of sound. Rob moved up beside him and they crouched there, wide-eyed, listening and tense. From within came a murmur of voices and they could see a thread of light from a crack in the

14

boarded-up window. A few inches below, a shaft of light streamed from a knothole.

They moved forward from tree to tree until within a dozen yards of the house, then stopped again. Now they could distinguish the words of the men inside.

"You took long enough."

"Hutchins is there, and he's travelin' alone. Ridin' one horse, leadin' another. From the way he bulges at the waist he's wearin' a money belt."

"He's packin' two, three thousand in gold. Harry was there in the bank, seen him pick it up."

"Sam, I seen a kid out there. Settin' by the bee tree."

"He see you?"

"Nah . . . but what's a kid doin' in the swamp?"

"Well, what was he doin'?"

"Settin' . . . like he was waitin'."

"All right, then. He was waitin'. What more do you want? Maybe his pappy was huntin'."

"Nobody hunts in this swamp. Nobody."

"Probably LaBarge's kid. LaBarge built hisself a cabin over next the woods. I recall his woman used to collect bloodroot an' such to fetch down to the store. Made a livin' at it."

"You mean *Smoke* LaBarge?"

"You scared?" The tone was contemptuous.

"He never set much store by me. What you lettin' us in for, Sam?"

"Forget it . . . Smoke's dead and gone. Last I seen of him was on the Yellowstone, but at Fort Union folks were tellin' it the Blackfeet killed him."

"Take some doin'."

"Well, they done it."

There was a sound of breaking sticks and then a fire crackled and a few sparks ascended from the squat chimney. The good smell of wood smoke came to the boys. Jean got carefully to his feet. If these men were mountain men as their conversation implied, they would be able to hear the slightest sound. But Jean had to look into that knothole; he had to see those men.

Signaling for Rob to stay where he was, Jean crept forward in the darkness. At the window he lifted his head slowly, holding it to one side of the knothole. He peered through, first from one side and then the other, and saw not two men, but three. The third man lay on a bunk asleep, his face in the shadows. The stranger whom they had followed Jean recognized by the boots he wore and the size of him. He was huge, awkwardly built, and dressed as a farmer would be dressed. His face wore an expression at once stupid and cunning. The man called Sam was hunched over the table, a shorter, broader, thicker man than the big one. His was a brutally strong face, but it possessed a hard, cynical cast that indicated a certain grim humor. Jean shuddered to see as he turned his head that there was an inch-wide scar through his eyebrow.

The stone house was as Jean remembered it, the old fireplace, a table, two benches and a barrel chair. The floor was of hard-packed earth. On the wall there now hung various articles of clothing. Several guns were within view.

The big man looked around the room. "This is a good place. Too bad we had to leave."

"It was time. We use some sense this time we can stay here for months before anybody gets wise. Hutchins, he's from out of state, an' he's headed west, so nobody will miss him."

"What about the body?"

"What d' you think? Right in the swamp where we should have put them all. The Rings was too careless."

Jean listened, his mouth dry with fear. Everybody in the village knew Captain Hutchins by sight. He had kin in the village and had visited there several times, but now he was going west to California and the lands on the Pacific, and he was carrying gold to buy furs along the way.

He remembered hearing them talk about it in the village. "Country's growing out there," Hutchins had said that very day, "and I want to grow with it."

"Ain't that Spanish land?"

"It is now," Hutchins agreed, "but unless I miss my guess it won't be very much longer. Someday the United States will span the continent. Might even cover all North America."

"Foolishness!" That was what old Mister Dean had said. "Pure foolishness! The country's big enough as it

16

is. No sense taking in all that no-account land. Ain't worth nothin', never will be."

"There are folks who believe otherwise," Hutchins replied mildly. "And I know there's rich, black soil there, miles of fine grass, and a country that will grow anything. There's future in that country for men with the will to work and the imagination to see it."

These had seemed but the echo of words Jean had heard before. Had his father said them, long ago when he was too young to remember? Or had his mother repeated them to him? Whatever the reason or occasion, the words had struck fire within him and he listened avidly, knowing inside him that westward lay his destiny, westward with a land growing strong, westward with a new nation, a new people. And now these men within the house were planning to kill and rob Captain Hutchins.

Jean knew at once that he must get away to warn him, to tell him of these men and their plans. He got up, too quickly, and when he stepped back his foot slipped and he scrambled wildly for a foothold, then fell flat. Inside there was a grunt of surprise, and then a clamor of movement.

The door slammed open as Jean got to his feet and he was touched, just barely, by the shaft of light from its opening. He darted for the brush . . . once inside that brush, within its blackness . . . he tripped and fell flat, then crawled, scrabbling in the grass to reach the undergrowth only a few feet away. He was just about to make a final lunge when a large hand grasped his ankle. He kicked wildly, but the hand was strong. Inexorably he was drawn back and jerked to his feet.

The man with the scar grasped his arm. "Snoopin', were you? We'll be larnin' you better."

3.

SAM GRIPPPED HIS ARM and led the boy into the light from the open door. "This the one you saw?"

"Looks bigger," the big man said doubtfully. "I tell you, Sam, I ain't sure. He was settin' down. Could be, though."

Sam shoved Jean into the house and they followed him in, studying him thoughtfully. Jean stood very straight, his heart throbbing heavily. He was caught, and he had no idea what was to happen now; but he returned the man's stare boldly, although his mouth was dry and he felt empty.

"You're the LaBarge kid, ain't you?" Sam asked.

"I am Jean LaBarge." His voice was steady. For some absurd reason he was sorry his hair was not combed, that he was not wearing his other shirt. These men had known his father and he would not like them to think him unworthy.

"What you doin', sneakin' around here?"

"I was not sneaking," Jean lied. "I was coming to the door. I saw the light and wondered who was there. Nobody," he added truthfully. "ever comes here."

"What were you doin' in the woods?"

"I run a trap line." He tried to make his voice matter-of-fact. "And I collect herbs." From their attitude they apparently believed he had been alone, and therefore had no idea Rob Walker was outside. And they must not know.

"Pretty dark for that, ain't it?" Sam's voice was mild.

"I sold the herbs in the village. It is closer to the cabin if I come through the swamp."

"He's lyin', Sam." The big man had an ugly voice. "He lies in his teeth. When I seen him he was just a-settin'."

18

"What about that, boy?" Sam asked.

"I was studying the Honey Tree," he said. "I been aimin' to get me some of that honey."

Sam chuckled. "I studied some on that, too," he said. "It ain't easy." Sam ignored the bigger man, sizing Jean up with careful eyes, noting the shabby, often-patched homespun pants, the torn plaid shirt and the uncut hair. Sam found himself admiring the boy, for he put on a good show. He seemed wary all right, but if he was scared he managed to hide it. This was quite a boy. Old Smoke LaBarge would have been proud of him . . . but too thin, much too thin, and poor as a Digger Indian.

"Ain't you afraid of the swamp?"

"I grew up in it."

Sam had an idea but he was a slow man with his thinking. He took his time now, turning the idea slowly on the spit of his mind, studying it from all sides. They could kill the boy . . . that would be the easiest way, but it was a pity to kill a lad with his gumption. Also, if the boy failed to show up around the town folks would be sure to become curious and start looking for him. And Sam could stand for no snooping around. On the other hand, this boy was obviously very poor, probably making just enough to keep eating. A little extra money would look mighty big to him. If this lad was as smart as Sam was beginning to believe he would fit perfectly into their plans. Folks would become suspicious if an unemployed stranger hung about the tavern, but this youngster could go anywhere and nobody would think anything of it.

"Were you listenin' at the window, kid?"

"Not yet." Jean rightly guessed that frankness could hurt him none at all, and might win their friendship. "But I intended to. I'd have listened before I came around to the door."

Sam chuckled. "I'd have done the same, boy. I surely would."

The big man shifted his feet impatiently. "Sam, this boy means trouble. We've got to do something."

Sam gestured irritably. "Take it easy. I think this boy's on our side, Fud, and I've an idea."

Jean sat very still, waiting. Outside Rob would be

19

creeping away, until he got far enough from the house to climb to the top of the ridge without being heard. Once atop the ridge he could follow it along to the road, but what if he took the wrong direction and became lost in the forest? For the ridge was but an offshoot of the higher land back of the swamp, and there was forest there, almost untouched, without track or trail of any kind.

Sam finished stoking his pipe and lighted it at the candle. The strings of his shirt were untied at the collar showing the thick black hair on his chest, and his big hands were thick and powerful. From time to time as he moved about he glanced at Jean. "Fud," Sam finally said, "you got to use your head. We can get rid of this boy a month from now as well as now, but on the other hand, he's not apt to run to the law, bein' he's dodgin' it himself.

"Oh, yes!" Sam grinned wisely at Jean. "You might fool those folks in town, but Fud an' me, we know you're livin' alone in that cabin. Your Uncle George ain't home, an' what's more, he ain't comin' home. Now if those folks in town knew that they'd have you in the workhouse. I know these here good folks, they can get themselves mighty busy about a poor little boy livin' all by himself. I know them, lad, an' you know them, too.

"Those folks, they'd never figure you liked it here in the swamp. They'd want to mess up your life makin' a home for you. Now I ain't sayin' a boy shouldn't have a home. Mighty good thing, homes are, but these fussy folks they get to watchin' over a boy, expectin' him to make mistakes, or tryin' to make him somethin' he ain't. You, f'r instance, you're a woodsman. Anybody can see that. Take after you pa, you do."

Jean waited, his attention on Sam. Instinctively he knew his only hope lay in Sam's suddenly aroused interest. Moreover he was fascinated by the obviously brutal strength of the man, by his big, hard-knuckled hands, so broken and scarred from fighting. Fud was the bigger of the two, but when it came to strength he was not in the same class with Sam. Suddenly Jean realized that Sam had said Uncle George was not coming back. How could they be sure of that unless . . .?

"You get the idea, Fud." Sam was addressing his partner but he was talking to Jean also. "This here's quite a boy. He rustles his own living out of the woods, and as a body can see, he likes it. Of course, if folks knew he was alone they'd take him to a workhouse or 'prentice him to somebody. Either way they'd work the hair off him."

"Get to the point," Fud insisted irritably.

"Sure . . . this boy's on our side. We could tell on him, too. We could get him sent to the workhouse, and if he tattled on us we could say he was lyin' to save his own hide, usin' his imagination, the way kids do. We could even tell he'd been sneak-thievin' around, and maybe see something was found in his cabin to prove it. And who's to deny it?"

People would believe it, Jean knew. They would believe it because it would make them seem right for denying him the companionship of their children. Yes, they would believe it all right.

By now Rob would be climbing the ridge, and it would not be easy, in the dark like it was, when a body had no chance to choose a way. Soon he would be passing by the cabin along the ridge, and what if a rock rolled down?

"A boy like this," Sam continued, drawing deep on his pipe, "could do us some good. Got big ears, see? Good eyes, too. An' nobody suspects a kid. By now they're used to him comin' it around an' they would hardly notice he was there. He could find out who was carryin' money, how they traveled, and I'd bet he knows more hidin' places in this swamp than any catymount."

The climb up the ridge was steep, and Rob might slip back several times. He might fall headlong and get turned around in the dark when he got up. It had happened to Jean . . . but Rob had a good head and he had grit. He never took foolish chances. As soon as he got to Mill Creek Road, he would run. He would keep going, too: once Rob began on a thing he wouldn't let up.

"You got any real good friends in town, boy?"

"No, sir."

"How about the youngsters?"

"They say my mother was a gypsy."

"Right." Sam chuckled. He was pleased with himself.

21

He had guessed that a boy living like this one would be at outs with the town. He had been a poor boy himself. He leaned forward. "Boy, is there anything you want real bad? I mean something for your very own?"

"A rifle," Jean replied promptly. "I'd like a rifle so I could go west."

Sam's laughter boomed and he slapped his heavy thigh. "That's it! There it is! By the Lord Harry, Fud! There's the LaBarge cropping out in the boy! A rifle so's he could go west, now doesn't that beat all?"

He sat back on his bench against the wall, puffing at his pipe. He held the pipe in one corner of his mouth and puffed from the other side. Fud looked bored and impatient, but the man on the bunk merely snored.

Rob should definitely be on the ridge by now. He would be frightened and breathing hard from the climb so he would stop to catch his breath. Up there on the ridge it would be bright moonlight, stark and clear. Below him on this side would be the swamp, and on the other, the forest. All he had to do was pick his way carefully along the top of that comblike ridge until it played out at Mill Creek Road.

How long would it take him to get to town? Two hours? Three? Rob was cautious, and on the ridge he would take his time. Up there among the jagged rocks and brush it would be rough going and to hurry might mean a sprained or broken ankle. Once out of the woods and on the road he could run. But how far could a boy run without stopping?

Rob would be frightened up there in the moonlight with a vast sea of darkness below him, a sea whose waves were the moving tops of trees and whose bottom was swamp and forest. It would be very still up there, except for the wind, and a sudden noise would stop a man, make the hair prickle on the back of his neck. The air would be cool, but there would be that strange odor of dampness and decay, the smell from stagnant pools, of rotting vegetation mingled with the fresh smell of pines and hemlock. Somewhere a night bird would call, an eerie sound that would make Rob stop, shivering. But then he would hurry on, perhaps falling, skinning his knees, rising again and going on . . .

"So you want a rifle? Now that's smart. A good rifle

is a thing to come by, and mighty handy, but a good rifle costs money. Now you try selling herbs to buy a rifle and it would take quite a spell. You stick with us, do what I tell you and use that noggin of yours, then we'll get a rifle for you, and the best of the lot, too."

"What would I have to do?"

Sam chuckled again. "See there, Fud? No nonsense about this lad, comes right to the point. Business, he is, strictly business." Sam leaned his hairy forearms on the table. "Do? Nothing but what you've been doing, boy. You take your herbs to town to sell. On'y sometimes you go to Sunbury or Selinsgrove, too. And you sell 'em . . . what else? You listen. Just that. You listen. Sometimes folks passing through carry a sight of money, more'n is good for 'em. Well, we mean to he'p out, Fud, me, an' him.

"You see somebody with money, you just come to us. No townsfolk, mind you. Only travelers, folks goin' through on the pike or the river."

"Those folks who travel," Jean suggested tentatively. "Don't they have rifles sometimes?"

"Now" Sam slapped his leg again. "There's a lad! Eye right on the main issue!" Sam chuckled, winking at Jean. "Make a team, you an' me. We might even go west together, that's what."

"I can see that!" Fud sneered. "Sam, you're talkin' fool talk."

Sam lifted a thick, admonishing finger. "Don' take the boy lightly, Fud. Nobody in town is friendly to him, slurring his mother like they do, figuring his father no good, ready to clap the boy in the workhouse. No, sir! The boy's with us, aren't you, boy?"

"I hear things," Jean agreed, "an' folks don't pay me much mind."

Sam puffed on his pipe, his mind far away. The fire crackled on the hearth and the man in the bunk turned over, moving uneasily in his sleep, like a cat. Jean's ears strained into the darkness, striving to hear sounds he did not wish to hear. Was Rob safely out of earshot? How much time had passed?

"While you're doin' this plannin'," Fud's voice was sarcastic, "s'pose you figure what we'll do with him while we're gone. You goin' to leave him loose?"

23

Sam shook his head regretfully. "Not that I don't trust you, boy, but for safety's sake we'll lock the door."

Outside the wind was lifting. Sam got out a deck of worn playing cards and shuffled them. The man on the bunk fumbled at his face with a lax hand, and then his eyes opened and he lay for several minutes adjusting himself to the scene, his eyes continually returning to Jean. He was younger than the others, a lean, savage young man with dark hollows beneath his eyes and a yellowish cast to his face. He sat up finally, watching Sam handle the cards. Fud gestured Jean from the chair and sat down himself. The younger man, scratching his ribs and yawning, joined them.

"You slept long enough," Fud commented.

The young man turned his black eyes on Fud but made no comment. Sam began dealing the cards and Jean guessed that Sam was wary of this man. Fud he treated with casual contempt but there was something about this young man no one in his right mind would treat casually.

"Who's the boy?" he asked suddenly, without looking up from his cards. Sam explained, taking his time and attempting to make all the details clear. The young man did not look up nor did he interrupt, he just listened.

"We got to have information," Sam finished, "and we can't keep showing up in town. Certainly not you, nor me with this scar. There's men in town will remember how I come by this scar."

"They've never seen me."

"They know your family, Ring. They saw your father and brother, and you're like them as can be."

Jean's head nodded wearily, then jerked awake. The others still played cards. Sam glanced at him kindly, then nodded his head toward the corner. "Take a rest, boy, you'll need it."

There was nothing he could do. Wherever Rob Walker was, all was in his hands now, and Jean was terribly tired. His head no sooner touched the blanket than he was asleep.

A long time later he opened his eyes and the house was dark. He listened, but he heard no sound of snoring or breathing. Carefully, he sat up and looked around

24

in the darkness. He was alone . . . the stone house was empty but for himself.

Rising quickly he went to the door. It was fastened on the outside. The earthen floor was packed hard, like cement, and he knew the stones of the house were sunk deep into the ground. Even if he had something with which to dig it would require hours to make a hole big enough for him to crawl out. The window was solidly boarded and too small, anyway. When he had exhausted all the possibilities of escape he sat down on the floor and stared at the small opening left by the knothole. Outside it was still night, but he must have slept a good long while. Soon it would be growing light.

4.

WHEN ROB WALKER REACHED Mill Creek Road he was sobbing with fear and exhaustion. The ridge had proved to be a wild tangle of bramble, broken rock and wind-wracked pines. Under the white light of the moon it lay lonely and desolate and nowhere could he find the path which Jean had mentioned once, months ago.

Ghostly shadows of sentinel pines loomed about him, and he began scrambling over the jagged rocks and pushing through the brush toward the road. Branches tore at his clothing and twice he fell, skinning the side of his face on a rock. Briars snagged his clothing, yet he pushed on, knowing Jean was in danger, that he must bring help.

When at last he reached the road he was out of breath, his skin scratched and bruised, his clothing torn. The road lay wide and white in the moonlight with the black wall of the swamp on his right, on his left a rail fence bordering a pasture. Beyond the pasture was Mill Creek itself, and the air was damp and cool. He started to run, his short legs making hard work of it. Already breathless from his scramble over the ridge, pain stabbed at his side, but within him was a terrible fear that made a lie of his weariness.

He had no idea of the hour. It had been late after-noon when they started to follow the stranger, and dark when they lay outside the cabin. To circle around and climb the ridge must have taken at least an hour, for he had crept some distance before he trusted the noise not to reach the men in the cabin, and it had taken an-other hour to creep by the cabin. It must have taken him at least two hours to reach the road, maybe more: he had stopped many times to catch his breath and listen for sounds in the night.

It was the first time he had been away from home

after dark and his folks would be frightened. They were not lenient, and it was understood he must either be in the house or his own yard before dark. Finally, unable to run farther, he began to walk. He wanted nothing so much as to stop, to sit down, to lie down. Never had he been so utterly exhausted. This morning his mother had put out a clean shirt for him and now it was soaked with sweat, bloodstained and torn by brambles.

Far up the road he glimpsed a light. That would be the old Chancel house, and not a quarter of a mile beyond was the tavern, and only a little farther, a few steps only, was his own home. At last he ran up the path and burst into the door.

His mother started to her feet, her face tear-stained, and his father, who had been pacing the floor as he always did when worried, turned sharply, ready to scold. When he saw Rob's face and the condition of his clothing the words died unspoken.

"What is it, son? What's wrong?"

The story spilled out in sobbing gasps, and for the moment he forgot that he had been forbidden to go into the swamp or to associate with Jean LaBarge. His father listened, his eyes on Rob's face, seeing more than was being said. He knew his own son, and sometimes had wondered about the boy. Now he saw courage there, and if there was fear also, it was fear for Jean. Rob had always been frightened of his father, a quiet, stern man. Suddenly, for the first time, he felt they were on common ground. His father asked no foolish questions, wasted no time on angry complaints.

"You can take us back there? Do you know the way?"

"Yes, Father."

"Three men, you said? And Jean thought they were the Carters?"

"Yes."

"Come." Walker put his hand on his son's arm. "We'll go to the tavern."

"But can't you take care of it without him?" Rob's mother protested. "The child hasn't eaten, and look at his clothes! He . . ."

"He will have to come with me. Anyway," Rob's father added, "it is his story and I believe he had better tell it."

Side by side they walked to the tavern. Rob had rarely been inside, only when he and Jean had slipped in to listen to stories being told, when some traveler was there from the west, or going west. It was a large room, low-raftered and smoky. On the right was a huge fireplace and near it a dozen men sat about a worn black table with mugs of beer or rum, smoking their pipes. The place had a dark, rich smell that was always exciting, and the glint of light on burnished copper. As they entered, all eyes swung to them. Across the table Captain Hutchins lifted his level blue eyes and looked at Rob, then nodded to Rob's father.

"Hutchins," Walker said abruptly, "my son has something to tell you."

Rob began to speak, hesitantly at first, and then remembering Jean he spoke more boldly and swiftly, telling the story from the beginning. He repeated what conversation they had overheard from within the stone house, and Jean's whispered report that three men were inside. Captain Hutchins listened without speaking, his eyes never leaving Rob's. When Rob finished, Walker got to his feet and knocked out his pipe.

"I believe that is plain enough," he said. "How many of you are with me?"

There were nine in the group who rode out from the village. Four were from the local company of militia, and even old Mister Dean, armed with a tremendous double-barreled shotgun, had come along.

"Will there be time to reach the cabin?" Hutchins asked, turning in his saddle to look at Rob.

"No, sir. I don't think so. And with so many men there would be noise."

Walker spoke up angrily. "By the Lord, Captain, if they've killed that boy . . .!"

"Hsst!"

They drew up sharply at the signal, stopping in the black shadow of a roadside tree. They heard a murmur of voices and an oath as somebody stumbled. Men were coming through the brush.

Hutchins swung to the ground, very cool, very businesslike. Rob's father tossed his reins to Rob and dismounted. "Hold the horses, Rob," he said, "and don't be frightened."

Breathless with excitement, Rob watched his father. He carried a rifle, and from somewhere he had gotten a large pistol which was thrust into his waistband. Moreover, he seemed completely at home with both weapons. Rob had noticed with pride the businesslike way in which his father loaded them.

The four militiamen disappeared into the trees opposite the noise in the brush. Hutchins stood his ground, in the middle of the moonlit road. Some twenty feet farther along, standing partly in the shadow, was Walker. The other men had scattered themselves, two slipping into the brush, planning to come in behind the Carters and cut off any attempted escape.

Fud was the first Carter to reach the road. "Right across here there's a rock," he was saying. "We can wait there until Hutchins . . ."

His voice broke off sharply as he saw the slim, erect figure standing in the light of the sinking moon.

The others emerged from the woods, Ring pausing on the edge of the brush, warned by the sudden breaking off of Fud's speech.

"Stand where you are, men," Hutchins spoke clearly. "You're well taken."

A rustle of movement in the brush behind him made Sam start, then relax slowly. Fud was weaving uncertainly as his slow brain attempted to cope with the situation, a situation already beyond him. The shock of the trap was too much for Fud.

"You'll drop your weapons!" Walker's voice was crisp. "If you do not comply at once, we shall shoot to kill!"

Fud found his voice. "What's this?" he blustered. "Can't a man travel the high road 'thout bein' held up?"

"Our point exactly," Hutchins replied cheerfully. "I'm Hutchins, if you'd like to know. I understand you planned to meet me later. Now tell us: where's the boy?"

"What boy?" Fud tried to seem surprised.

"Don't pretend, man." Hutchins walked up to him. "You have been found out so you'd best tell us. If that boy has been harmed I shall personally attend to your hanging."

29

Rob's attention had been riveted upon the tense scene in the road's center. All at once his eyes swung to the edge of the road. Sam was still there, a man behind him with a gun at his back, but the third man was gone.

"Father!" he called sharply. "The other man's gone!"

Before anyone could speak, Sam lifted his voice. "Hutchins, you'd better get to the cabin and save that boy. Ring's got away and he hates the lot of you. He'll kill that lad. I know Ring. He'll kill him certain sure."

Fud turned his heavy head to glare at Sam. "Why don't you keep shet?" he demanded.

Sam shrugged, smiling wryly. "You heard the man. If anything happens to that boy, we hang. Do you want to hang, Fud?"

"Did you say *Ring?*" Walker crossed the road to Sam. "I thought we'd killed the lot of them."

"This here's Bob Ring. You killed his father and brother. They were the first of the Carters."

Walker turned to his son. "Rob, can you take us to the cabin? I don't like to ask you. I know you're tired, but . . ."

"I want to go!" Rob slid from his horse. "I know the way."

Four men took Sam and Fud, their hands tied behind them, and started for the village. The others followed Captain Hutchins and Walker into the woods, and Rob led the way. Out there in the stone house Jean LaBarge waited for help, and he was bringing it.

The light outside the knothole slowly turned gray. Unless Rob had reached them in time Captain Hutchins would now be approaching the place where the Carters lay in wait for him on Mill Creek Road.

What if Rob was not believed? But he would be, for Rob was a serious boy, not given to pranks, and he had a way of making people listen to him. He knew how to talk, and had the words for it. That was because he read books. Jean made a mental resolution to read more . . . if he got out of this.

He got to his feet and went to the door. The cabin smelled of dirty clothes and stale tobacco smoke. He tried to get his fingers into the crack between the door and the jamb but there was no space for them, nor could he budge the heavy planks at the window.

Somewhere out in the woods there was a sound, and he went to the knothole, peering out. The grass of the clearing beyond the hemlocks was gray with morning dew; with the rising sun it would turn to silver. A bird came out of a tree and sat on a stump, preening his feathers. There was no sound, there was no other movement.

Yet there was . . . a stirring of leaves, a branch that moved, and a man peering furtively out. The bird, frightened, took off in a low swoop for the trees, and the man named Ring came from the forest and started toward the house.

Jean's throat tightened with fear. Ring was back and he was alone. He had been running: his breath came in ragged gasps and he walked with swift, jerky steps. That meant something had happened—

Ring hesitated, staring back at the forest and listening. His lank black hair hung around his ears, his eyes were wild and staring. There was a pistol tucked in his waistband. He ran on to the stone house and Jean heard him fumbling with the hasp on the door.

Frightened, his mouth dry, Jean hid where the opening door would conceal him until the last moment. They would be coming. Rob must have gotten help; Ring was being chased. If only he could . . .

The door slammed open and Ring stepped into the room, glaring about like a wild animal, looking for Jean. Gasping hoarsely from his run, the man was beyond reason, beyond thought, filled with murderous rage. He stepped on into the room, and instantly Jean ducked around the door and ran.

Wheeling with amazing swiftness, the black-haired man grabbed for him. Jean felt the fingers clutch at his arm, slide off. Then he was out of the door and around the corner of the house. The man was like a cat. He sprang after him, but Jean ducked behind a hemlock and froze in place, eyes wide, fear choking him.

Ring stood in the clearing before the house and looked around him slowly. When he spoke it was in an amazingly cool, almost conversational voice. "You surely needn't try to get away. I know these here woods better'n anybody. My name is Ring and I growed up here."

Jean looked toward the brush, judging the distance. The black-haired man would not want to use his gun and draw the pursuers to him. The brush was only fif- ten feet away, yet for the time it took to cover that dis- tance he would be in full view.

"I'm surely goin' to kill you, boy. They done kilt my daddy, an' I'm a-goin' to kill you."

Jean sprang out and leaped for the brush.

Ring swore, a shrill, whining scream, then lifted his pistol. Realization of what it might bring made him lower it again. He raced after the boy, but Jean LaBarge was already into the woods and once more in his own element. He ducked, dodged, then plunged out into an unexpected little clearing. Behind him Ring yelped a cry of triumph. And then out of the bushes ahead of them stepped Captain Hutchins. "It's all right boy," Hutchins said quietly. "Let him come."

5.

THE HARDEST PART had been saying goodbye to Rob Walker, for they had always planned to go west together, and now he was going and Rob was staying behind. The next hardest part was to leave the swamp.

Before he left he walked alone to the Honey Tree, and he sat down there where he and Rob had sat so many times together, and where he had sat so many times alone. Around the towering tree millions of bees hummed unceasingly, and he watched them, a lump in his throat.

He told himself he would come back and take that old Honey Tree yet, but deep down inside he knew he never would, and suddenly he found himself hoping that nobody else would, either . . .

Neither Rob nor he had felt like talking. They just stood there, and he kicked a clod out of the grass on the Walker lawn.

"Guess you'll be seein' Indians, and everything," Rob said.

"I guess so."

"You going to write me? You going to tell me all that happens?"

"I'll write . . . maybe won't see any post carrier for a long time, but I'll write."

It was his first goodbye, and he did not like it. A long time later, sitting under the cottonwoods and watching the campfire on the little creek west of Independence, he thought of that. He missed Rob, and he missed the swamp, too, but he missed them only a little now because there was so much to see.

Not that there was no trouble, for trouble seemed to go with him wherever he went. He remembered what had been said when the others of the westward-bound company discovered he was a boy. The objections had been violent and profane. But Captain Hutchins faced them, his feet a little spread, cool as he had been that morning when he killed Bob Ring. "The boy goes or I do not. I've a notion he's worth the lot of you, and he'll walk as far or trap as much fur as any of you."

Captain Hutchins owned most of the horses, and Captain Hutchins had been free about providing powder and ball and the others knew they would be a while finding a man to replace him. It finally simmered down until only one man objected and Captain Hutchins faced him. "If it's a choice between you or the boy," he said coolly, "I'd rather have the boy beside me. If you don't like his going, I'd suggest, sir, that you find a party more suited to your temperament."

A man named Peter Hovey, leaning on his elbow against a wagon wheel, had said, "Was I you, Ryle Beck, I'd back up an' set down. I've a notion you've overmatched yourself."

Beck glowered and grumbled, but after a little bluster he shut up and went back to the fireside.

Captain Hutchins turned to Hovey. "Thanks, man. It'd be a bad thing to begin a journey with trouble."

"Aye, an' trouble enough for us all will be seen before we've found our bait of fur." He glanced at Jean. "Are you a trapper, boy?"

"I caught my living at it, furs and herbs, more'n four years now," he said, "but it was swampland and not the mountains. I'd be obliged if you'd teach me."

"You'll do." Peter Hovey grinned. "I've a thought you'll do your share."

And so it began.

Days later, moving westward, Captain Hutchins swung a wide arm at the country about them. "One man, Jean, a man with a vision, gave us this. If Tom Jefferson hadn't gone ahead, overriding the little men without vision, all the frightened little men, we'd not have this. By signing the Purchase agreement he risked his political future, but he doubled the size of the nation. You might even say he created a nation. Before the Louisiana Purchase we were a cluster of colonies; after it we became a world power."

"Is that good, sir?"

"Who knows, Jean? But nations and men are alike: they go forward or they stagnate and die."

There was new respect for him when it was learned he was the son of Smoke LaBarge. Peter Hovey had known him, had trapped with him on the Upper Wind River. Smoke had been killed by Blackfeet the following year, Hovey thought. But you could never be sure. He had a way of turning up.

They went to Pierre's Hole and traded there, and for the first time the others began to see that young Jean LaBarge knew fur. He had learned it by selling his own, and had learned trapping, too. Although only a boy, his take for the season was almost as good as the men's.

With Captain Hutchins and a party of twenty mountain men they went up through the country along the Wind River and the Teton Peaks, and then floated down the Missouri to St. Louis. It was the biggest town Jean LaBarge had seen, and it was there, from old Pierre Choteau, that he first heard the magic name . . . Alaska.

"Alaska," Choteau said, "you know . . . Russian America. Talked to a man who had been there to trade with Baranov. A rich land he said, the furs are thicker there because of the cold. Untrapped country. If I was younger . . ."

Alaska was an exotic name like Kashgar, Samarkand and Bagdad, but different, stronger, stranger. It was wild, untamed, lonely . . . or so it sounded to him.

That night he had written to Rob Walker about it, his first letter home, after so long a time. He told him, in pages of writing, what they had done, of the mountain men he had met—Jim Bridger, Milton Sublett, Peter Hovey. But he wanted to go to Alaska. Rob must meet him in San Francisco and they would go together.

Was that when their love for Alaska began? Or had it begun in that other so-called wasteland, the Great Swamp? Others despised and feared it, yet Jean had lived there, made his way there, known its richness and its beauty. The experience made him wary of the term wasteland.

Now he was seeing great western lands that old Mister Dean had disparaged. He was seeing millions of geese, millions of buffalo, streams with beaver, forests of splendid trees, and the waters of the Missouri. He remembered a big, hairy-faced trapper who grinned at him and said, "Takes a man with hair on his chest to drink from the Missouri. Cowards cut it with whiskey!"

Rob had been away at school when Jean next heard from him, receiving the letter at Astoria, and a package containing a translation of Homer. Captain Hutchins had already given him a Bible. Later, a drunken trapper gave him a copy of Plato's *Dialogues*.

He read his books at night beside the campfire, and read them lying in his bunk at Astoria, and later in San Francisco. Several times after they arrived there he took trips with Captain Hutchins back into the Sierras or the Rockies, and each time he took a book with him.

At sixteen he had read just seven books, but had read them over and over, and at sixteen he was a veteran of nine battles with Indians, and victor in a man-to-man fight with a drunken trapper.

When his seventeenth birthday came around, he had read only one more book, but had read it, Plutarch's *Lives*, four times. He had a fight with Comanches under his belt by that time, carried the scar of his first wound, and had recuperated in Santa Fe.

By the time he was twenty he had covered the length of the Rockies and the Sierras, had nearly died of thirst, carried the scar of another wound and was over six feet tall, lean as any savage warrior, and stronger than any man he had so far met. That was the year he lost all his furs on the Green River when his canoe upset, and lived two months with Ute Indians while they made up their minds whether to kill him or not. By the time they decided he had chosen his horse and rifle, and the night before his captors came for him, an Indian who had befriended him loosed the rawhide bonds they had finally tied him with, and he slipped out of camp in the darkness and rode south until he struck the trail from Santa Fe to California. Two months later, broke, ragged and hungry, he had showed up at Captain Hutchins' office on the wharf at San Francisco.

The following year he bought furs for Captain Hutchins, read twelve more books and tried prospecting in the gold fields without luck. Twice he made strikes but both petered out.

Returning one night from the wharf he heard a woman cry for help from an alley in Sydney Town. He rushed into the alley and something struck him a terrible blow across the back of his head. He came to, to find himself lying in a stinking bunk in the fo'c'sle of a windjammer bound for Amoy and Canton, China. The mate, a burly ruffian with tattooed arms and a heavy chest, came down the ladder with a marline spike and jerked men from the bunks. Tentatively, Jean LaBarge swung his feet to the deck.

"Hurry it up, you!"

He looked up and started to speak and the mate hit him. His head still throbbed from the night before and this second blow did him no good. He painfully got to his feet, as tall as the mate when standing, lean and hard as a wolf, but he only choked back his anger and went on deck.

By the time they reached Canton he knew his way about a ship. He learned fast, paid attention to his job, and bided his time. Captain Swagert eyed him doubtfully, but the mate, Bully Gallow, shrugged it off. "Yellow. He's big, but he's yellow."

At trappers' rendezvous Jean LaBarge had won a dozen rough-and-tumble fights, and had lost one. He found that he liked to fight, there was something savage and wild in him that reveled in it. One of the trappers who worked for Captain Hutchins had once been a bare-knuckle bruiser in England, and he added his teaching to what Jean had learned the hard way. And now Jean's time came in Amoy.

It was a waterfront dive where sailors went, and it was filled with sailors the night Jean LaBarge went hunting. He knew all about the back room at the dive, the place reserved for officers, and it was there he found Captain Swagert, and beside him Gallow.

A big man, Gallow was, with two drinks under his belt and his meanness riding him like a devil on his shoulders. He saw LaBarge and LaBarge grinned at him. Gallow waved a hand. "Get *out!* This room is for your betters!"

"Get up," Jean LaBarge told him. "Get up. Stack your duds and grease your skids because I'm going to tear down your meat-house!"

Gallow left the chair with a lunge and learned for the first time the value of a straight left. It stabbed him in the mouth as though he had run into the butt end of a post, and it stopped him in his tracks. What followed was deliberate, artistic and enthusiastic. Jean LaBarge proceeded to whip Bully Gallow to a fare-thee-well, dragging him from the back room for the entertainment of the common sailors and when the job was finished he went into the back room again where Captain Swagert sat over a bottle and a glass.

"Captain Swagert, sir," he said, "you'll be needing a new mate. I'm applying for the job."

The older man's eyes glinted. "You'll not get it," he said abruptly. "You'll not get it at all. One more trip and you'd be after my job. You're through, lad, and you're on the beach in Amoy, and I envy you not one whit."

So that was the way of it. And Jean wrote to Rob from Amoy but he did not tell him he was on the beach there, only what the port was like, and that he was staying on awhile.

There was no love in Amoy for the white man since the Opium Wars, and for a month Jean LaBarge lived a hand-to-mouth existence, then signed on with a four-master sailing north to the Amur. It was a Russian ship, clumsy on deck and dirty below, but it was a ship, and when they had discharged cargo in the Amur they sailed for Fort Ross on the California coast. There, evading a guard who walked the decks by night, he slipped over the side into the dark water and floated ashore with an arm over a cask.

Once back in California, Jean had a long letter from Rob. His friend had gone far since the Great Swamp days. He had borrowed money and gone to college. He had graduated from the University of Pennsylvania at the age of eighteen and paid the money back by his own efforts. Then he had married the granddaughter of Benjamin Franklin and moved to Mississippi. A successful lawyer, he was now rapidly gaining eminence as a senator . . . Rob had always had a gift for words and a way with people.

Jean LaBarge settled down in the growing city of San Francisco, buying furs and selling supplies to the

Alaska traders and other seagoers. On the foundations of their first efforts Captain Hutchins had begun a thriving business, ignoring the gold rush and building for the future when the boom would be a thing of the past. Not only did Jean know furs, but his sea experience had given him the knowledge to talk equipment and supplies with the best of them. And always in the back of his mind was the thought of Alaska.

It was waiting there, a great subcontinent, almost untouched, overflowing with riches, and all in the hands of a greedy, self-serving company under a charter from the Russian government, a company that kept out all interlopers despite regulations and international treaties. Yet soon Jean LaBarge discovered that nobody had any exact information about Alaska or the islands off the coast to the south. For the greater part they had never been explored and no proper charts existed. The smattering of Russian he had picked up was quickly improved by conversations with the few Russian shipmasters who came to Captain Hutchins' chandler's shop or to trade privately a few furs they had purchased on their own. From these casual conversations and further talks with seamen from the ships, he gleaned what information he could.

Later, on a ship of which Captain Hutchins and he were part owners, he sailed down the coast of Chile and to the Hawaiian Islands. There they picked up an old man, a survivor of Baranov's ill-fated attempt to capture those islands many years before. Relatives of the old man still lived near the abandoned Fort Ross, and on Jean's authority the old man was transported back to California. For hours each day and night Jean's interest kept the old man yarning about his own trading days in the vicinity of Sitka.

Not long after his return Jean learned that Rob Walker had led an attempt in the Senate to buy from the government of Mexico all of Baja California and fifty miles deep into Chihuahua and Sonora for a price of twenty-five million dollars. The Mexican government was prepared to sell, and Walker desperately urged the purchase, but an economy-minded Congress turned down the offer. Wasteland, they said.

The letters were not many but they continued. No

longer was there talk of the two going to Alaska together, although Rob did plan to come to California where he had clients, and there was some talk of a trip to China, but neither trip materialized as the growing demands on Robert Walker's time increased, and his own importance to the nation he served.

From time to time Jean LaBarge heard of his father. He was dead . . . he was not dead . . . he had gone to Canada . . . had been seen in the Yukon country. The swamp on the Susquehanna seemed far away now, but Alaska was closer. What he needed was a ship.

6.

WHEN THE LIGHTER CAME alongside the dock with its load of furs, the man in the blue jacket sprang ashore, then turned to look back at the harbor. Crowded with shipping though it was, he had eyes but for one vessel, a low-hulled black schooner that lay some three hundred yards off the landing.

Jean LaBarge looked what he was, a man born to the wild places and the tall winds. The mountain years had shaped him for strength and molded him for trial, the desert had dried him out and the sea had made him thoughtful. His boyhood in the Great Swamp near the Susquehanna had given promise of the man he had become.

His eyes traced the lean, rakish lines of the schooner, making a picture of her as she would appear against the fjords and inlets of the northern coast. She would do well in that trade where the number of skins one took was less important than the number one successfully brought away. With that color, and with her low silhouette and slim masts, she could easily lose herself against the changing greens and browns of the iron coast. And with her shallow draft she could hug the shore so closely as to be almost invisible from seaward.

Jean knew that if he expected to trade in Russian America and avoid capture or sinking she was just the craft he required, and he intended to own her.

The man suited the ship as the ship the man, for Jean had about him the same lean look, big though he was. His were the hands and shoulders of one who had worked much against the sea and wind. His eyes measured the schooner, studying her lines and guessing at her speed and capacity. She had come into the harbor and dropped anchor while he was bartering for furs aboard the Boston ship, and his first glimpse of her had come as he started for shore. Obviously she was strongly as well as lightly built, fashioned for speed and durability by a knowing hand.

It was a raw morning with a cold gray sky above a slate-gray sea, and a wind blew in through the Golden Gate with a hint of rain. Nevertheless, he remained on the dock studying the schooner. She lay too far off for him to make out the port of registry, but he remembered no such schooner in these waters since he had first come to San Francisco.

With such a schooner, if a man steered clear of the Russian capital at Sitka and its immediately neighboring islands he might trade along the Alaskan coast and be gone before the Russians were aware of his presence in the area. With luck he might slip in and out of that network of channels like a dark ghost ship, for the Indians were not apt to talk to their Russian masters, preferring to deal with the "Boston men" as all Yankees were called by them. The Russians were all too willing to let the Indians have a touch of the knout.

Yet trading among the islands was not a simple thing, and within the past few years a dozen ships had vanished there, ships mastered by men who knew the waters, the bitter offshore winds and fogs. Furs were not coming out as they had been, and prices had risen. Now if ever was the time for a private venture.

There are men who give their hearts to a horse, a boat, or a gun, men who are possessed by all these things, absorbed by them to the exclusion of all else. Jean LaBarge was such a man, but he was absorbed by a land. To the north lay a country vast and unpeopled, without cities, a land of glacier and mountain, of icy inlet and rocky fjord, of long grassy valleys and canyons choked with snow, of endless tundra and mile upon mile of mighty timber. It was a land with broken shores where the icy tongues of an Arctic sea licked at gaping mouths of rock, while above it the sky was weirdly lit by the vast play of color that was the northern lights. Long before he had seen the land he had loved it, for he had felt its strength and beauty in the richness of its fur, in its timber and gold.

He knew of the gold. There had been a trapper who

had come to him with furs, a man who had wintered with the Tlingit Indians north of Fifty-four. Jean had bought furs from him, wondering at their richness, and he asked the man when he was going back.

The trapper turned sharply around, his face flushed and angry. "Back? Are you crazy? Who'd go back to a country that freezes the eyeballs in your skull, the marrow in your bones, where the bears grow tall as horses and heavy as bulls? The Russkies can have it, and welcome. I wouldn't even go back for the gold."

"Gold?"

The trapper dug into his pocket and drew out a bit of tanned hide, unrolling it to reveal a nugget of walnut size. It gleamed there on his calloused palm, heavy as sin in the heart of a man. "If that isn't gold, what is it?"

Jean remembered the feel of it in his own palm, the weight of it and the brightness. This was gold, all right, raw gold, of which he had seen plenty here in California. Yet this was from Alaska.

"Found it in the shallows of a mountain stream when my canoe tipped over. I was picking my gear off the bottom when I saw it lying there, and could have picked up a dozen more. Only the country was freezing up and my grub was gone.

"Rough gold, see? Means it wasn't carried far from the lode or it would have been worn smooth by rocks and gravel. The Tlingits have gold but they value it less than iron." He made a brushing gesture before his face. "I'd set no value on it either, if I had to go to Alaska for it."

Yet a year later Jean LaBarge heard the trapper had been killed in Alaska in a fight over a Kolush squaw. They were all the same, these men who went to the north country, they claimed to hate it, but they went back. And Jean knew it was not the furs or gold nor was it the wild, free life. It was the land.

Thoughtfully, he considered the problem presented by the schooner, her probable cost and the additional expense of outfitting her. Beyond the trim, black-hulled schooner was a big square-rigger flying the Russian flag—it was almost a challenge. He grinned thoughtfully, thinking of the places that schooner could go where the square-rigger could not hope to follow.

Few Russian ships came to San Francisco since the closing of Fort Ross, yet occasionally they made their way down from Sitka to buy grain or other food even as they had done in the days of the Dons when they had bought much from the missions. The square-rigger had come into port only a short time ago.

Glancing around at an approaching footstep he saw a short, thickset man with a captain's peaked cap shoved back on the hard knot of his head. Despite the damp chill the man had his coat over his arm and his shirt open at the neck. In his mouth was a short-stemmed pipe. "That schooner, now. She's a pretty thing, isn't she?" He slanted a shrewd, measuring glance at Jean. "And the beauty of it is, she can be had. In a week I'd make no bets on it, but right now, for hard cash, she'd be a real bargain."

He made a thrusting gesture, his pointing finger held waist-high, like a pistol. "Right now her owner's got a touch of the yellow . . . he's discouraged."

"Discouraged?"

There was a hard competence about the man, and a scar on his cheekbone, scarcely healed. His eyes, however, held a quizzical humor that belied the toughness. "Bad luck in the Pribilofs. The Russkies got him."

"They didn't take the schooner?"

"He hadn't the schooner with him. That time he was sailing a barkentine. They didn't take her, either, just the cargo. Six thousand prime sealskins. Six *thousand* mind you." The man spat. "And lucky, at that. Had it been Baron Zinnovy he'd have been lucky to be alive, to say nothing of ship and crew."

"Zinnovy?"

"If you're in the trade it's a name you'll know soon enough. He's out from Siberia to command the Russian patrol ship, the *Kronstadt*. And none of your vodka-swilling scenery bums such as they've been sending out, but a tough man, one chosen to do a bloody job and put the fear of the Lord in such of us as sail north."

"He's already on the north coast?"   ,

"He's right here . . . in Frisco." He indicated the square-rigger. "He came aboard of her, but as a passenger, mind you.

"If I'm to fight a man, give me a brute every time,

44

but this one is cold and he's smart, and fresh from the Russian navy with a lot of ideas. I've heard them say his idea is to end the free trading with a rope, a knout for the Indians and a noose for the Boston men, and the deep six for their ships."

"That's a large order."

"Ay, but this one's man enough, don't you be doubting that. I say it as hate to, he's man enough."

The square-rigger had lowered a boat that was coming shoreward. Jean strained his eyes against the distance, making out but one passenger aside from the boat crew.

"You've been sizing up the schooner, and she's a likely craft, but you'll be needing a skipper, a man who knows the islands. You'll find none who know them better than myself, from Vancouver Island to the Circle."

He gestured at himself. "You see me now, name of Barney Kohl, standing in the middle of my property. But wealth, man? 'Tis not property that makes a man rich, but what's in his skull, and I've a pretty lot upstairs. You'll be needing a man with more in his head, Jean LaBarge, than mincy ways and nancy talk. You'll be seeking a man who knows the way of a ship and the sea, and the tricks of the Kolush prominent among them. You'll be needing me, LaBarge, if it's yonder schooner you'll be buying."

Kohl was a name well known to shipping: a tough rascal by all accounts, not above cutting a corner or two, but a good man with a ship, and a fighter. He had bargained with the Kolush and dealt with the Eskimo, and had a couple of running battles with Russian patrol ships.

"You know the kind of man Zinnovy is and you'd still go north?"

Kohl took the pipe from his teeth. "That's why I want to go. There was a ship lost up there, and I know what happened.

"You've heard of the mosquitoes on that coast? They'll cover every naked bit of a man and eat him alive. I've seen a man after being left naked by the Kolush, black with them, driven crazy by them.

"Well, there were six men left alive when their ship was taken, and Zinnovy had the six whipped with

45

cat until the muscles were laid bare and then tied them, bloody as they were, to trees. Then he left them for the mosquitoes, and I was the one found those men—or what was left of them."

"You're hired," Jean said, "if I can buy the schooner."

"You'll get it. I'll see to that . . . you'll have her within the week."

7.

THE SECOND LIGHTER HAD now reached the dock, piled high with bales of furs. It bumped alongside and a heaving line was tossed shoreward. A dockside hand started for it, but LaBarge was nearer and snared the monkey's-fist on the end of the line with a one-handed catch. Barney Kohl grasped the line beside him and together they hauled it in, hand over hand, then the heavier line to which it was belayed. They threw three fast turns around the bollard and topped it off with a half-hitch to complete the tie. Stepping back, they grinned at each other.

"I've a thought where the owner may be," Kohl suggested, "so let me handle the deal. He knows I'm on my uppers and I can wrangle a better price than you."

A dozen husky longshoremen moved toward the lighter and began tumbling bales within reach of the crane. Jean LaBarge ran an appraising eye over what he could see of the skins. Without breaking a bale he knew they were prime stuff; he had broken enough bales while he was aboard the Yankee ship to assure him of his judgment.

A few spattering drops of rain fell, and he stood on the dock, liking the feel of them on his face. Beneath the wharf the waves slapped against the piles, a pleasant sound, a sea sound. He liked the damp, chill morning and the salt air, the ships lying out there on the waters of the bay, the black-hulled schooner he hoped might soon be his own.

"Go ahead," he said finally. "You'll be sailing as mate."

Kohl had started away, but the words brought him up short. "What?" Obviously he did not believe what he had heard. "Me? As mate? And who'll sail as master? What man is fitted to—"

"I'll be in command."

Their eyes met and held, measuring each other. Kohl was astonished, then angry. For fifteen years he had sailed as master of ships, and half that time aboard his own vessel. And now he was expected to take a back seat.

"You've commanded before?" he asked skeptically. The thought of sailing as second-in-command to a man who, so far as he knew, had never gone to sea was not to be borne.

"I have. And I can use a mate if you've a liking for the job. If you haven't, I'll get another man."

"Oh, I'll take it!" Kohl was exasperated. "What else can I do? I've no liking for the beach, that's certain, and a man must eat. You've got me over a barrel."

"I'll have no discontented man aboard my ship," La-Barge said flatly. "If you're shipping with me because you're broke, I'll stake you so you'll have no worries until you get another ship."

Kohl's irritation waned. "Well," he grumbled, "that's fair enough. It's more than fair. No, I don't want your stake, I'd rather have the job even if I am stepping down. I'll go to sea."

"Good . . . you're on the articles as of now. Come see me tonight and sign them—or as soon as you've lined up a deal for the schooner."

Kohl turned away, still a little angry, yet as he walked away, his irritation waned. He was going to sea again and in a schooner that was as sweet a bit of seagoing merchandise as he had ever seen. He was no dockside sailor who did his seafaring when talking to the girls, but a deep-water man who liked it out where the big ones rolled. Besides, around Frisco there was every chance he'd some night have a drink in the wrong place and wake up, shanghaied aboard the ship of some lubber who couldn't navigate a dory in a millpond. Anyway, he reflected with a grim pleasure, after a trip north LaBarge might lose his stomach for those waters and be only too happy to turn the ship over to him.

Jean LaBarge smiled as his eyes followed Kohl's broad shoulders down the dock, then he turned to watch the crane swing shoreward with several bales of hides. As it swung in to the dock he saw one of the bales slip, realized instantly it was improperly slung, knew the whole load was going to fall. At that moment a young woman stepped around a pile of lumber directly into the path of the sling. The crane jerked and the bales broke loose and there was a shout of warning from the lighter, but Jean was already moving.

Scooping the girl into his arms he lunged for safety. One of the bales struck him a glancing blow that sent them both rolling. The bales of furs tumbled to the dock, and Jean sat up, shaken by his fall.

The girl sat beside him, flushed and angry. The scarf that bound her hair had come loose and the wind blew a strand of dark hair across her face. Angrily, she brushed it away, glaring at him. She was younger than he had first thought, and uncommonly pretty. At that moment, her face flushed and her hair blowing, she looked . . . he leaned over and kissed her full on the lips.

For an instant, startled, she stared at him. Then her lips tightened and she drew back her hand to slap him, but he rolled swiftly away and got to his feet, grinning. He offered his hand.

She took his hand and he drew her to her feet, and when she was standing properly she slapped him. There was a whoop of laughter from one of the men on the dock and Jean LaBarge turned. His hat had been knocked off by the fall and his dark hair fell over his brow. "If the man who laughed will step out here," he invited, "I'll break his jaw."

Nobody moved, all the faces looked equally innocent, and carefully they avoided each other's eyes.

The girl was brushing a few slivers of the dock from her clothing, "Ma'am," he said apologetically, "you were in the way of being hit by those bales, and—"

She straightened to her full height, her chin lifted. Coolly, imperiously, she said, "I have asked for no explanation, and I expect no comment. You may go."

He was puzzled. "Sure," he agreed doubtfully, "but if you'll accept a suggestion you'll take a carriage. This is no place for a woman to walk without an escort."

Her eyes straight ahead, she said quietly, "You may call a carriage."

Gathering the folds of her skirt, her chin lifted, looking neither right nor left, she walked to the edge of the

49

street. Jean glanced at her profile, so perfectly carved, and her hair, rumpled now, showing dark from beneath her scarf. When the carriage for which he signaled drew up before them she disdained his offered hand and got into the carriage and drove off without a backward glance.

He stood alone on the edge of the street, staring after her. She had spoken with an accent faintly foreign. He knew of no woman, even in this town of San Francisco, who dressed so well. There was some vague difference in her manner, some inner poise and awareness that puzzled him. He turned his back on the street and walked slowly back to the growing stack of bales.

There was no reason why he should think of the girl, yet he did. He knew many girls, for in San Francisco a rising young man as tall, ruggedly handsome, and as well off as he was, was naturally an object of attention. He had kissed her strictly on impulse, but the more he thought of it the more he was glad that he had done it.

The black-hulled schooner was stern-to now, and looking along the line of her hull he sharpened his eyes with genuine pleasure. What a craft she would be for the fur trade! How easily she would slide through the water in those narrow channels to the north!

From the beginning both Hutchins and Jean had looked to the furs from the north for their business. They had supplied the mines with equipment as they had supplied ships, but they knew the fur industry was the coming thing.

Now, if ever, was the time to go. Rumors had been affecting the market, and he had an idea prices on fur were going to rise drastically. Just such stories as Kohl had told him were sure to have their effect.

Theoretically there were no restrictions on the trade with Russian America. Actually, the Russian American Company exercised complete control over Alaska and the coast islands; the authority of the Company was subject only to the Czar himself, and as they said in Sitka, "God's in his heaven and the Czar is far away." The governor of Siberia was a stockholder in the Company, and like most stockholders concerned only with profits. The Boston traders had cut deeply into those profits, with better offers for furs, and with ways that were generally more considerate of the natives.

The claim of the Russian American Company to exclusive trading privileges in Alaska and the neighboring islands was a claim not many Americans were prepared to admit. The Boston men had been encroaching on the area for years just as the *promyshleniki,* those free-roving hunters and traders from Siberia, had been moving into Canadian or American territory when opportunity offered. Under Baranov, trading in the Russian-American area had been distinctly dangerous unless that trade was carried on with Baranov himself, then the government of Russia had interceded and opened Russian America to free trade. The ruling was still in effect, but it meant no more to the Company than many another, and they waged open war on all who dared trade in their territories.

Restrictions of the Company, or even of a far-off Czar, had little effect on Americans, a people impatient of any restriction, and trade with the Pribilofs continued.

The seal islands did not interest Jean LaBarge. The risk was great for the profit involved, but the coastal islands were a veritable maze. Charts of the area were sketchy and inadequate and what knowledge of its waters existed was only in the memories of those shipmasters who had cruised the channels and traded in the islands, or among the Indians themselves.

With such a schooner as the one in the harbor a man might slip in and out of those channels with small chance of encountering a Russian patrol ship. The furs of the coast were excellent and Jean had made it his businesss to learn which villages were outlets for the furs of the interior. Tonight he would learn more. Tom Herndon's parties were a clearinghouse for news. Whoever was somebody in San Francisco might be found there on Tuesday nights. Herndon's wife came from the Carolinas with southern ideas on entertaining, and with money enough to gratify her every whim, she entertained on the grand scale.

The face of the girl on the wharf kept forcing its way into Jean's thoughts. A connoisseur of accents, as everyone in San Francisco must eventually become, he could not place hers. There were many German and French settlers now, but her accent was not German or French. Suddenly, he remembered the square-rigger recently arrived in port. But what would a girl, and such a girl, be doing on a ship from Sitka? During the Russian occupation of Fort Ross there had been several girls of good family there, and others had visited with their husbands or fathers, but Fort Ross had been long abandoned.

Disturbingly, her face remained in his mind, and the feel of her body in his arms. There had been that brief instant when she rested, passive, in his arms, an instant when it seemed natural and right, as if she would always be there. When she had realized the situation she had straightened quickly away from him. Yet for that moment. . . .

The Herndon party was an hour old when Jean entered the crowded rooms. Hutchins was there, a tall, handsome man of soldierly bearing with a shock of pure white hair and a dignity few could match. Royle Weber was there, too, a small, fat man, very busy and very talkative, always gesturing and smiling. Weber was an agent for the Russian American Company, buying and selling for them locally. Perhaps, Jean suspected, a spy for them also. That might explain the disappearing ships.

As he was passing Sam Brannan, the latter stopped him. "We've been wanting to talk to you, LaBarge. We may need your help."

"Thanks, no. I appreciate the problem, but I'll skin my own cats."

"There is power in organization, LaBarge," Brannan said seriously. "Alone, a man is helpless."

"They've not bothered us so far."

Brannan nodded. "You've been fortunate. The hoodlums from Sydney Town are growing bolder every day."

From the beginning Sam Brannan had been one of the most intelligent and far-seeing citizens of the town, and one of the few willing to stand up to the Sydney Town thugs. He had been one of the original leaders of the first Vigilante organization, and it had been successful largely because of the men Brannan had selected, and because it had been no incoherent and hastily assembled mob. The men he had chosen were solid citizens as well as men of courage and integrity.

When LaBarge had passed them, Brannan turned to his companions and said, "If there's trouble again, I want him with us."

Charley Duane lifted his eyebrows. "Why? I've not seen any of his graveyards."

Brannan knew enough about Duane not to like him. "No? Next time try Nevada."

Royle Weber was emphatic with his nod of agreement. "I know the story, Charley. It was an attempted claim jumping, and two men lost out in a gun battle with LaBarge, but LaBarge didn't stop there. He went to town to see the man who sent them."

"And . . . ?"

"He sent *him* out of town—walking. He had only what he stood up in, and a broken arm."

Duane was thoughtful. His friends from Sydney Town had been wary of LaBarge, and this might be the reason.

"I hear he's growing wheat," Herndon commented.

"He bought property from you, didn't he, Sam?" Weber asked.

"I handled the sale. Yes, he's growing wheat, which more of us should be doing. He'll sell his crop this year for much more than many a miner will get from a claim. If you're doing business with them it isn't a good idea to underrate anything either Hutchins or LaBarge are doing."

Weber turned a cigar in his fingers, then bit off the end, his manner thoughtful. "What," he asked then, "is all this interest in Alaska? I hear he's forever asking questions about it."

"You'll have to ask him," Brannan replied shortly.

Jean LaBarge moved from group to group, pausing only briefly here and there. More than one pair of feminine eyes lingered on his broad shoulders and his dark, lean face with its high cheekbones and scar. His manner and dress was that of a gentleman, but his face was that of a pirate. He was carefully dressed: well-tailored suit, ruffled shirt and a black tie; but no matter how carefully he combed his hair it soon resumed its natural tumbled curliness. His boots were of Spanish leather, handmade. Turning away from the group where Hutchins stood, he came to an abrupt stop, audibly catching his breath.

Before him, wearing a satin evening gown surely from Paris, was the girl from the wharf . . . and as his eyes found her she turned slightly and saw him.

For an instant their eyes held, then moved away as if by agreement. Jean felt a queer excitement. His mouth was dry. He turned to answer some comment from Hutchins, and replied to the question without really knowing what he said. The man who stood beside the girl was tall, much older, with iron-gray hair and the thoughtful face of a scholar. There was something about his poise, his dignity that commanded attention. But it was the other man who immediately drew Jean's attention so that he scarcely noticed Royle Weber, who stood between them.

He was an inch taller than Jean's six feet two inches, as broad of shoulder as Jean himself and somewhat heavier in the body. His hair was blond clipped high on the sides and close-cropped on top. His eyes were gray-white and closely set. He carried himself with a military bearing; his white uniform coat was ablaze with decorations. His trousers were black with a thin white stripe down each leg and he wore black boots. Yet the insignia he wore, despite the uniform, was of the Navy. This could only be Baron Paul Zinnovy.

"Mr. LaBarge?" Weber spoke loudly. "May I present Count Alexander Rotcheff? You were asking about wheat, sir. Jean LaBarge is one of the few, these days, who think of planting. If anyone will have wheat to sell, it will be Mr. LaBarge."

The older man bowed slightly. "It is good to know, Mr. LaBarge. It is the reason for our visit. We must have wheat at Sitka."

"Well, we have the wheat," Jean answered. At once his mind seized upon the idea. Wheat for Sitka? Free, unquestioned access to the islands? It was just what he had been hoping for, planning for. "I am sure we can reach an agreement."

Rotcheff turned to include the girl and the tall blond

officer. "Mr. LaBarge? May I present my wife? And Baron Zinnovy, of the Imperial Russian Navy."

Some of his dismay must have been evident, for there was something in her eyes that responded to his . . . was it regret?

"Baron Zinnovy," Rotcheff continued, "is in command of the patrol ships at Sitka."

"To a dealer in wheat that will not be important. If Mr. LaBarge dealt in fur it might be very important indeed."

Jean smiled, but his eyes held a challenge. "But I am a dealer in furs, Baron Zinnovy! Wheat is just a sideline with me. My real business is in fur. In fact, Captain Hutchins and myself are among the largest buyers of fur on the coast."

"No doubt," Zinnovy said, his voice arrogant, "you have bought many Russian skins. For the future, if I were you, I would put no trust in that source."

"Russian skins?" Jean furrowed his brow with exaggerated perplexity. "You have the advantage of me, Baron. I have taken the skins of fox, marten and mink, but so far I've never had to skin a Russian."

The girl laughed outright and Count Rotcheff smiled. "Let's hope you never do," he said agreeably. "There are furs enough for us all without our skinning each other. Don't you agree, Baron?"

"I think," Baron Zinnovy replied distinctly, "this merchant is insolent."

Count Rotcheff started to interrupt, obviously uncomfortable and hoping to turn the conversation. Jean spoke quickly.

"You use the term 'merchant,'" Jean said, "as if you considered it an insult. I think of it only as a compliment, for it was the merchant adventurers of the world who opened the roads and discovered continents and developed the riches of the earth while, if Count Rotcheff will forgive me, the titled lords were mainly concerned with waging petty wars or robbing priests and women."

Zinnovy's face was pale. Never had he been spoken to in this manner, and although he despised Count Rotcheff for his diplomacy and political views, to be openly insulted before him was insufferable.

"If we were not guests—"

"But we are!" Rotcheff interrupted sharply. "We are guests, Baron Zinnovy, and this visit is of great importance to our colony at Sitka. We can have no quarrels here."

Zinnovy bowed slightly, his eyes coldly furious. "I regret my haste, Count Rotcheff. As for Mr. LaBarge, I hope he makes no further attempt to open his merchant roads to Russian America."

Jean feigned surprise. "But Baron, you forget! Count Rotcheff has just been discussing a purchase of wheat. If he buys my wheat I'll have to deliver it."

"It will be a delivery I shall watch with interest." His cold gray-white eyes met Jean's. "Who knows but that we shall meet when neither is a guest of the other?"

"I'll look forward to it." Jean turned. "Countess . . ."

"The name," Rotcheff interposed, "is Princess. My wife is the Princess Helena de Gagarin, niece of His Majesty, the Czar of Russia."

"Oh . . . of the Czar?"

"And the niece of the Grand Duke Constantin also—you may have heard of him."

"A lot of us Americans admire the Grand Duke for his liberal views . . . naturally, they would be popular here."

"If you approve of the Grand Duke," Zinnovy suggested, "then you must approve the policies of Muraviev?"

"If he were an American I might approve. As he is a Russian, I do not."

"You approve his territorial claims against China? As you might approve of your own government if they laid claim to Russian America?"

Jean shrugged. "I don't know anything about statecraft, Baron, but I have heard of no claims made by the United States on Alaska. As to purchase, that is another thing. We might be interested in that question."

Count Rotcheff studied Jean more carefully. This young American was no fool . . . or did he speak with information of some sort? There had been talk in St. Petersburg of a bargain with the United States. It was most interesting that it should be mentioned here.

Rotcheff had been listening to the discussion with

irritation. The Russian colony at Sitka was dependent on foodstuffs from California and Hawaii for its very existence. Russian ships were received without undue warmth and any dispute might bring an end to trading; the success of his own mission depended on friendship with the business interests of San Francisco. He seized the moment to change the subject. "My wife is very interested in your country, Mr. LaBarge, and I would be honored if you could show her something of the state outside the city."

Rotcheff led Zinnovy aside, anxious to break up the circle and avoid a discussion that could lead to trouble. The music started and Jean led Helena de Gagarin out on the floor. For a time they danced without speaking, each content with their own thoughts. She danced lightly, gracefully, moving easily to the waltz. And he could only think that being a princess as well as a wife she was doubly lost to him.

The thought brought irritated amusement to his eyes: he had never before thought of a woman in terms of marriage, and now he had chosen someone as remote as a star. Yet he had never seen a woman so beautiful and desirable.

She looked up at him. "You've not said you were sorry."

"That you're married? Of course I'm sorry."

"I did not mean that. I meant for what happened on the wharf."

He grinned cheerfully. "Sorry? I'm not a bit sorry. I liked it!"

Late that night, Jean LaBarge climbed the stairs to his rooms and opened the door. He felt gay and more excited than he could remember, and although it was two o'clock in the morning he was not in the least sleepy. All the way home through the poorly lighted streets he had thought of nothing but Helena. Throwing off his coat he sailed his hat to the settee against the wall and as he lighted the lamp he glanced at the map that covered the wall.

Not even Captain Hutchins knew of his map. It was on canvas and was six feet wide by nine feet long, and it had been pieced together, bit by bit, fragment by fragment, for six years. It embodied information acquired from ship's masters, common seamen, hunters, trappers, traders and occasional Indians. Each day or so Jean added another bit of information to the map or checked something already there.

In his business of buying he had occasion to do much listening and to ask many questions, and most of the traders or mariners were eager enough to talk of their successes or discoveries. Yesterday he had added an inlet to the map, two days before it had been a rocky ridge with pine trees at the tip. Beside the map, on a small desk, was an open book. It was one of a number of such books, and each item of information on the map was also entered in the books, along with much more. Descriptions of landmarks, tides, currents, timber, people, customs, weapons and living conditions. Without doubt his knowledge of Russian America was greater than the knowledge of men who had lived there for years. Each of those who lived in Alaska knew their own area and perhaps a little more, but Jean LaBarge's books contained knowledge gleaned from thousands of men, and it was gathered by himself, who knew how to ask questions, how to make leading remarks, and who could ask those questions from a broad base of already acquired knowledge.

He knew the depth of water and best anchorage in Yakutat Bay, the best place to anchor and trade on Kassan Island. He knew by name the Indian in each village who was the best trapper and therefore most likely to have furs. He knew each chief by name and reputation, and knew his relations with other tribes. He knew of a fine salmon stream that flowed into Humpbacked Bay, and of the waterfall about a half mile back from the beach. He knew the channels where tidal currents were most dangerous and where lay hidden rocks likely to rip the bottom from a ship.

Most of all he had made discreet inquiries about landlocked harbors, hidden channels, portages, and places likely to offer concealment from a patrol ship. Not one of the men to whom he talked knew very much, but in the aggregate they could tell him a great deal. No hunting story was too long to listen to, and any drunken trader or trapper found LaBarge a willing audience.

The few charts of the Sitka area were woefully inadequate, but he secured copies and studied them. No day passed that he did not review the information he had gathered, for it was not enough that he had it in books; all he had gathered must be in his own head. Only one other man knew of that map, and that man was Robert J. Walker.

After all these years, the two friends still occasionally corresponded, keeping track of each other's progress. Rob Walker's success continued to be striking. After his term in the Senate he had returned to his law practice, but always with a strong interest and influence in political circles.

Jean LaBarge knew that Walker's interest in Russian America was different from his own, which was strictly commercial. To Jean, the Alaska fur trade offered a great chance for wealth, and once the country was opened to American interests, there might be much more that could be done. He already knew of the gold; there was no way of guessing what else the cold land might ultimately yield.

Rob Walker thought of Alaska in terms of their childhood dreams, as another potential Louisiana Purchase. Jean LaBarge's view was simpler and more immediate: Alaska meant money and adventure. That was enough for him.

Now, after all his planning, it looked as if he would at last gain access to that northern land. If Rotcheff bought wheat from him he would himself transport it to Sitka or it would never leave the farm. It was for just this sort of opportunity that his wheat had been planted. True, he was always sure of a local market, but north was where his interest lay, and a cargo of wheat was a sure passage to Sitka.

This was his chance, and there must be no mistakes. A cargo of furs in San Francisco three months or even two months from now would bring premium prices, but he must be wary . . . Baron Zinnovy would be sure to keep him under his eyes. Yet much might happen in those northern fogs and that maze of channels. He must select the most likely places for a quick cargo of furs, slip in and out and then run for it, a fast voyage south, and—

He got up and paced the floor, considering tonnage, arms, trade goods.

His thoughts turned to Helena. He remembered the gray eyes, the dark hair drawn back, the quiet poise and beauty of her . . . he was a fool to waste thought on her, even for a moment. She belonged to another man. She was a niece of the Czar! Yet he did think of her, and he was not likely to stop thinking, for he was, he realized it suddenly, he was in love.

There was a light step on the stair outside his door. Jean dropped his hand to the pistol he always carried, and waited. The Sydney Town toughs had broken into more than one home, robbing and murdering as they would. Outside the door there was a creak, then a light tap. With his left hand, he opened the door. It was Barney Kohl.

He was grinning widely. "I think we've got it! I've bought us a schooner!"

8.

COUNT ALEXANDER ROTCHEFF FOLDED his *Alta Californian* and placed it neatly beside his plate. He was a tall old man, finely featured, with graying hair and a pointed beard. He glanced thoughtfully at his wife. Helena, he observed, was unusually quiet this morning.

Moreover, she was up earlier than usual. She seemed younger, somehow, and fresher. The ribbon around her hair was attractive, and he wondered absently how she would look with her hair disarranged, and decided the effect would be even more charming. If only he were a few years younger. . . .

He sighed. Unfortunately some things did not comport with the dignity of an aging diplomat, courtier, and emissary of the Czar. It was a pity.

He smiled, remembering that some philosopher, he could not recall the name, had said that no wise man ever wished to be younger. Obviously the man who made such a remark had not seen Helena in the morning, fresh from the bath. And this morning there was a glow in her eyes as well as on her cheeks. A pensive glow.

Whatever else the years had taken from Count Rotcheff they had not taken his knowledge of women. His marriage had come late in life, and had been largely a matter of expediency, joining two powerful families in an even more powerful alliance. The marriage had served him well and had been successful in itself, beyond expectation, and that success had been due quite as much to Helena as to himself.

She had given him companionship, tenderness, and a well-managed home, she had given him intelligent understanding of his problems, approaching their life together with a maturity of judgment that would have been surprising in one of her years to any other person

61

than Rotcheff. The Count, although this had been his first marriage, had successfully survived numerous less formal attachments, and had learned thereby. He was aware that it did not necessarily take years to make a woman practical, or experience to make her wise. To a fool time brings only age, not wisdom.

Helena's understanding of diplomacy and statecraft was scarcely less than his own, and it is a business in which a beautiful and intelligent wife is the greatest of assets. She had used her talents, her knowledge and connections to a superlative degree. She listened well. Men talk easily of their plans to a beautiful girl, and Helena had the faculty of making the most horrendous bore feel brilliant. What was even more important, she could remember what she heard, and no one could guide a conversation more skillfully without seeming to do so.

She was warm, lovely and exciting, yet beneath it there was steel. It was one thing, he reflected, to love a woman. It was quite another to admire her and respect her judgment. Yet he admired her most of all because she was successful at being a woman, she was always and forever feminine.

He tasted his coffee and found it too hot. Putting down his cup, he got out his pipe. That young man . . . what was his name again? LaBarge . . . Jean LaBarge. For an American he seemed uncommonly well informed. The other Americans he had met were absorbed in their own affairs, their own country to the exclusion of all else, knowing little of the problems of other countries and peoples. That was one of the benefits of being a secondary power, for it is only when a nation becomes a world power that it becomes imperative to understand other peoples or fail in its objectives. One rules by knowing. Russia had never learned and that was why Russia had always remained on the outer fringe of world affairs. England, France, Germany, and Spain, even Austria-Hungary and the Netherlands, all helped to shape the destiny of the world while Russia sat astride a great and integrated empire and was rarely consulted.

LaBarge had been correct, of course, in his comment on titles of nobility. Too often such a title was won by a man of energy and used thereafter to mask the indolence and complete uselessness of his descendants. In the

United States a man could not rely on a family name to carry him through, although that unhappy time might come as it did to all aging countries. In his own Russia too many of the old families were producing effeminate, idle, and extravagant young men more preoccupied with fashion and gaming than with the destiny of their nation. He smiled ironically, realizing that none of this was true of his political opponent, Baron Zinnovy, nor of Muraviev of Siberia. Say what one might of them, they were able and dangerous men. And Zinnovy was basically more dangerous because he was a man without honor or conception of it. He lived to win, and cared not one whit how it was done nor who suffered from his actions.

It was a credit to LaBarge that he had faced Zinnovy so calmly. Not many either could or would dare to do so.

"I believe," he commented aloud, "the Baron would have challenged LaBarge in another minute. I have never known him to anger so quickly."

"What do you think of him?"

Rotcheff put down his pipe, smiling to realize that they both understood of whom she was asking. "LaBarge? A damnably handsome man, and an able one, I'd say."

There was something about that lean, dark face with its scar that sent a thrill of excitement through her. The way he had looked at her!—she flushed at the thought. But she had been most impressed by the confidence with which he replied to Zinnovy. "He is a dangerous man," she said thoughtfully, "and a man who knows where he is going."

Something prompted Rotcheff to say, "Dangerous to Zinnovy, you mean? Or to me?"

"You?" She looked up quickly, then gathering his intent, she blushed again. "No one is dangerous to you, my love."

He was embarrassed. "I am sorry." He waved a hand, dismissing the comment. "I had no reason to say that. Only, he is very handsome, such a man as any woman would notice."

"I did not believe you saw such things."

Rotcheff laughed lightly. "When a man has a beautiful wife he had damned well better!" Dropping the bantering tone he added, "He can help us. Weber informed me that the wheat LaBarge has to sell is the only wheat available."

"He will bring it to Sitka?"

"I doubt if other ships will be available. We have no real right to trade here, you know."

Rotcheff drank his coffee and smoked, the paper at one side. There was more to his trip than even Baron Zinnovy guessed. Reports had reached St. Petersburg that the Company was victimizing the natives, inflicting many cruelties upon them and hesitating at nothing in their grab for profits. If these rumors were proved true then the charter of the Company would not be renewed, nor would another charter be granted.

Alaska had long represented a problem to Russia, lying outside the continental limits as it did. Russia was a land rather than a sea power. War would leave Alaska exposed to seizure, and it was well known that Great Britain looked upon Russian America with acquisitive eyes. If war with Britain and France should again develop Alaska would be vulnerable and its loss a serious blow to Russian prestige in the Far East.

Rotcheff believed as did the Grand Duke that it was better to sell Alaska than risk its loss with the accompanying loss of face. And he knew California might be just the place to lay the groundwork for such a sale. There were men here accustomed to thinking on the grand scale; to men who have crossed a continent, won a state, and ripped open the earth for gold, the buying of Alaska would present no great problem.

LaBarge . . . the man might actually be a government agent. No, he was thinking like a Russian again. The Americans were naïve, something only time would cure, time and some great hurt. As yet they were unaccustomed to intrigue on the great scale. All but that man Franklin; too bad he was dead. The old Quaker had been a master in the field, perhaps the equal of Metternich. But in general American diplomatic success had so far been largely due to their bluntness of manner and the obviousness of their motives. It was a method calculated to cause the more subtle Europeans to suspect them of hidden objectives.

It would be wise to talk to that young man again, even at the risk—he glanced at Helena—but it was no risk.

The cynics said a man was a fool to trust a woman. Perhaps. Yet he trusted her.

"My husband?"

"Yes?"

"Be careful of the Baron. I have a feeling he know why you are here, and that he has been sent here for the express purpose of defeating you."

"You could be right." He pushed his empty cup away. "Helena, I wish you would arrange for me to talk to that young man . . . in private."

She was thoughtful. "Alexander, does it strike you at all that it might be significant that he owns wheat? The only wheat available?"

He glanced at her curiously. "What do you mean?"

"I am foolish, of course. But in a place where all seem to think of seeking gold or raising cattle it is surprising to find a man growing wheat on such a scale. And such a man. Suppose he wished to make a trip to Alaska? He must know that we buy supplies both here and in Hawaii, and what better way to come to Alaska unsuspected?"

Rotcheff rubbed his chin. Helena was thinking in European terms herself. On the other hand, in the case of LaBarge it might be the right way. "Are you merely surmising?" he suggested. "Or have you something on which to base this feeling?"

"Mrs. Herndon told me her husband tried to buy wheat from Mr. LaBarge, and he would not sell. And the offered price was good."

"I see . . . of course, as he himself said, he is in the fur trade."

"To let his wheat be wasted? No, I think he had other reasons. He might be saving his wheat for a wedge."

It was easy to understand a man who wanted something. Those were the obvious ones with whom it was simplest to deal. It was the idealists who worried him. He said as much.

"What of the idealists who pursue profits along with their ideals?"

"They are worst of all," Rotcheff said. "The worst to deal with, I mean. They drive a hard bargain."

LaBarge might be just such a man, but the only fact they possessed was that he was a fur trader, and without doubt there was fur in Russian America. That was motivation enough.

"Mrs. Herndon was telling me that Jean LaBarge has an obsession: he asks qustions about Alaska."

"She told you that?"

"It's common knowledge. And there is something else. Mr. LaBarge has a very old friend with whom he corresponds, a former senator named Robert J. Walker."

The Count was pleased—pleased to have the information, pleased with his wife for discovering it, and pleased at finding here in America what seemed to be some genuine European duplicity. This innocent young man, who looked like a professional duelist and who bought furs, this young man was an associate of one of America's ablest politicians.

"You know the name?"

"Robert Walker," Rotcheff said quietly, "is one of the least appreciated of American statesmen, but one of the most able and tireless."

"Mrs. Herndon said he was no longer in office."

"My dear"—Rotcheff filled his coffee cup again—"such a man is never out of office. Once tarred with that brush they are never free of it. I've no doubt that politics is Mr. Walker's lifeblood, and his country is his life." He chuckled. "It pleases me that our young friend is not so naïve as one might suspect."

"It may be a coincidence."

"He has wheat which he will not sell to a friend, but will sell to Alaska. He has a political friend to whom he writes. He asks questions about Alaska, and he has a friend who would gladly see the Yankee flag flying over the whole continent. I think, Helena, this young man may help us. He may help us very much indeed."

9.

JACKSON AND KEARNEY STREETS met at an intersection known locally as Murderers' Corner. The Opera Comique faced Denny O'Brien's Saloon across this corner and there was but little to choose between them. The saloon was the hangout for Sydney Town hoodlums and later for those toughs known as the Barbary Coast Rangers. It was burned and rebuilt with few added features and no change in clientele. In the cellar beneath the saloon were other forms of entertainment than the usual drinking and gambling. In a pit situated in its center dogs were fought against each other or a variety of other animals. A man who had a job to be done by tough men could be sure of finding them at O'Brien's.

On the Tuesday following the meeting between La-Barge and Zinnovy, three men sat at an inconspicuous table in O'Brien's. Charley Duane, Royle Weber and the Baron Zinnovy had scarcely seated themselves when O'Brien himself appeared. Weber and Duane he knew very well, especially Duane who was a fixer, a politician, and a man with a hand in a number of illegal pies. These two were enough of a magnet; but the elegantly cut clothing of the Baron smelled of money, an odor calculated to draw immediate attention from Denny O'Brien. He went to the table rubbing his fat hands on his vest front. "Somethin' for you, gents?"

"A bottle of Madeira," Zinnovy said. He measured O'Brien with his cold eyes.

O'Brien smiled. "Yes, sir! We have just what you want. We cater to all tastes an' kinds, don't we, Mr. Duane?"

He brought the wine and the glasses himself and lingered over the decanting, for Denny O'Brien was a knowing man and these three had not come here without a reason. O'Brien had had his dealings with Duane and Weber. He was, after all, known to them both as a man who could be counted on to deliver five hundred votes at election time, provided several of the boys repeated their voting. He could also be counted upon to deliver almost anything else.

O'Brien leaned his fat hands on the table. "Girls, maybe? Got any kind you want. You just name it, and—"

"No," Duane came to the point. "We want to talk to Woolley Kearney."

O'Brien did some fast thinking. Kearney was a former Australian convict who made his boast that he could whip any man alive in a brawl. He had killed a fellow prisoner, then killed a guard in escaping, and in San Francisco he had killed at least one man publicly, with his fists. If it was Kearney they wanted it was a beating somebody was to get.

Kearney would hog all the money and O'Brien would never see a red cent of it. "Kearney?" he said doubtfully. "The man's not been seen around, last few days." He lowered his voice. "Who be the gent you want called upon? I know just the lads for it."

Weber shifted in his seat. He was sweating a little. Duane glanced at Zinnovy and the Baron shrugged. "It will be Jean LaBarge."

Zinnovy was surprised at O'Brien's sudden change of expression. The saloonkeeper drew back a little and touched a tongue to his lips. "LaBarge, is it? You'd want Wool Kearney, all right. Or maybe three of my boys."

"Three?" Zinnovy lifted an eyebrow.

"He's a skookum man, that LaBarge. Most of those about town will have no part of him, but I know three lads who'll do just the job for you, and no kickback."

Zinnovy's eyes were chilled. "If there *is* a kickback, as you phrase it," he said quietly, "I'll have you shot."

Startled, O'Brien looked at Zinnovy again. The man was not joking. "Is it a beating you'll be wanting?" he asked.

"I want him out of business for a while." Zinnovy did his own talking now. "A beating, but a broken arm or leg included. Also, I want the warehouse that holds his wheat burned to the ground."

68

O'Brien hesitated. "It will cost you one thousand dollars," he said at last.

Baron Zinnovy looked up, his gray eyes showing no interest. "You will be paid five hundred. If LaBarge gets a very severe beating, five hundred more. If the warehouse is destroyed, another five hundred."

O'Brien took a long breath. "It'll be done tomorrow night."

Zinnovy pushed a small sack across the table. It tinkled slightly as O'Brien's fat hand closed over it. "See to it," Zinnovy ordered.

Duane lingered as they started for the door, and whispered, "Don't slip up. He isn't playing games."

"When did I fail, Charley? Ask yourself that—when did I fail?"

10.

CAPTAIN HUTCHINS STOOD at the window of the small office above the warehouse. It was late afternoon and a dismal, rainy day. Now, for a few minutes, the rain had ceased and the waterfront lay wet and silent. The sea in the harbor was a dull gray and the hulls of the vessels had turned black. Here and there a few anchor lights had appeared. There were two windows in the office, and the one at which Hutchins stood, hands clasped behind his back, looked out over the edge of the dock and the bay. The other window looked across the street and up the length of the dock to where the shore curved away into distance. The office held little furniture. A roll-top desk, a swivel chair, a bank of pigeonholes on the wall, each stuffed with invoices or receipts, a black leather settee and two captain's chairs, very worn.

From the window there was nobody in sight but a tall man who stood looking out over the water, yet several times he turned and glanced back at the warehouse. Hutchins frowned. In a city practically ruled by hoodlums such a fact was not to be overlooked. Behind him, Jean was outlining his plan for the trip north.

The man at the dock edge turned again and for the first time Hutchins got a brief glimpse of his face. "Jean, do you know Freel? The fellow who hangs out with Yankee Sullivan?"

"I know him."

"What would he be doing on the dock at this hour?"

LaBarge got up and walked toward the window. Freel, one of the Sydney Ducks, was known to him as a thoroughly vicious character, figuring in a number of knifings and assaults. He stepped closer to the window and noticed a flicker of movement farther up the waterfront. After a moment he saw that two men stood in the sha-

70

dows near a darkened warehouse about a block away. "He's not wasting his time looking at sunsets. He's got something else on his mind."

"They've left us alone so far."

Jean walked back to the center of the room and drew his pistol, checking the loads. "If they start trouble, Cap, I'm taking it to them. We've been lucky so far, but if they start it—"

"That's quite an order, son."

"Coyotes run yellow in the pack. I've hunted them before."

He turned to his lists. Spare sails, heavy cable, lines. He had never done this for a ship of his own, and it was a wonderful feeling. Item by item he went down the list. The heavy gear was his own idea. Kohl had questioned the usefulness of the heavy blocks and wire rope, but Jean had been adamant. What lay before them they could guess, but there was always the unexpected, and they might need to make repairs somewhere in those strange channels to the north. He wanted to be prepared for any emergency. And if a man had enough blocks and tackle he could move the world.

The men on the dock came briefly to mind. Ben Turk and Larsen would be staying in the warehouse, and neither was a man to back up from trouble.

"It's late, Jean, and that work will keep."

"Are they still out there?"

"Yes."

The door opened and Larsen came in, followed by Ben Turk. Larsen was a rawboned Swede with thick blond hair that fell over his brow and curled over his collar at the back of his neck. His shoulders and arms were massive and blue anchors were tattooed at the base of thumb and forefinger of each hand. Ben Turk was a man of slight build, a compact and swarthy man with a black, handle-bar mustache. He was lean, alert, and dangerous. He had served on whaling ships and had made three voyages to the sealing grounds of the Pribilofs. He had trapped in Canada and Oregon.

"Where's Noble?"

"He's strutting it around Bartlett Freel, trying to egg him into a fight."

"Get him in here."

71

Briefly, he gave them their instructions. One was to keep awake at all times. Hutchins' carriage came and Jean walked to the door with him. Hutchins hesitated with a foot on the step. "Sure you won't come with me?"

"Later." LaBarge glanced at Freel who was looking unconcernedly across the bay. "I'll walk up." He deliberately spoke loud enough for Freel to hear. If Freel wanted him he wanted him to know exactly where he could be found, but if Freel followed Hutchins, LaBarge could be right behind.

There was nothing reckless about Jean LaBarge. He avoided trouble when he could, never sought out a fight until the proper moment for it. He considered the situation tactically. The men up the street, and there seemed to be two of them, were at least sixty yards away. Freel was close.

There are times when trouble cannot be avoided, and he knew that if they wanted him, they could get him. The thing to do was to choose his own ground, and he was ready now. The way to be left alone was to let them know what the alternative was.

He knew that Larsen, Turk and Noble would relish a fight. None of them had any love for Freel and his crowd, who frequently shanghaied and robbed seafaring men, but Jean did not want help. This was a situation he wanted to handle himself. He wanted it understood that he did not need help, even when it was ready to hand.

"You fellows sit tight," he told them when he was back inside. "Watch if you want to, but don't interfere. And stay inside."

"There's at least three of them out there." Turk looked at him curiously. "That Freel is bad with a knife."

LaBarge dropped his hand to the latch. Suddenly he felt very good. He felt better than he had for a long time. There was too much fear in San Francisco, too many people were afraid of the hoodlums, of their beatings, their murders, of their looting. "Just stay out of it, boys. This one's my show." He pulled the door shut after him, and stood on the dock.

The edge of the wharf was perhaps fifteen steps from the door of Hutchins & Company. And Bartlett Freel was standing over there under a dock light. A light rain was falling, a fine mistlike rain. The hour was not late but due to the clouds it was already dark. There was a faint light showing from the front window of the warehouse, and besides the light under which Freel stood, there was another light on the street corner a dozen yards away, and there was a light up the dock, perhaps a hundred yards off.

Obviously they would not attack near the warehouse where help waited, but would follow him up the street into the darkness. They would have no reason to doubt their success and little reason to expect retaliation, and certainly there was nothing to fear from the law or the corrupt political machine behind it. Since the Vigilante movement the town had shown little disposition to fight back.

Without too much reason Jean decided the attack had been instigated by Baron Zinnovy. Freel moved to the dictates of Yankee Sullivan who was a henchman and friend of Denny O'Brien, and O'Brien was a man who would arrange beatings, murders, disappearances for a price. Neither LaBarge nor Hutchins had had trouble with the hoodlums, neither had antagonized any of them, and neither had any local enemies. The attack that he could see shaping up came immediately following his trouble with Baron Zinnovy. True, there had been only a few words passed between them, but Jean's hunch was that Zinnovy had other motives. Suppose Zinnovy, for reasons of his own, did not want wheat shipped to Alaska? Or did not want Jean LaBarge taking it there.

As Jean LaBarge moved away from the building Freel turned. Up the street the two men started to move; Jean heard a foot scrape up there in the darkness.

The reading of Greek history might seem a dull occupation, but there is an axiom to be found there that suggests the military principle of "divide and conquer." It was a good thought . . . Jean started for the corner and when Freel moved to follow Jean turned quickly and faced him, his hand gripping his left lapel.

"Looking for me, Freel? The name is LaBarge. Jean LaBarge."

Freel hesitated. Why didn't those fools *hurry?* "And if I am?"

"Who sent you, Freel?"

Bartlett Freel was a lean, savage man, surly even among those who knew him best, but more intelligent than most of his kind. He had a flaring temper and he both envied and resented LaBarge. "You won't know," Freel said, "you'll never know. You been comin' it mighty big, and now—"

There was a time for words, but the other two men were coming swiftly now. LaBarge's left hand gripped his lapel lightly and when he struck he struck from that position and he stepped in with the punch. He felt Freel's nose crumple under the blow but before the man could even stagger, Jean hit him hard with his right fist.

The other men ran up. Grabbing Freel, who was badly hurt, Jean turned swiftly and threw him into their path. The nearest of the oncoming men tripped and fell and Jean kicked him in the head, and the second man, holding a knife low down in his right hand, took the moment to move in.

Jean struck swiftly with the barrel of his pistol, hastily drawn. The descending weapon caught the knife-wrist and the knife clattered on the dock, the man dropping to his knees clutching a broken wrist.

The man he kicked was on his feet now but Jean had him stopped with the gun muzzle. "Can you swim?" Jean asked pleasantly.

"Huh?"

"I hope you can," LaBarge continued. "because you're jumping in."

"I'll be damned if—!"

"Jump." LaBarge spoke conversationally. "If you can't swim, you can drown, but don't try climbing back on this dock or I'll part your hair with a bullet."

"You won't get away with this!" The man was impotent with fury. "Yankee will—!"

"Jump . . . I'll talk to Yankee."

"He'll smash yer!" The man shouted from the dock edge. "He'll blind yer! He'll bash yer bloody fyce! He'll—"

The pistol lifted and drew a line on the man's head. The water would be cold but a grave was colder still. As Jean's arm straightened the fellow jumped.

There was a splash and then the floundering of a poor swimmer. Jean LaBarge turned and walked to the others.

Freel was sitting up, trying to staunch the flow of blood from his nose. The knifeman clutched his broken wrist, moaning.

"Yankee shouldn't send boys to do a man's job," he said, and catching Freel by the coat he jerked him to his feet. Twisting him around, Jean began to go through the hoodlum's pockets.

Freel tried to pull away but Jean threatened him with the gun barrel. "You can take it standing still or lying on the dock with a split skull. Make up your mind."

"I'll stand," Freel said hoarsely.

There were several gold coins in his pockets, and the coins were Russian. Jean pocketed the lot, then went to the man with the broken wrist. "Yours, too."

"I ain't got a thing!" he protested. "They wasn't to pay me—"

"Stand up!"

Shakily, the man got to his feet. There were three gold coins in his pocket. The man began to curse bitterly.

"You didn't do the job," LaBarge told them. "I'll return these to Yankee."

"I wish you would!" Freel's voice was bitter. "I just wish you had the guts."

That area of San Francisco of the 1850's and 60's that lay back of Clark's Point was a hellhole of dives and brothels. Robbery was too frequent to warrant mention, and murder a nightly occurrence. To walk that area in safety one must be a pimp, a prostitute, or a thug, and along such streets as Pacific, Jackson, Washington, Davis, Drum, Front, Battery and East (the Embarcadero) moved some of the choicest rascals unhung. The shanghaiing of sailors was a major industry, engaged in by at least twenty gangs who worked in close association with keepers of brothels and cheap saloons.

Another closely allied gang was that which specialized in claim jumping within the city. The absent owner of a lot might return to find a thug in possession who enforced his point of possession with a pistol. Litigation was a long-drawn-out affair and more often than not decided in favor of the claim jumper. All of this Jean LaBarge knew and like most residents accepted it as part and parcel of a booming seaport with gold in the back country. Trouble had so far avoided him and he had avoided trouble.

Freel and his men had acted, without doubt, as directed by Yankee Sullivan. Now the lads of Sydney Town must be taught, once and for all, that action against Hutchins or himself would meet with immediate reprisal. One sign of weakness and they would be stripped of all they possessed. He could move against Denny O'Brien, but such a move would not be nearly so effective as against Sullivan himself.

Yankee Sullivan, born James Ambrose, in County Cork, Ireland, had grown up in the slums of East London. As a hard-fisted young Irishman in Whitechapel he won a reputation by defeating Jim Sykes, Tom Brady and a man named Sharpless in brutal bare-knuckle prize-ring battles. On a brief trip to the United States he defeated Pat Connor, then returned to England to whip the great Hammer Lane in nineteen grueling rounds. After a term in Australia as a convicted criminal he escaped and appeared in New York where he whipped Vic Hammond in fifteen minutes, fought his great fight with Bill Secor and beat him in sixty-seven rounds at Staten Island. He won four other fights and then was soundly beaten in his own saloon by Tom Hyer, son of a former heavyweight champion. However, this was a rough-and-tumble brawl, no more, and the unsatisfied Sullivan met Tom Hyer in a ring at Rock Point, Maryland, for ten thousand dollars as a side bet, and lost again. Later, a losing fight with John Morrissey, soon to be heavyweight champion, broke up in a riot after thirty-seven rounds.

Throughout this period Sullivan had been a criminal and an associate of criminals. In Sydney Town he carried an authority backed by his own malletlike fists and his former Limehouse and Whitechapel associates. Whatever else he was, Yankee Sullivan was a first-class fighting man. Powerful, brutal, and without either scruples or mercy, there was no man in Sydney Town more influential than he. He was a known center of criminal activity.

Jean LaBarge had no doubts that the job he had set for himself would involve him in the most brutal fight he had known, yet the fighting of fur traders' rendezvous had been the dirtiest kind of rough-and-tumble fighting.

Opening the door of the warehouse, he stuck his head inside. "Slip a couple of pistols under your jacket and come along, Ben. We've a job to do."

Turk glanced at the men on the dock. "I'd say a job had been done. Will it take more?"

Denny O'Brien's was in full swing. At the bar were a dozen of the Sydney Town toughs, and among them Jean could see the massive shoulders and bull neck of Yankee Sullivan. He looked as invulnerable as a battleship. Also at the bar, talking to a sour-faced man in a stained canvas jacket, was Barney Kohl.

Ben Turk stopped beside the door and leaned against the jamb, a cigarette between his lips. A music box was jangling and somebody in a corner was singing an old sea chantey in a loud, off-key voice.

Jean LaBarge walked across the room and took Yankee Sullivan by the shoulder and spun him around. Yankee threw up a hand an instant too late. Jean hit him.

The blow was unexpected, and it had been years since anyone had tried to hit him outside a prize ring. He was stunned by that quite as much as by the punch. The man facing him was big, lean and tough-looking, his black eyes blazing. The blow slammed Sullivan against the bar and before he could get his hands up, LaBarge knocked him down.

In an instant they were surrounded by a milling, shouting mob. Jean drew back and gave Sullivan a chance to get up. It was foolish to give the man any break at all, and he would get none. At that instant there was a pistol shot.

Ben Turk had a gun in either hand and he was smiling. A thin thread of smoke lifted from the left-hand gun. "Let 'em fight," he said. "If anybody interferes or gets between the fighters an' me, I'll kill him."

Sullivan got up slowly. He had been hit, and hit hard, harder than John Morrissey had hit him, harder than Tom Hyer. The man before him looked like a rough evening. Yet Yankee had whipped some tough men. He

77

came up fast and went in, punching with both hands. Shorter than Jean, he was wider and thicker, and aside from his prize-ring skill he was a brutal barroom fighter.

As Sullivan attacked, Jean met him with a left to the mouth, and then struck again as Sullivan went under his left and hooked viciously to his ribs. They clinched and Sullivan back-heeled him to the floor, trying to fall on him and drive his knees into his belly. Jean rolled away and got swiftly to his feet and met Sullivan as he came in. The blow landed hard and Jean saw Sullivan go white around the eyes. Sullivan lunged, landed a glancing blow and Jean went under him, throwing Sullivan over his head to the floor.

This had won many a fight at Pierre's Hole but the Irishman had the agility of a boy. He had tucked his head under and taken the fall on his shoulder.

With blood streaking Sullivan's face they fought for several minutes, smashing, kneeing, gouging. Both men went down but neither could be kept down. Yankee's lips were puffy from stabs to the mouth and Jean had a swelling on his cheekbone half as large as an egg. He felt better. He could never really fight until he had been hit hard, and now he walked in, finding he could punch a little faster than Yankee. He feinted a side step and smashed the Irishman in the mouth with a right.

There was little sound but the heavy breathing of the fighting men, the dull smack of blows and an occasional grunt. For the first time the Sydney toughs were seeing their hero in a fight he might not win. There was something grim and terrible about LaBarge. Yet it was grueling and bitter. LaBarge's years of living in the forest and on ships stood him well now. He absorbed the punishment that came his way, hooked and smashed and heeled. Sullivan, boring in, thought he saw a good chance at Jean's chin and put all he had into a right-hand.

Something exploded in his mid-section and he grunted with pain as his knees buckled. Setting himself, LaBarge swung both hands at Sullivan's unprotected face. Sullivan swung a hand to wipe the blood from his face and Jean caught the wrist and with his other hand, grabbed Sullivan's wide leather belt. He bent one knee, turning slightly, then threw Sullivan bodily into the crowd. The fighter lit on his face and skidded with a jolt against the wall.

LaBarge's shirt was torn, revealing the powerful muscles of his arms and chest. He wiped a smear of sweat and blood from his face.

"I wanted no trouble," he said, "and he sent trouble to me." Jean LaBarge lifted a hand. "Ben!"

Turk slid a pistol behind his belt and tossed a bowie knife. Jean caught it in mid-air and faced the crowd. "Anybody else? I'll open any of you lads to the brisket if you want to back the Yankee's fight."

Nobody spoke. Jean held the knife low, cutting edge up. Somebody sighed and shifted his feet and LaBarge turned to Denny O'Brien. The saloonkeeper had never seen steel that looked so sharp, and he was a man who had seen many knives, and seen them used.

"I've a thought, Denny O'Brien, that you've taken some Russian money. Don't ever spend it, Denny, for I'll hear of it and have your heart out and lying on your own bar. You hear me, Denny?"

O'Brien swallowed, muttering something inaudible. Jean flipped the point of his knife . . . once, twice. Each move slashed a suspender and O'Brien's trousers fell around his boots, yet he did not move, breathing hoarsely, knees trembling, his face yellow-sick. Sweat stood on his brow and cheeks, it dripped from his fat chin.

Jean continued to smile, a wolfish smile that turned O'Brien's insides to jelly. With flick after flick of the knife he took the buttons from O'Brien's waistcoat. It was a moment long-treasured on the coast, a story told many times in Sydney Town, and in the fo'c'sles of many a ship outward bound. It was a story men loved to hear, of the click of falling buttons and the sweat dripping from O'Brien's fat jowls.

"And Denny," LaBarge warned, "tell Charley Duane to be careful. Tell him if he crosses me again he'll be getting his tail in a crack. You hear me, Denny? You tell him that."

11.

BY NOON of the following day the story of the battle at O'Brien's was being repeated in excited whispers in every boudoir on Rincon Hill, where the name of Jean La-Barge was well known in other fields of endeavor. At the Merchant's Exchange they could talk of nothing else, and the click of those falling vest buttons was heard wherever even two people happened to meet.

Count Rotcheff even found a brief reference to the fight in his *Alta Californian*. "Your friend LaBarge seems to possess a variety of talents," he suggested.

Helena looked up quickly. "The maid told me while I was having my bath." She paused. "She also told me something else. There is a rumor the original attack was paid for by a Russian."

Rotcheff rustled his paper angrily. "The man's a fool! Why would he get involved at a time like this?"

Helena put down her cup. "Do you actually believe he would do something of that kind merely because he was angry?"

"You think it was done because LaBarge was to sell us wheat? But why would he do that? The wheat was for the Company."

"And we both know he is interested in a new charter, for another company."

He was too trusting—though not of foreign diplomats, only of his own countrymen. It was a fault from which all the Russian liberals suffered. Alexander knew how to cope with duplicity, but the Renaissance type of violence used by Paul Zinnovy was beyond the realm of his consideration; this Helena told herself. Her husband was a gentle man, and Paul Zinnovy was cold, efficient, deadly.

"Another thing," she warned, "you must yourself be

careful. Paul wants two things: to get a charter for the new company and to return to St. Petersburg with a brilliant coup behind him. You stand in the way of both goals." She put her hand on his. "Alexander, you must be very careful! Your report can ruin him, and he knows it!"

Rotcheff shook his head. "You exaggerate, my dear. He would not dare use violence against anyone as close to the Czar as I am."

"You are a thousand miles or more from any Czarist official, you are many thousands of miles from St. Petersburg. Who is to know what happens out here?"

Somehow the idea had not occurred to him, yet instantly he saw that she was correct. He was far from the capital and no longer young, and accidents could be arranged. If he were murdered out here it would be months before the Czar even heard of it, and years before any investigation could be conducted to a conclusion. For the first time he was uneasy, less for himself than for Helena.

"Why, Alexander, was Paul Zinnovy sent here? Stop for a moment and think of that."

"He was in trouble"—Rotcheff was worried now—"and of course, he is a capable officer."

"Do you remember Paul's last duel? Rodion announced he was going to demand an investigation into some of the Company affairs, and three days before he was to appear before the Czar he was challenged to a duel by Zinnovy over some fancied slight. And Rodion was killed."

Rotcheff was silent. There was much to be said for Helena's interpretation of the situation although he was hesitant to admit that Paul Zinnovy might have been sent out for the express purpose of removing him. Three groups were involved in the affairs of Russian America. The Grand Duke's party, of which he was one, wanted to sell the territory of Alaska to the United States, if they could be induced to buy. The Russian American Company were bleeding the Indians white to pay dividends, but they were also bleeding their own stockholders and the government as well. The third group, of whom some were stockholders in the present company, wished to secure the lucrative charter for their

81

own group who were establishing a new company with even greater dividends in prospect.

Suppose he were murdered by a drunken native? Or fell overboard in a storm? Or was suddenly taken ill? Who but Zinnovy would prepare the report? Even at Sitka, it would be Rudakof, who would do what Paul Zinnovy told him.

Count Rotcheff knew that if the investigation he was conducting brought out the evidence the liberal party believed it would, if it substantiated the complaints the government had received from parties in or visiting Russian America, then the Company's charter would not be renewed nor would another be granted.

"Helena," he said abruptly, "I believe you should return to St. Petersburg. If the situation is as serious as you believe, this is no place for you."

"On the contrary, it is all the more reason I should be with you." She glanced over her teacup. "Have you thought of Jean LaBarge? He might help us."

In his rooms, Jean sat over the books spread out on the table before him. He ran a finger over a small map, searching for Kootznahoo Inlet. He had checked all the reports of furs bought in San Francisco in the last four months and nothing had come from Kootznahoo. He listed it as a likely call, then added four more names to the list.

This first trip must be fast. The places he visited must be near the accepted route but where he could lie at anchor in concealment, and every stopping place must have more than one opening so that if discovered he could get out fast.

The deal for the schooner had been consummated, the rifles, ammunition and trade goods had been loaded. Kohl wasted no time, and the schooner was a tight, ship-shape craft, easily handled and loaded. She would carry but one gun, and despite her strength and capacity she was a "light" ship with none of the bulky, overweight gear that characterized so many ships.

The sour-faced man who had been in the saloon at the time of the Sullivan fight appeared and was signed on as second mate, and the last two members of the crew were signed. Gant was a broad-built man, and Boyar was tall, stooped in the shoulders, and spoke fluent Russian.

Kohl looked at him without favor. "You a Russky?"

"I'm a Pole. But I worked for the Company."

Kohl turned to Jean. "Cap'n, you sure you want this man?"

LaBarge turned. "Take off your shirt, Shin."

Shin Boyar shucked off his shirt and turned his back for Kohl and Captain Hutchins to see. Scars lay like livid bands across his back, scars like twisted cords of white. Kohl glanced at them, then at Boyar's face.

"I served in the Navy under Zinnovy. That was ten years ago." The tall man pulled on his shirt. "I have a good memory, sir, a very good memory."

"We can use you," Kohl said.

"After that I was *promyshleniki* for the Company, and I smuggled gold out of Siberia to China for a while. I was thrown into prison, but escaped."

"No argument," Kohl said. "You'll do."

"After Monday," LaBarge told Kohl, "I want the crew kept aboard. No more than two men ashore at any time, and ready to sail at a moment's notice. When a man goes ashore, you know where he'll be, just which place. No last-minute delays."

When all were gone he concealed his invoices under a board behind a bookshelf. Then, finally, he wrote one of his rare letters to Rob Walker. He was, he told Rob, going to Alaska himself. When he came back—

Behind him there was a slight rustle. An envelope had been slipped beneath his door.

He ripped it open. From the feminine handwriting and perfume he knew at once who it must be.

Can you come to see us? It is important.
Helena

"Us" she wrote. She wanted him to come and see them both, but nonetheless, it was signed Helena.

He got up and walked to the window. Outside the street was empty and still. It was now Friday, and by Monday he wanted to be at sea, sailing north, and the master of his own ship To Alaska . . . to Sitka.

They would be leaving soon, and he might even see them there.

He remembered how Helena had looked that first day, flustered, mussed, and angry. He grinned at the thought. And then how prim, with her lifted chin, her too precise English.

She was charming, and so lovely, and he was in love with her and it would do him no good at all. She was married, and to a good man, a man of her own kind, her own rank.

He was a fool. . . .

But on Monday there would be the sea, the wind and spray in his face, and beyond there the places where nobody would mind, and where at night in the lonely hours, watching the seas roll aft, he could remember or forget.

12.

THE TAWNY SLOPE of the hill lay before them, dull gold in the afternoon sun, and beyond the hill the blue Pacific waters rolled to the horizon. When the two riders reached the trail's end high above the waters, Jean drew rein and relaxed in the saddle.

It was their second ride in two days, and might be their last. When riding Jean wore a tight-fitting Spanish-style jacket of buckskin, fringed in the Indian manner. It molded itself against his wide shoulders and was, Helena decided, most becoming.

"You ride like a vaquero," she said.

He pushed his flat-crowned Spanish sombrero back on his head and hooked a knee around the saddle horn. Filling his pipe, he watched her profile against the sky. "What about the plans for Alaska?"

"It is really the Baron who interests you, isn't it?"

"Of course. But when Count Rotcheff leaves, you will leave."

"We have more reason to fear the Baron than you, Jean. He is our enemy also."

"But you are the niece of the Czar!"

"You know what they say? 'God's in His heaven and the Czar is far away.' "

Far out at sea a windjammer was beating in toward the Golden Gate, and they watched it for several minutes without speaking. There was intimacy in the silence, and it was such moments they had come to treasure above all else. There was no need to use words to build a fence about their emotions; during those long silences the barriers were down and something within each of them reached out to the other.

"You see, Jean, any investigation of what happens in Russian America would require a great deal of time. And any investigator they might send from Siberia would be corrupt, and whoever came from St. Petersburg would have to ask questions of the very people who have most to conceal. Paul has power even in St. Petersburg, Jean. Actually, he was sent out here because he was in trouble, but it is temporary only, a mild punishment, a means of keeping him out of the way for the time being. I believe he was sent here for other reasons as well. I believe his friends decided to accomplish two objectives with the one move. Get Paul Zinnovy out of the way of more severe punishment, but also place him where he could be of use to them."

She paused. "You know, in Russia he is considered very dangerous. He has killed several men in duels. And sometimes these duels are not exactly what they seem. Often it is not a case of offended honor but simply that some powerful person wishes to be rid of a man."

"Suppose," Jean suggested tentatively, "the charter is not renewed, nor another granted. What will become of Alaska then?"

"Who knows? It might be sold, but certainly not to England. Perhaps to the United States."

Jean lit his pipe, which had gone out. "I suppose it could be done if the negotiations were handled carefully. But it wouldn't be easy. There are a lot of Americans who think that Alaska's only a wasteland, not worth a penny."

The sailing ship was closer now, making slow time of it against the strong current and a wind that helped little. They watched the ship while the afternoon trailed away like distant smoke, fading slowly. Soon it would be dusk.

"You've never married, Jean? I wonder why?"

He swung his horse a little. "For a long time I couldn't find a girl I wanted, and when I did find her she was married to another man."

"But there must be others, Jean. You're very attractive, you know."

"Oh, I've known girls . . . here and there."

"You would lose your freedom, and a man like you should be free, free to fly far and high, like an eagle. A wife would tie you down, she would hold you."

"Maybe. It might not even be so bad. I've been alone

all my life, never known a real home. If you want to find a man who will love his home, find a man who never had one."

"I should think a man would always long for freedom. It is hard, I'd think, for a man who has known freedom to give it up."

He watched the ship. "Hard? With the right woman most men will settle down easy enough. Oh, sure! They look at the geese flying south, or maybe some night their eyes will open into the darkness as they lie in bed beside their wives, and they'll lie awake in the darkness and remember how native drums sounded, or the surf along a rocky shore, or how the bells ring from the temples . . . but they stay where they are."

"Why?"

The ship was taking in sail now, approaching the passage gingerly, for many a fine ship had been wrecked in the Golden Gate.

"Because they've . . . accepted their destiny, I suppose. They might think about the great world outside, but they wouldn't trade it for home."

"Not you . . . I believe you would go."

"I'd be the easiest of all, Helena. I've never known a home, so even the faults would seem virtues to me. As for love, who doesn't want it? To love and be loved in return?"

"I think, Jean, you will find what you want."

"Will I, Helena?"

The sea was darker now. The last of the color was deepening reluctantly into darkness.

"We'd best be going back."

Swinging their horses they put the sea behind them. Jean's gelding tugged at the bit, eager to be running. Helena's mare started and then both horses were running. Over the tawny hillside, still faintly tinged by rose from the sun that had set, a hill that changed as their horses ran to an inverted bowl of burnished copper against which drummed the racing hoofs. Laughing together, they cantered down the long hill and something trailed off behind them like whispered laughter. Abruptly, as they rounded a bend, the city lay below them and a column of smoke lifted from the waterfront. Jean drew up sharply, standing in the stirrups.

"It's my wheat, Helena," he said. "They're burning my wheat. The warehouse is going and everything in it."

He touched the spurs to his horse. The gelding left the ground in a tremendous leap, and with Helena beside him they raced neck and neck down into the city and through the empty streets. Their hoofbeats echoed from the false-fronted buildings and thundered in the empty channels of the town, stripped of people by the demands of the fire.

Helena rode magnificently. Rounding a corner he caught the glow of reflected flames on her flushed cheeks and parted lips, and then they were running their horses down another chasm between buildings. As they thundered out upon the dock he knew this must have been a planned effort to destroy the wheat.

Squads of men with buckets were wetting down the buildings around, and two long bucket brigades were passing water from the bay to the fire. One engine was working its pump near the wharf, another in the street behind the warehouse, yet he saw at once the building was doomed.

Swinging down from the foam-flecked horse, he pushed through the crowd and saw Captain Hutchins shouting to Ben Turk above the crackle of flames. Close by, Larsen and Noble were busy with a bucket brigade.

"Anybody in there?"

"No . . . thank God!"

The roar of flames all but drowned the reply, and Jean watched his wheat go up in flames, the black smoke shutting out the stars and sending the dark banners of its anger streaking across the bay, shrouding the silent ship in sudden clouds, then whisking away to leave the ship standing, amazed at the sight before it.

There was no wind. Had there been wind the whole of the waterfront would have gone, and nothing could have saved Sydney Town or any part of the city back of Clark's Point. Yet no wind blew, and there was only the crackling flames beating their great red palms together above the bay's black water.

His first impulse was to find Zinnovy for a showdown, but this would lead to nothing and might close all doors to Russian America. Wheat was the answer. The importation of wheat into Sitka was obviously something Zinnovy wished to prevent, but it was also his own open sesame to the northern fur trade. Staring at the fire, he began to think.

Sutter had grown wheat but had none now. How about Oregon? Many farmers had settled in those fertile valleys and they would need bread. Despite its proximity less news reached California from Oregon than from Hawaii; still there was a chance. The settlers of Oregon were a more substantial lot than most Californians. There would be wheat there, there had to be wheat.

Swiftly, he pushed through the crowd, searching for Barney Kohl. When he found him Kohl was standing with the new second mate. "Tomorrow night," Jean said. "You sail tomorrow night."

"Without a cargo?"

"Fitzpatrick has some goods for Portland and has been looking for a vessel for a month. I don't care how you do it, but be loaded and under way by five tomorrow afternoon."

"If you say so," Kohl said. "Damn it, man. I was ready for Alaska. I was all ready."

"You'll go . . but meet me in Portland first."

Oregon . . . Jean watched the wall of the warehouse fall in, saw the flames and the smoke puff up, saw the great smoldering ball of his wheat. Sparks showered upward. No need to think of that. What was done was done.

He went swiftly to his horse and swung into the saddle. "Helena"—he turned the gelding—"I'm taking you home. Tell Count Rotcheff he'll have his wheat in Sitka as promised. Tell him not to worry."

"But *how?*"

"Leave that to me." They were walking their horses away from the fire. "I wish I knew I'd see you again. I wish—"

"So do I," she said simply. "Oh, Jean! I do, I do!"

At the door of the house on Rincon Hill he helped her from the saddle and watched the boy lead the horse away. For a moment they stood together before the empty eyes of the dark building. He could hear her breathing, smell of the faint perfume she wore and which he would never forget. Together they looked back at the red glow of the dying fire. "It's been a good day," he said at last, "a good, good day."

"Even with that?" she gestured.

"Even with that."

He gathered the reins. If he looked into her eyes he knew he would take her into his arms, so hastily he stepped into the saddle. She took his hand briefly. "What is it they say here, Jean? *Vaya con dios?*" He felt the quick pressure of her fingers before she released them. "I say it now, Jean. Go with God. Go with God, Jean."

At his rooms he paused only a moment, throwing things into his saddlebags, packing some small bags of gold, filling a money belt. He took his rifle and his spare pistol, then for a long moment he stared at the map. He would not see that map for a long time.

There was a rush of feet on the stairs. Hand on his gun, he swung wide the door. It was Ben Turk.

"I knew it!" Ben was ready for the trail. "You're riding! I'm comin' along."

"I'll travel faster alone. You go to the schooner." He stuffed extra ammunition into the saddlebags.

"Nothing doing. I ride along or I quit. There's nowhere you can go that I can't."

Turk was a good man, a very good man, but . . . "All right. We leave our horses at the river landing. We're taking the first boat for Sacramento, and if you can't ride a thousand miles you'd best head for the schooner."

Ben Turk stared at him. "Mister LaBarge . . . Cap'n, you . . . you ain't goin' to ride to *Portland?*"

"It worries you?"

"There ain't no trail, Cap'n! The Modocs will kill a man as fast as look at him! That's outlaw country. Why, man—I'm comin' with you!"

"You're inviting yourself. You're a damn fool."

"Why, now." Ben chuckled. "I just figure we're a couple of damn fools."

The riverboat was already moving when they raced their horses onto the dock. Jean swung his horse alongside and tossed his saddlebags. Then, rifle in hand, he sprang for the boat's deck and lit, sprawling.

It was a bare four feet of jump, but both horse and boat were moving. Ben Turk hit the bulwark, caught it with his hands and swung himself over to the deck. Together they looked back. The fire was only a sullen red glow now.

McCellan yelled at them from the pilothouse. "Law after you, is it? I been expectin' it for years!"

"Shut up!" Jean yelled genially. "Get a move on this crate! I've business in Knight's Landing!"

"Turn in," he yelled. "I'll call you!"

The last thing Jean LaBarge recalled as sleep took possession was the pressure of Helena's hand, the expression on her face. He remembered how she had ridden beside him through the dark streets, how she had waited to be with him after he realized his wheat was destroyed, his hopes ruined. She had waited for him as a man's woman would, only she was another man's woman.

He opened his eyes. "Don't forget, Mac. Knight's Landing."

13.

A ROUGH HAND on his shoulder awakened him. Mac's florid face and blond hande-bar mustache bent over him. "Rise an' shine, boy. We're comin' up to the Landing now."

Ben was already on his feet rubbing the sleep from his eyes. Through the murky light the Landing was visible, right ahead.

Jean LaBarge got to his feet and hitched his gun belt into position on his lean hips, then threw the saddle-bags over his shoulder and took up his rifle. McClellan peered over his shoulder at him. "I hope you don't need those guns, boy."

"We'll have to be lucky."

If anyone had ridden the route they were to follow La Barge was unaware of it. There would be settlers here and there and a trail of sorts, but it would be sheer luck if they got through without fighting.

Thirty minutes later they rode out of Knight's Landing headed north. The day was bright and clear, the horses eager. A few hours from now they would be less eager, Jean reflected, yet the horses proved gamer than he expected and it was almost midnight when they sighted a fire ahead of them. As was the custom of the country they drew up and hailed before approaching.

A shadow moved but for an instant there was silence, then a cautious voice called, "What do you want?"

"Name's LaBarge. We're hunting a couple of fast horses. Can you help us?"

Walking their horses into the firelight they waited. There was a wagon here, and a small camp, such a camp and wagon no outlaw would be expected to have. Six head of mules were in sight and some good-looking saddle stock.

Two men, both armed and spread wide apart, emerged from the shadows. At the edge of the brush LaBarge could see two women who no doubt believed themselves concealed in shadows.

"You ridin' from the law?"

"No." LaBarge got down on the far side of his horse. A man could shoot better from the ground and there was no telling what might happen. "But we need horses mighty bad."

The bearded man was a thin, high-shouldered fellow in torn shirt and homespun jeans, but he looked like a man who could use the rifle he carried. He sized up their horses with shrewd, appraising eyes. "Reckon I'll swap. You got boot to offer?"

"Look, friend," Jean smiled, "we want horses, but not that bad. I'll trade our horses for that Roman-nosed buckskin and the gray. You can throw in a couple of sandwiches and some coffee."

The man glanced at the horses, both fine animals. "I reckon it's a trade. Sal"—he looked toward the woods —"fetch these men some supper."

While Ben switched saddles, Jean faced the fire and the two men. The bearded man had been studying Jean's expensive boots and drawing conclusions. The boy could be no more than half-witted and the women were hard-faced.

The coffee was black as midnight and scalding hot, and the sandwiches were slabs of bread inclosing hunks of beef.

"Anbody comes along," the man suggested slyly, "what should I say?"

Jean grinned at him. "Tell 'em you saw two men nine feet tall riding north with fire in their eyes. Or tell 'em whatever you want. If anybody was chasin' us, we'd stop an' wait for the fun, wouldn't we, Ben?"

"Those who know us well enough to come after us," Ben agreed, "are too smart to try."

Ten hours out of Sacramento, they rode into Red Bluff, and ten minutes later rode out again, their extra saddlebags stuffed with food. Twenty-five miles farther they stopped at a lonely cabin for coffee and when they rode out they were astride two paint Indian ponies.

The air was cool and damp. Twice they glimpsed

campfires but their horses seemed no more tired than at the start and they pushed on farther into the night. Once a dog rushed out to bark, amazed and angry that anybody should be moving at all. The night air, cool as a freshwater lake, washed them as they dipped into a hollow of the hills, and then for twenty miles they saw no one, nor any human sound save their own.

At daylight, for forty dollars, Jean swapped for a black stallion with three white stockings and a trim bay gelding. The stallion had an edge on his temper but distance robbed him of his urge for trouble.

They were climbing steadily through country where they saw few houses and no settlements. Before them and on their right was Mount Shasta, sending chill winds down across the low country, winds that blew off the white, white snows of her peak.

This was Modoc country and they rode with rifles across their saddlebows. The Modocs had been slave traders among the Indians long before the coming of the white man. At nightfall they reached Tower House, beyond which point there was no road and little trail. At daybreak, on fresh horses, they were moving again. Glancing back, when farther along the trail, Jean saw a rider at the edge of the trees, and later after they had crossed a clearing, he watched long enough to see three riders come out of the trees, then swing back under cover.

"Look alive, Ben. Trouble coming up behind."

A dim trail suddenly turned into the trees, a trail that by its direction might intersect with their own somewhere beyond the valley. They turned off, then obliterated their tracks as best they could in the few minutes they could afford and rode down through the forest. When their path turned off in a wrong direction they cut through the trees until they reached the main north-south trail once more.

At Callahan's they switched horses again, and Jean found himself with a tough line-back dun. Taking the old Applegate wagon road, they reached the mining village of Yreka just seventy hours of Knight's Landing.

Putting their horses up at the livery stable, Ben nudged Jean. "Look," he said, low-voiced.

Two men were riding into town on blown horses, one wearing a short buffalo coat they remembered as worn by one of the men seen behind them on the trail. As they watched the third man rode into town and the three went along the street, examining all the horses.

Jean led the way into the saloon and they stood at the bar, cutting the dust from their throats and some of the chill from their bodies for the first time on the trip. At a casual question from the bartender, Jean explained, "Riding north, buying wheat for a ship that will meet us at Portland, and there are three men following us, hunting trouble."

A man in a dark suit standing near them, backed off. "Not my fight," he said.

Taking his drink, Jean motioned to Turk and they crossed to a table and sat down, facing the door. The bartender brought steaming white cups filled with coffee and, of all things, napkins. Jean slid his Navy pistol from his belt and laid it under his napkin. The other gun was in plain sight in his holster.

When the three men pushed through the door they glanced sharply at LaBarge and Turk, then walked to the bar. The three were obviously thieves, trailing them to rob and murder. No honest man ducked off a trail as they had. After a quick drink they turned and started out.

"You in the buffalo coat!"

The three stopped abruptly at Jean's call and turned slowly, spreading out a little as they turned. They could see the gun in LaBarge's holster. Ben's gun was belted high and out of view.

The last man in wore a fur cap, the one in the buffalo coat had a thin, scarred face. The third was short with a wide, expressionless face. "You talkin' to us?" he asked.

"You followed us out of Scott Valley, and you followed us into town. Now get this. If we see you anywhere close to us again, we'll kill you."

"G'wan!" he said irritably. "You ain't seen nobody! We ain't even goin' your way."

"How come you know which way we're going? Look, when I see men dodging in and out of the brush on my back trail I get suspicious, and when I get suspicious, I get irritable, and when I get irritable I'm liable to start shooting, so just to avoid trouble, stick around town a few days."

"We'll go where we like!" The man in the fur cap was growing red in the face. "We wasn't dodgin' in no bush, either!"

Jean smiled pleasantly. "And I say you're a liar!"

The man's face seemed to swell. "By God!" he shouted. "You can't call me a liar!"

"I just did," Jean replied coolly. He was determined to bring the matter to an issue now, on ground of his own choosing. "Furthermore, you're a couple of thieves." He took a wild gamble. "As for you," he looked right at the man in the fur cap, "you stole that red horse you're riding at Callahan's."

The man in the fur cap was a coward, but he could see Jean with a cup of coffee in his right, hand, and Jean knew the instant he started to reach for his gun.

"You called me a liar!" he shouted. "And by the Lord—!"

The gun cleared leather as Jean shot. He fired with his left hand, from under the table. The man jerked sharply with the impact of the bullet and dropped his gun. He fell, rolling over on his side with his knees drawn up.

Ben Turk was on his feet, watching the man in the buffalo coat.

Jean gestured at the third man. "Take your hand off that gun. I never like to kill more than one man while I'm eating."

The fat man seemed about to speak but Jean interrupted. "Bad company for you, mister. They'll get you into trouble."

"I guess you're right."

The wounded man was cursing now, in a low, monotonous voice. Gingerly, the others picked him up and helped him from the room.

At the bar the man in the dark suit turned to face them. "That was mighty cool," he said to Jean. "I don't know whether I like it or not."

"I don't like dry-gulchers trailing me."

"We don't know they were dry-gulchers."

"You'll have to take my word for it, and if you have any thinking to do, do it quietly. I'm hungry."

At the bar there was subdued muttering and glances cast in their direction. More men drifted into the bar, but a difference of opinion was obvious. Jean knew there would be no chance to sleep here now. They must ride, and at once.

The man in the dark suit turned on them. "You two stay in town until we decide what to do about this, you hear?"

LaBarge got to his feet. "Listen to me, mister. You said before this wasn't your fight, so don't make it yours. Those men were trailing us to rob us, and if any of you want to keep us here, you just stand out in the street. In ten minutes we'll be riding out with our rifles across our saddlebows."

He paused, letting it sink in. "And, mister, if you feel lucky, you just try stopping us."

Ten minutes later, mounted on a horse loaned him by Charley Brastow of the stage company, Jean LaBarge rode out of town with Ben Turk beside him. The man in the dark suit stood on the steps of the saloon chewing on a cigar, several men around him, but he made no move.

"I seen them come in," Brastow had said, "an' I can smell a bad one further'n most. They sized up your horses and asked where you went."

He looked over their horses. "I'll credit you with fifty apiece for the horses and you can leave mine at Johnson's Camp on Hungry Creek. Tell him you're to have the two grays."

Johnson met them at the corral as they rode up. He was a tall man with no chin and he came from his clumsily built log cabin on the run.

"Get the grays for us, will you? Brastow said we were to have them. We're riding on to Portland."

Johnson's Adam's apple bobbed against his frayed collar. "That's crazy, stranger! Pure dee crazy! Them Modocs killed a trapper up the crick yestiddy, and burned a couple of farms! Mister, you two wouldn't have a chance against 'em!"

Jean took a rope from the corral post and shook out a loop. One of the grays shied but he swung his loop and made an easy catch. Both were magnificent horses, and

97

as he roped them, Ben stripped their gear from the others. Still protesting, Johnson watched them mount up and ride off.

Both men were dead tired. Their plan to sleep in Yreka had been blasted by impending trouble. Jean's eyelids felt thick and heavy, and he rode as did Ben, in a sort of stupor.

Hours later they were walking their horses along Bear Creek bottom when a bullet struck water ahead of them and whined away into the brush. Glancing around they saw five Modocs come out of the trees on their right rear, and fan out as they came down the meadow at a dead run, whooping shrilly.

"Make the first one count, Ben." Jean lifted his rifle and looked down the barrel. He was wide awake now. He took a long breath, let it out easy and tightened his finger on the trigger. The rifle jumped in his hands and the foremost Modoc fell face forward from his running horse. The report of Ben's rifle was only an instant behind his own, and a horse fell, spilling its rider.

Both men were using the Porter Percussion Turret rifle, .44 caliber, firing nine shots. Steadying himself, Jean fired twice more and saw Ben's second man swing away, clinging to his horse with only a mane-hold, his body slumped far forward. The Modocs drew off, two men gone, another wounded, and shaded their eyes after Jean and Ben Turk. Accustomed as they were only to single-shot rifles, the burst of firing was too much for them.

At Jacksonville they stopped for coffee and sandwiches, and an hour farther along they mounted a tree-covered knoll and caught an hour's sleep, trusting the horses to awaken them if Indians approached. Twice more they exchanged horses, giving up the grays with reluctance, knowing such horses were rare. They passed the place called Jump-Off Joe, and later, crossing Cow Creek, they saw more Indian signs. At Joe Knott's Tavern they exchanged horses again. After a meal and a short rest they pushed on.

An hour out of Knott's it began to rain and with less than two hundred miles to go they spotted a cabin, barn, and corrals. Beyond was some forty acres of stubble. They rode toward the cabin, hallooing their presence.

A man with yellow side-whiskers stood in the door, rifle in hand. "Light an' set, strangers," he invited, "you're the first folks we seen in two weeks."

"Modocs are raiding," Jean explained, then jerked his head to indicate the stubble. "What was that . . . wheat?"

"Uh-huh."

"I'll buy it. How much have you?"

"Done sold it, mister. Feller name of Bonwit from Oregon City bought wheat all through here. Why, he must have upward of two thousand bushels headed for the Willamette."

A meal and thirty minutes later they stepped into the saddle. Bonwit of Oregon City was the man to see.

He was a stocky man in a store-bought suit and a cigar clamped in his hard mouth. His face was wide, his hair sparse and rumpled. He rolled his dead cigar in his jaws and spat into a brass spittoon. "I'll sell," he said flatly, "for cash!"

"I'll take two thousand bushels, delivered in Portland," LaBarge said, and began counting out the gold.

Bonwit rolled his cigar again and shot a glance at La-Barge from astonished eyes. "You carried that over the trail . . . just you two?"

"Part of the way we had Modocs with us."

They sold their horses in Portland and pocketed the money. They had ridden six hundred and sixty-five miles in one hundred and forty-four hours.

14.

Baron Paul Zinnovy sat at his desk in a San Francisco hotel. The wheat had been destroyed but LaBarge had vanished, and it worried him. A close watch had been kept on the schooner until it sailed; LaBarge was not aboard.

He paced the floor, scowling. Rotcheff seemed willing to remain right here in San Francisco, and as long as he did so, he would be safe. He had his instructions as to Rotcheff but nothing could be done here. If Rotcheff was lost at sea farther north there would be no investigation but his own. Or at a landing on one of the lesser islands they might be attacked by the Kolush . . .

Officially, the Russian American Company was losing money, but actually a few key men were doing very well indeed between paying low prices to the *promyshleniki* and padding expenses in stockholders' reports. If Rotcheff succeeded in getting wheat to Sitka conditions would be alleviated and prices could no longer be held down.

It was dangerous to leave Rotcheff unwatched. There were Boston men here in San Francisco who could offer evidence on the cruelties of the Company, and Rotcheff could choose his own time to come north—perhaps one inopportune for Zinnovy.

None of his agents had learned anything of LaBarge. On the evening of the fire he had been seen riding with Helena de Gagarin, but had dropped off the world right after that, and whatever she knew she was keeping to herself. Without wheat LaBarge could not really cause any serious trouble, and yet it was strange that he should have disappeared. Still, the thing to do was to take one thing at a time and the first was Rotcheff.

The *Susquehanna*, as Jean LaBarge had renamed the schooner, arrived in Portland only a few hours after he did. Knowing that if he reached Sitka before the Baron Zinnovy his chances would be greater to get the cargo of fur he wanted, he laid his course for Queen Charlotte Sound as soon as the last of the wheat was aboard.

Clearing the mouth of the Columbia with a cold wind kicking up whitecaps around them, the *Susquehanna* lay over on her side and took the bone in her teeth, pointing her bows into the cold northern seas as if anxious for the green water that lay ahead.

LaBarge, his wind-brown face wet with flying scud and spray, stood beside Larsen at the wheel, watching her move along under a full head of sail. His sea boots and oilskins were shining wet, the sky was gray and lowering with clouds, but the wind was good.

"How was the trip up the coast?"

"Flying fish sailing . . . it was good time."

"How about the Russian ship?"

"I think she go to sea soon. We see her loading stores."

He went below to study the charts again, glancing at Kohl asleep in his bunk, his body moving slightly to the roll of the schooner. If the wind held. . . .

Hours later when he came down to shake Kohl awake, the mate opened his eyes at once. "How is she?"

"Holding steady, and we're making knots." He took off his sou'wester. "She's raining a little, and we're catching some spray, but the wind is right. Just what the doctor ordered."

Kohl shrugged into a thick sweater. "You figuring on trouble in Sitka?"

"Not if we can get out before Zinnovy gets there. Sitka should be glad to see the wheat."

"What then?"

"We discharge as quickly as possible, stock with whatever we can get of food and water, then lay a course for Cross Sound. With luck we'll have our furs and be on our way south before Zinnovy can get his patrol boat to watching us."

"We'll be lucky to find furs that fast. There'll be ships ahead of us."

Jean grinned. "Don't worry about it. I know where there's furs to be had . . . plenty of them."

101

Kohl cocked an eye at him. "Seems to me you know a lot."

LaBarge shugged. "I know enough. Listen, Barney, I hired you because you're one of the best men with a ship on the west coast. I hired your ability, all your knowledge, but this much I know. You may know things I don't about particular bits of this northwest coast, but I know more about the *whole* coast than any man alive. I've made it my business to know."

"That won't help if Zinnovy gets you."

"One thing at a time."

LaBarge rolled in his bunk. Outside the hull, just beyond his ear, he could hear the whispering wash of the sea, rustling by with its strange secrets, its untold tales. On deck the sky would be gray with the last of the day's light, and there would be phosphorus in the water. There would be no stars tonight, or if any, a mere glimpse between rifted clouds. Yet he was strangely content.

This was the world he wanted, this was the way. Sailing north in command of his own ship to trade along that coast that had so long held his thoughts.

Rising some hours later, Jean shrugged into a sweater and his oilskins and went topside. A pale-hearted moon hung above the fo'm'st and the sea rushed past in the half-darkness. Spray blew against his face and he put out his tongue, tasting the salt.

Walking forward along the deck he watched the black, glistening water as the great waves rose and then slid away beneath the hull. Aft there was no sign of anything else upon the sea; they were a tiny microcosm, a little lost world of their own, moving upon the sea with their own heart beating in tune to the sea's great rhythm and the talking of the wind in the shrouds.

Far behind him there was a girl with green eyes and dark hair, a tall and regal girl who had walked beside him briefly, a girl who was not his and could never be his, yet a girl who held his heart now and would hold it always.

He walked aft and found Kohl, wide as a door in his bulky clothes, standing by the port rail.

"How does she go?"

"She's a dream ship, this one. If the Russkies get her, I'll shoot myself."

"See anything back there?"

"Once I thought I saw a light . . . probably a star."

For a long time Jean LaBarge watched the sea behind them, and saw nothing; if there was a ship back there it was almost certainly the square-rigger.

If Zinnovy was following him, would he have Helena aboard? Could that light Barney thought he had seen be hers?

Helena. He wished he could drive her out of his mind. Wanting her did no good. She belonged to somebody else, and that was that. He had never thought of himself as a lonely man before, but Helena had made him realize just how alone he was.

No man should have to walk the earth alone. A man should have a mate, to share his luck and his strength, but his sorrows as well. He had seen a Blackfoot squaw fight to her death beside the wounded body of her mate, and he had come upon a Chinese woman alone in the hills, giving birth to her child while her man worked five hundred feet underground to earn money to support them. Life had flavor when people had such courage. Strange how it was always the spoiled who weakened and cried first, and it was the injured, the maimed, the blind, and the poor who fought on alone.

Perhaps there was a life hereafter, a man thought of those things at sea, but he had never worried much about it because if he was not himself—this same collection of good, evil, bone, muscle, and blood—it wouldn't matter anyway. This was what he was, the bad with the good, and if he was anything less than this he wouldn't be himself, not Jean LaBarge.

He knew his faults, or most of them. Knew the kind of sinning he liked and where to put his salt and he did not want to get acquainted with new likes and dislikes. As for sinning, most of the things he enjoyed were sins in the eyes of somebody. Except for reading . . . and most of his books were written by pagan authors.

He was what he wanted to be, a free man. With luck he would not only keep his liberty but sail south with a cargo of furs, all the more precious because he'd taken them from under the nose of Zinnovy. He shrugged

. . . here he was wasting his watch below. That was the trouble with the sea and the mountains, they made a man think. It was always the little men who huddled together in cities who believed themselves important, and they had a conspiracy among them to keep up the illusion. They huddled in cities because a man at sea, in the desert or mountains had time to know himself, to examine what he was . . . so they stayed in their cities, knowing they could not stand to ever really look at themselves.

Spray blew over the rain and against his face. It had a fine, briny taste to it. No wonder the great countries were seagoing countries.

It was late, and it was his watch below. . . .

15.

ON THE MORNING of the eleventh day the *Susquehanna* was skimming along through a bright blue sea with the sun just above the horizon when Jean came on deck. Barney Kohl came down the port side to meet him. "Cape Burunof is just astern, and that's Long Island over there."

Jean took the glass and studied the horizon astern, but there were no sails in sight. Evidently they were arriving well ahead of the Russian ship.

"Barney, we'll have to work fast and smart. I'll go ashore and see Governor Rudakof and try to get things moving." He studied the islands ahead. "As soon as I'm in the boat, start getting that wheat up. I'll try to have a lighter alongside before noon."

"They won't move that fast," Kohl advised. "We'll be lucky if we start discharging cargo before tomorrow afternoon." A glance at LaBarge's jaw line made him qualify the remark. "Unless you think of a way to start them moving."

"I will . . . I've got to. But in the meantime I want a man on deck with a rifle at all times. Nobody is to come aboard without written authorization from me, and I mean nobody. The crew is to stand by at all times—we may have to get out of here at a moment's notice."

"Suppose they try to keep you here?"

"They couldn't unless they arrested me on some charge, and we haven't done anything wrong yet."

"Suppose they arrest you anyway?"

"It could happen . . . then you head for Kootznahoo Inlet and I'll join you there."

"If not . . . what?"

Jean chuckled. "If I'm not there in two weeks, come back and break me out. I'll be ready to leave."

For a man who had never sailed these waters LaBarge knew a lot about them. Kootznahoo was a likely spot. A ship could lie there for weeks and never be observed. Of course, LaBarge had said he did know this coast better than anyone; it might not be just a boast.

Ordinarily American ships had no trouble in Sitka. The government's friendship varied according to its needs, for the diet in Sitka, even on Baranof Hill, was often restricted, and famine a risk. Rudakof had been friendly on the surface, and now, with grain purchased by Rotcheff, they should be welcome.

The *Susquehanna* dropped her hook in nine fathoms off Channel Rock. At this distance from the port LaBarge knew he would at least have a running start for open water.

The sunlight was bright on the snow-covered beauty of Mount Edgecumbe, and it shimmered over The Sisters, and to the east, over Mount Verstovia. Moving down the channel, LaBarge could see the roof of Baranof Castle, built in 1837, and the third structure on the site. The Baranov era had been a fantastic one, for the little man with the tied-on wig had ruled some of the world's toughest men with a rod of iron, and had just barely failed to capture the Hawaiian Islands.

Jean wore a smoke-gray suit with a black, Spanish-style hat. His boots were hand-cobbled from the best leather, and he looked far more the California rancher and businessman than a ship's master and fur trader. And he chose to look so.

With him in the boat were Ben Turk and Shin Boyar, aside from the boat crew. "You're to get around," he said to the Pole, "listen, and if it seems advisable, ask questions. I want to know the gossip around town, patrol ship activity, what ships have called here, conditions in town. Then return to the boat."

Boyar nodded solemnly. "It is a beautiful place. I who have suffered here, I say it." He gestured toward Mount Edgecumbe. "It is as lovely as Fujiyama."

A dozen loafers watched the boat come to the landing, their manner neither friendly nor hostile. Boyar disappeared into the crowd, and with Turk at his side, LaBarge started for the Castle. Leaving the old hulk that served for a landing, they walked down the dim passage through the center of the log warehouse and emerged on the street leading to the Hill. Along the way were booths where Tlingit Indians gathered to sell their wares, baskets of spruce roots, hand-carved whistles of rock crystal, beaded moccasins and a few articles of clothing. Jean stopped at one stand to buy a walrus-tusk knife for a letter opener. He would send it to Rob Walker when he had a chance: a souvenir of Sitka.

As they walked, people turned to stare. Jean's hat was unusual, and his dress elaborate for the place and time, although many illustrious visitors had come to the Castle.

On the terrace before the Castle, Jean paused to look back. The town itself was little and shabby, but the setting was superb! Tree-clad islands dotted the channels that approached the town, their fine shores rising picturesquely from the sea. All this . . . and behind them Alaska, the Great Land.

A stalwart Russian with close-cropped blond hair admitted them and they waited in an inner room while the servant took their names to the governor. The waiting room was, for this place at the world's end, fantastic. Here were statues and paintings worthy of the finest museum.

The Russian appeared in the door, holding it open. "If you please," he said in a husky voice, "this way."

Rudakof was a stocky, corpulent man with a round face and sideburns. He got up, thrusting out a hand, but his smile was somewhat nervous. "Captain LaBarge? I am mos' happy to see you." He paused, obviously anything but happy. "What can I do for you?"

Jean placed his papers on his desk. "I am delivering, as of this moment, a cargo of wheat, ordered for delivery here by His Excellency, Count Alexander Rotcheff, emissary of His Imperial Majesty, the Czar."

Rudakof's eyes bulged a little. The roll of titles had their effect but he was afraid of Baron Zinnovy, who had told him definitely that intercourse of any sort with foreign ships or merchants was to cease. Yet the wheat had been ordered by Count Rotcheff, and Rudakof was also afraid of him. Still, of the two he was most afraid of Zinnovy.

Jean guessed the sort of man he confronted. "There

was a crop failure in Canada where wheat was previously purchased, and so the Count acted without delay."

A crop failure in Canada? Rudakof had heard nothing of this, but then what did he ever hear? Nobody told him anything. If there was a crop failure it could mean a serious food shortage in Sitka . . . perhaps famine.

He mopped his brow. "Well, uh, there has been no message, Captain, no authorization. You will have to wait until—"

"I can't wait. The money is on deposit in a San Francisco bank, but if you aren't prepared to receive this cargo I'll have to dispose of it elsewhere. I imagine there are businessmen in the town who would jump at a chance to buy."

Rudakof's face grew crimson. "Oh, come now!" he protested. "It is not so serious, no?" He struggled to find any excuse to delay the decision. "You will have dinner with me? There is much to do. I must think . . . plan."

"I'd be honored to stay for dinner. But in the meantime you will order the lighters for us?"

"Wait, wait!" Rudakof brushed a hand as if to drive away an annoying fly. "You Americans are so impetuous. The lighters are busy, and must be requisitioned. They must—"

"Of course." LaBarge was firm. "But you are the director; the authority is yours. You can order them out."

Rudakof became stubborn. "Dinner first, then we will talk."

Realizing further argument at this point would be useless, Jean shrugged. "As you like . . . but we plan to be out of the harbor by tomorrow."

"Tomorrow?" Rudakof was immediately suspicious. "You are in a hurry." He rustled some papers on his desk. "You talked to Count Rotcheff in San Francisco. Did you also see Baron Zinnovy?"

LaBarge frowned as if making an effort to recall. "Do you mean that peculiar young officer? The one in the pretty little white suit?"

Rudakof blanched with horror at the description. "The man you speak of"—he struggled with emotion—"is Baron Paul Zinnovy, of the Imperial Navy!"

"I believe he did say something of the sort. But wasn't he the one who was in some kind of trouble in St. Petersburg? Such a young man, too!"

Rudakof refused to meet his eyes. He was more worried than ever. This infernal American knew too much. He, Rudakof, had heard whispers about Zinnovy, but he did not like to think of them. Even a disgraced nobleman could have friends in high places, and if there was any shake-up here, trust the Baron to emerge on top, with those who served him.

Yet Rudakof did not wish to be held accountable for refusing a cargo of wheat that might save Sitka from famine. The colony was too dependent, and some of the citizens, like that merchant Busch, had friends who were influential also.

Promising to return for dinner, LaBarge left the Castle. "Stalled," he told Turk, who had waited for him, "but I think we can get it done by tomorrow night."

"You might even have a week," Turk suggested, without much hope. "A lot could happen in Frisco."

LaBarge wasn't so sure. Without doubt Zinnovy would have left for Sitka soon after the *Susquehanna* cleared, and some time had been lost on the Columbia River, picking up the wheat.

Count Rotcheff might delay because he did not relish putting himself in the hands of his enemies, yet he was not a man to shirk his duty, and sooner or later they must come to Sitka.

Sending Turk to the dock with a message for Kohl, he strolled through the few streets of the town. The dark-skinned Tlingit women, picturesque in their native costumes, gathered along the street, each with some trifle to sell, and each walking with a pride of bearing that belied the menial position into which they were placed by the Russians. The Tlingits had been a warlike people, an intelligent people, physically of great strength, who were in no way awe-struck or frightened by Russian weapons. They had wiped out the first colony at Sitka in 1802, and given the right opportunity, believed they could do it again.

Pausing before the clubhouse built by Etolin as a home for employees of the company, Jean watched two husky *promyshleniki* stagger by, drunk and hunting trouble. Shin Boyar was across the street, but he waited until the *promyshleniki* were gone before he crossed.

He stopped near LaBarge and without looking at him, said quietly, "You kicked up a fuss, Cap'n. Feller from the Castle hustled to the waterfront, jumped into a boat and took off for that new patrol ship, the *Lena*."

Rudakof was acting with more intelligence than he had given him credit for possessing. He must have come upon a plan that would place him in a better bargaining position before they met at dinner.

"Found a man I know," Boyar continued, "told me Zinnovy threw a scare into Rudakof. Officially, the director outranks him, but Zinnovy has frightened Rudakof with his influence in St. Petersburg."

"Go back to the boat and tell the boys I want a close watch. At the first sign of that Russian square-rigger I want to be notified, no matter where I am or what I'm doing."

They could leave now, but payment depended on delivery of the wheat, and moreover, he needed the cargo space. The schooner was small and lightly built, and without that space he could do nothing.

He walked to the knoll and seated himself at a table in one of the tearooms. A girl came to his table, smiling in a friendly way, and he ordered honey cakes and tea. Sitting over the tea he tried to surmise what Rudakof was planning. Obviously, he wanted neither to lose the wheat nor see the schooner leave before Zinnovy returned.

The waitress was a pretty blonde with braids wrapped around her head and dark blue eyes that laughed when her lips smiled. Her mouth was wide and friendly, and as she refilled his cup, her eyes caught his. "You are Boston man?"

"Yes."

"You have beautiful ship." She spoke carefully and chose her words hesitantly. "When I was small girl a Boston man gave me a doll from China. He said he had a little girl like me."

"I'll bet," Jean smiled at her, "he'd like a big girl like you."

"Maybe. I think so." Her eyes danced. "Most Boston

men like to have girl." She wrinkled her nose at him. "Even Eskimo girl."

An idea came to him suddenly. How much pressure could Rudakof stand? Suppose a little pressure could be generated?

He spoke casually. "Count Rotcheff ordered a cargo of wheat for delivery here on my ship, and now Rudakof won't accept it."

"He is a fool!" She spoke sharply. Then what he had said registered. "You have *wheat?* Oh, but we need it! You must not take it away!"

"I'd like to unload tonight or tomorrow," he said, "but I doubt if I can get a permit."

"You wait!" She turned quickly and went into the kitchen, and listening, he heard excited talk. A few minutes later a stocky, hard-faced Russian emerged from the kitchen and stalked angrily out the door.

LaBarge sat back in the chair. The tea was good and the honey cakes like nothing aboard ship. He had a feeling something had been started that not even Rudakof could stop. Sitka was a small town. In the several hours before he was to meet Rudakof at dinner everyone in town would know he had a cargo of wheat, and if a wheat shortage existed, the director should begin to feel the protests.

When he had finished his tea he placed a gold coin on the table. When she handed him his change, he brushed it aside. "You did not tell me your name?"

"Dounia." She blushed. "And you?"

"Jean LaBarge."

"It is too much. I cannot take the money."

He accepted the change, then returned half of it. With a quick glance to see if anyone saw, she pocketed it. "You might," he suggested, "whisper something to the man who just left."

"My father."

"You might whisper that if Rudakof does not unload the cargo promptly, I shall be forced to leave. Unless . . . and this you must whisper very softly, unless someone came at night to unload it, someone who could sign for it, someone reliable, whose name Count Rotcheff would accept."

111

16.

RUDAKOF'S ROUND FACE was beaming when Jean came into the room; he seemed a little drunk and very pleased with himself. It appeared that the problem the arrival of the *Susquehanna* presented was deemed to be over. He grasped Jean's hand eagerly. "Come, my friend! Sit down! Whatever else our Castle holds nobody ever complains of the cellar! What will you have? A bottle of Madeira?"

Jean was pleasant but wary. Rudakof was too sure of himself. "Thank you," he said, glancing swiftly around the room.

At Rudakof's signal the servant came with two glasses. "Dinner will be served at once," Rudakof explained, "and we have a few guests."

Jean tasted the wine. "You have a very interesting city," he said, deciding to strike a blow at Rudakof's new confidence. "I walked about a good deal, and talked with some of your people."

The smile left the Russian's face. Obviously this did not please him, but his spirits were too high to be undermined so easily. They toasted their respective governments and the glasses were refilled. "To the Grand Duke Constantin!" Jean proposed.

Rudakof hesitated, obviously startled, then repeated in a dull voice, "To the Grand Duke." He drank, but some of the bounce was gone out of him. Jean guessed that when one worked for the Russian American Company there were some to whom it was not good politics to drink.

The other guests were arriving. A French botanist and a German geologist who traveled in company, and a young Russian naval lieutenant named Yonovski, a handsome youngster with blond curly hair. "You have a fine schooner, Captain," Yonovski told him. "Have you had a chance to visit any of the islands?"

"We came by open sea. Count Rotcheff wished us to arrive as quickly as possible."

"Oh?" Yonovski was surprised. "You know the Count?"

"He is in San Francisco, but he'll soon return to Sitka."

Several of those at the table exchanged glances, obviously surprised. Rudakof, his face growing redder, filled Jean's glass. "Come, come!" he protested. "No business! The Captain is our guest!"

The conversation turned to California, the sudden westward advance of the United States due to the gold rush, and the somewhat similar movement in Siberia. Yet several of those at the table seemed preoccupied, and one of these was a tall man, stooped in the shoulders. He was a lean, hard, capable-looking man who was later introduced as Busch, a merchant-trader.

All were much interested in the American attitude toward Russia. Obviously with the situation in Europe growing serious this was becoming a major factor at Sitka.

When they moved into the next room for brandy and cigars Rudakof was beaming and jovial; the numerous drinks were having their effect. He opened his collar to give his thick neck more freedom and became involved in a lively discussion with the geologist.

Almost accidentally, LaBarge found Busch at his side. The tall man studied him out of cool, intelligent eyes. "Is it true, Captain, that you have wheat aboard? And you have not received permission to discharge the cargo?"

"That's right." Rudakof's broad beam was turned to them; he did not notice their conversation. "In fact, the director seemed upset instead of pleased, and when I asked to have lighters at once, he created delays."

"This wheat . . . how much is it worth?"

"That's just it. The wheat was ordered by Count Rotcheff and the money for payment is on deposit in a San Francisco bank. I can collect payment by showing a receipt signed by the governor, or"—he paused—"by other responsible parties who will see the wheat used for the benefit of the colony."

"Paid for?" Busch was astonished.

"Evidently," Jean suggested tentatively, "everyone is not anxious to see the wheat delivered."

For a few minutes Busch said nothing, then, "You will understand, Captain, that in our country as well as yours there are factions, and there are those who would make money even at the expense of their country. I realize this is hard to believe, but there are men who regard nothing as disloyal as long as the profits are large. Loyalty to their pocketbook or to their business firm is above loyalty to their country."

"It's the same in my country."

"I think men vary little the world over, but there are always a few who serve and ask nothing but to serve. The survival of the Sitka colony is of interest to me, and at this moment your wheat is almost the price of that survival."

Yonovski interrupted and Busch moved away. The conversation grew more desultory and more ribald. Finally, the party broke up and Jean started down the steps. His eyes swept the dark harbor, searching out the schooner. Another ship was showing her lights, anchored only a short distance from the *Susquehanna!* From her size she could only be the patrol ship.

He never recalled how he reached the boat. Boyar and Turk were sitting on the edge of the landing, smoking. Turk got up quickly. "No chance to do anything, sir. She just moved up and lay broadside to us."

Behind them in the dark passageway a boot scuffed. LaBarge stepped quickly out of the light and Boyar got to his feet. Light gleamed on a gun barrel in Turk's hand.

Two men stepped from the passage and walked to them. The first was Busch, the other the father of Dounia. "If we give you a receipt, Captain," Busch asked, "will you deliver to us the wheat?"

"The wheat was bought for Sitka. If you'll accept delivery, I'm agreeable. But you will have a problem." He indicated the patrol ship. "Have you an answer to that?"

"You underrate us, Captain." Busch spoke softly. "We

114

saw the patrol ship while you were still at the Castle, and the men who stand the night watch aboard her were still in town. They were at the tearoom, of course, for all men come to the tearoom to look at Dounia, who is the prettiest girl in Sitka.

"Dounia is a clever girl and when she told them it was her birthday they drank to her health in vodka. They drank many toasts, Captain, and naturally they were supplied with bottles by my friend here, Arseniev, the father of Dounia. They celebrated very well, Captain, and we gave them a dozen bottles to take back to the ship."

"Good . . . the cargo will be on deck, waiting."

Hours later, in silence and darkness, he watched the last sack go over the side into the big, flat-bottomed scow. The scow had made several trips, always careful to show no lights and to moor herself on the off side of the schooner. Busch came aboard and signed the receipt, then gripped Jean's hand. "Thank you, my friend! Thank you!" he whispered.

The scow slipped away into the darkness. A few lights sparkled from the Castle on the Hill, and the snows of Mount Edgecumbe glimmered faintly through the night. Barney Kohl came down the deck. "If it wasn't for her," he said, "we—"

"Get everybody on deck. No lights, no noise. Then haul us up to the anchor."

"You going to slip the anchor?"

"And lose it? Not unless I have to."

A soft wind was blowing over the bay as the *Susquehanna* came swiftly and silently to life. Clothes rustled, a knot struck the deck, a board creaked, ghostly hands moved on a line.

Kohl spoke. "Over the anchor, Captain."

Several of the crew were beside Jean, busy with a queer contrivance. He looked around at Kohl. "All right, take her in. Gently now."

Their only worry was the patrol ship; the watchers there might be drunk or might not. There was no sound now from the *Lena*. Earlier there had been loud laughter and occasional singing.

"Ben?"

"Yes, Cap'n?"

"Ready?"

"Sure as you're alive."

Several of the crew moved up beside him and together they lowered the contrivance over the side and anchored it in place. It was a long, narrow raft that supported two thin masts and a boom. On the end of one mast and on the boom, lights were mounted. From a distance, if the observer was drunk enough, it would look as if the schooner were still there.

"Douse your lights, Kohl. Then light these."

The tide was setting northward toward Channel Rock. Jean let the schooner drift, and there was no sound above the ripple of water past her hull.

"When she comes abeam of the Rock," Jean said, "shake out a jib. I want no noise. Sound carries too well over the water at night."

There was, for several minutes, no other sound. Then across the water on the patrol ship somebody moved and spoke. Kohl swore softly and Jean held his breath. The schooner seemed to lie still on the dark water, and ashore on Japonski Island, an Indian chanted. Behind him, higher in the forest, a lone wolf howled inquiringly into the night. The night gave back its echoes to his repeated question.

"We're movin'!" Pete Noble whispered hoarsely. "Look at them lights!" Astern of them, almost fifty yards off, were the lights that simulated the schooner.

They were moving but the movement was desperately slow and at any moment some drunken sailor aboard the *Lena* might realize something was wrong. The crew stood in silence, almost afraid to breathe, wondering what a Russian prison would be like.

"Channel Rock ahead, Cap'n. Shall I shake out the jib?"

"Hold it."

The minutes walked by on cat feet. A star appeared through a veil of cloud, then was quickly banished behind a dark mass of rolled black-cotton cloud. The patrol ship was well astern now. Somewhere ashore and far off, a dog barked.

Channel Rock was abeam. "All right, Barney," Jean said, and watched the white flag of the jib shake out and fill itself with the light breeze.

"Stand by the mizzen," he said, after a minute. Channel Rock fell astern and the dark bulk of Battery Island loomed on the port side, yet they were still far from free. There was no more time. "All right, Barney. Get some sail on her!"

Smartly the mizzen was hauled aloft, then the mains'l. The *Susquehanna* gathered speed. Out from behind Japonski Island the wind filled her sails and she heeled over and began to dip her bows deeper. With luck they would soon have a full cargo and a ticket home.

"Sail, ho!" The call, from the lookout in the bow, was low and desperate.

Jumping to the bulwark, Jean strained his eyes into the darkness. A big square-rigger was coming up the Western Channel, headed into port under a full head of sail, although even as they sighted her she began to take in canvas.

Barney swore. "Look at that, would you?"

"I'm looking."

She was bearing down upon them and coming fast. The man at the wheel turned and glanced at Jean but LaBarge shook his head. To change course now would be to lose distance they could not afford, yet the big windjammer was headed as if to run them down.

"Cap'n!" The man at the wheel had a pleading note in his voice.

"Hold your course!"

Kohl drew a sharp breath and looked up at the towering heights of canvas. Before he could speak he was interrupted by a shout from the square-rigger and a command to put the wheel over. The big ship sheered off and a man ran shouting to the rail. A dozen faces joined him, peering over the side of the schooner.

A rough voice hailed them. "What ship is that? Who are you?"

The hail was in Russian, then in English. LaBarge ignored the shouts and then suddenly, in the white light from a scuttle, he saw a face, and it was the face he could never forget, that would always be with him. There it was, not more than heaving-line distance away, and for a moment as the two ships passed their eyes met across the space, and then as they drew apart, he lifted a hand.

She hesitated, then waved back, a vague, sad gesture

in the night, and then the square-rigger fell astern and there was no sound, no light, and only a memory of a white face lonely in the light from an open scuttle, and the memory of a girl who had ridden beside him over the tawny, sunlit hills.

The schooner dipped her bow and spray swept the deck. On the wind there was a smell of open sea and of the far-off pine-clad islands to the north, those far green islands where the schooner was bound.

17.

Within a very short time Baron Zinnovy would realize that despite all his efforts the wheat had been delivered, and he would know that LaBarge and the *Susquehanna* were at large in the Alexander Archipelago.

The immediate problem was obvious. They must be where the patrol ship was not, they must pick up the cargo of furs as planned, and slip away to the south at the first opportunity thereafter.

The schooner carried eighteen men and three officers, all carefully selected men. A third of the number could have handled her, but the others were needed for trading, fighting, or any move LaBarge might make ashore.

"We're pointing for Cross Sound. Do you know it, Kohl?"

"As well as any man, which means nothing. I know there's glaciers north of it that keep feeding ice into the Sound, and there are bad fogs."

"Do you know a small cove with an island in its mouth? It's on the north coast of Chichagof?"

"That's old Skayeut's village."

"All right. Take us there."

Jean walked forward to the waist. There were no sails in sight and they could expect a few hours' grace. With the following wind they could make good time and farther north they could hug the coast. The wind was cold now, the sea choppy. From now on they would need luck, ingenuity, and every bit of their combined knowledge. Fortunately, the schooner was new, she could sail close to the wind and could carry canvas.

The shores of the island, when they reached it, were heavily wooded right to the water's edge. Here and there a small indentation, each with a minute section of beach,

119

broke the monotony of the forest-clad shore. The morning was bright and the day cold. Taking the schooner in past the George Islands they reached toward the cove, seeing no sign of life except a lone tern floating comfortably on the gray sea.

"The entrance is narrow," Kohl advised, "right abeam of the island."

It opened before them as he spoke and he conned the schooner into the opening between island and shore. Trees came down to the water and there was a fringe of ice along the shore. Inland, over the trees, they detected a column of smoke.

"This Skayeut," Kohl said, "he's a mean old blister."

"Can we go on in?"

"The passage is narrow, and there's only three feet of water over the rocks at low tide, but you could make it at high tide, and inside it's deep enough."

"We'll stay here."

Two canoes put out from shore and circled the *Susquehanna* just within hailing distance. There were four men in one canoe, two in the other, but no movement showed on the shore, although all knew Indians were there, studying the schooner. These Indians had suffered too much from the greed and rapacity of the Russians.

The dark green walls of the forest closed them in, and the schooner lay like a ship in a dream on the still, cold water. There was a faint slap of paddles on water as the canoes circled closer. The Indians stopped rowing.

"Where's Skayeut?" Kohl shouted.

The Tlingits said nothing. The schooner was new in these waters. One Indian shaded his eyes to stare at Kohl. "You Boston men?"

"Sure! Come aboard!"

They hung off, reluctant to risk it. One of the Tlingits indicated LaBarge. "Who that?" he called.

"LaBarge!" Jean called back. "You tell Skayeut that Jean LaBarge has come to see him!"

The paddles dipped deep and the canoe shot shoreward. Two of the men in the larger canoe turned to stare at LaBarge and Kohl turned to his captain. "They acted like they knew your name."

"They know it," Jean replied blandly, enjoying Kohl's mystified expression. "He knew me, Barney."

120

Just before noon a half dozen *bidarkas* shot out from shore, each packed with Indians. In the first was Skayeut, a tall man with a wide, deep chest and massive bones. He thrust out his hand to Jean and they looked into each other's eyes, and then they both smiled.

Trade was brisk. The Tlingit Indians were born traders. Even before the arrival of Captain Cook they knew the value of the land trade routes and their economic value to the tribe. At one time the tribe had traveled three hundred miles to stop the establishment of a Hudson Bay post where it would interfere with their own trade with tribes from the interior.

Of this Jean knew, and that old Skayeut could give him information about the interior. The old chieftain was about to learn that information itself could be a valuable item of trade.

For three nights they remained at Elfin Cove, and each night LaBarge noted down the results of his talks with the old chief and the procession of Tlingits and Salish the chief brought to talk of Alaska. Later, alone in his cabin, Jean noted down what he had heard for future reference.

. . . the gold is known to the Russians. An effort was made to mine it without success and for some reason further attempts were discouraged, probably they did not wish to attract attention to a territory so insecure in a military sense.

Old Skayeut knows where more gold can be had and will trade for iron. The iron here is in small deposits and difficult for the Tlingits to work. They are a superior people and the blankets they weave of dog hair or cedar bark are equal to the best, anywhere.

For a month the *Susquehanna* worked her way south, down Saginaw Channel into Stephens Passage, pausing at this island or that village. As planned, they touched a dozen villages where no traders had been in some time and soon the hold of the schooner was filled with prime fur.

Occasionally they sighted some native canoe, but heard of no other vessels in the area. Yet Jean was nervous, for the channels were narrow, allowing no

121

chance to maneuver, and steep mountains rose on either side to about fifteen hundred feet in solid banks of forest before giving way to bare rock or snow. The presents he had sent north were paying off, for everywhere he was welcomed as an old friend.

The seventh week of trading was ending when Kohl came to the cabin where LaBarge was busy adding more information to his books. "Cap," Kohl said abruptly, "I've mastered my own ships and I'm not one to butt in, but the crew are getting nervous. We've been lucky this far; now let's head for home."

"You know Kasaan Bay?"

"Sure."

"That's our last stop."

Kohl dropped into a chair and shoved his hat back on his head. "I'm not one to show the feather, Cap, but this trip worries me. Maybe it's the fool luck we've had, cutting that square-rigger so close aboard you must have scared them out of a year's growth. I know you scared me. You done it deliberate, too . . . and she couldn't have come around in a half hour, not to chase us, she couldn't. But it's fool luck we've had, every village loaded with prime fur, and no patrol ship in sight. You know what I think?"

"Let's have it." Jean tipped back in his chair.

"They're waitin' for us, Cap. Zinnovy will be to the south, knowing we've got to go that way, and he'll be lyin' where he can cover the best routes. He'll have both the *Lena* and the *Kronstadt,* and men staked out to cover every passage."

"I think you're right."

"Look." Kohl bent over the crude chart on the table before them. "We're heading down Clarence Strait. Once we cross the bay down here we'll be in Canadian waters, but that won't stop Zinnovy. Only right there some ships would head for open sea and a straight run to Frisco. So what does he do? He waits for us in the mouth of the Strait."

"Just where do you think he'll wait?"

"My guess is right off Duke Island, but maybe a little south so he can check both channels."

Kohl had made a point that disturbed him. LaBarge was not sure that Zinnovy had even bothered to make a search, for such news travels from island to island and village to village by swift traveling canoes. It was likely Zinnovy was doing just what Kohl suggested, patrolling the outlets to the south.

He did not tell Kohl that he had been, for days, worrying the problem as a dog worries a bone. "Barney, if you've got it figured straight, we'd better stand ready for action."

"You'll fight?"

"I won't be taken. We'll run if we can, but when we can't run any more, we'll fight."

Kohl went aft with a small grin on his lips. He had begun the voyage in a surly mood, hoping LaBarge would get his belly full and decide that San Francisco life was better. But as the voyage progressed he grew to like the man more and more. He had nerve, and he had brains. He still did not understand LaBarge's vast knowledge of the islands.

Later, they discussed the question again. "There are channels," Kohl said, "but too many dead ends and some of the channels are filled with ice. A man needs local knowledge."

The lantern above their heads swayed with the gentle roll of the schooner. Her timbers creaked and they studied the chart. It offered few alternatives.

"This island?" LaBarge put his finger on a large mass of land ahead and to the east. "That's Revillagigedo, isn't it?"

"Uh-huh. You can call it an island, Cap'n, but nobody knows whether it is or not."

"Ever see a Russian chart?"

"A dozen. On their charts it's part of the mainland."

"Good." He got to his feet. "That was what I'd hoped. Understand now, Barney, no fighting unless we have to. Until then we play hide-and-seek around the islands."

Suddenly, there was a shout from aloft, and running feet on deck. Then the cry, "Sail, ho!"

"Where away?"

"Dead ahead, an' comin' up fast!"

"Well." Kohl grinned at LaBarge and rolled his quid in his jaws. "Here's where we start to run."

Together they went up the companion to the deck

and studied the oncoming ship through the glass. A flag was climbing the halyard and when it was caught by the wind it was easily seen. It was the flag of Imperial Russia.

18.

THE *Susquehanna* FELL OFF before the wind. Standing in the waist, Jean LaBarge watched the oncoming ship. It was the *Lena*. Although a patrol ship she was only a middling fast sailer, quite fast enough for the average ship in these waters but not in the same class with the schooner.

He wanted to draw her deeply into Clarence Strait, for from her present position she could cover both the Strait and Revillagigedo Channel, a position fatal to his plans.

On the east side of the Strait, only a short distance off, there was the mouth of a channel opening between Gravina and Annette Islands, which in turn opened on Revillagigedo Channel. From there several openings offered themselves, but of five possible openings three were dead ends. If he could win to the head of Nicholas Passage and disappear, the *Lena* would have small chance of finding him unless Zinnovy was shrewd and patient enough to return to the former position and wait. And once the quarry was sighted, Jean did not believe Paul Zinnovy would be patient.

The sky was overcast, the sea gray. Lying close off-shore he waited, hoping to draw the Russian ship deeper and deeper into the Strait. The shores were thick with forest except where cliffs of gray rock jutted out. White water broke over Hidden Reef. The wind was good and he allowed the schooner to loaf under reefed sails while the Russian ship came on. Jean waited, judging the distance.

"All right," he said suddenly, "let's go!"

In an instant Kohl was shouting orders and the crew exploded into action. Eagerly, as if welcoming the chase and knowing what was demanded of her, the schooner answered to the wind. There was a low cheer from the crew as her sails filled and she started to run for it. From the Russian ship there was the dull boom of a gun, a warning signal, an order to heave to. She was much too far away for a cannon shot.

Jean took the wheel from Larsen and when the schooner was rolling along he put the wheel over and headed into the passage that led to Smugglers' Cove. From behind them the gun boomed again, impatiently. Standing at the wheel Jean watched the shore line, and suddenly glimpsed the lightning-blasted pine of which he had been told. Three minutes later by careful count he put the wheel over and slid between Hidden Reef and another rock patch, unnamed as yet. Then he was in full channel and reeling off a good eight knots.

"If we can make the head of the Passage before he rounds the point," he told Kohl, "we'll be all right."

"I hope you know what you're doin'." Kohl was worried. "This is dangerous ground."

"I know."

He hoped he did. There was a chance despite his endless checking that the information in the little black book was wrong. Beside the channel the somber walls of timber closed them in, virgin timber, untouched by man or fire. Ahead of them the outlet was filled with dangers, and there would be little margin of safety, yet if he could make the turn. . . .

He glanced back . . . nothing in sight. Sweat broke out on his brow despite the wind. If they were trapped in a cul-de-sac they would have no chance, for Zinnovy could stand off and shell them to pieces, and with the greatest enjoyment.

He stood with his legs spread to the roll of the ship, taking his time. Whitecaps dotted the sea, and a cold wind came down off the mountains. Nobody said anything until Larsen, glancing over his shoulder, said, "I think we make it."

Momentarily, Jean resigned the wheel to him. He walked forward, scanning the sea and the marks on the cliffs. The distance was slight, but if the *Lena* had continued her pursuit she should be rounding into the Passage by now.

126

"Head her toward the island." He pointed. "We'll get behind it and out of sight."

Kohl was in the stern with a glass to his eye, anxiously watching the point on Annette Island beyond Hidden Reef, but there was no sign of the patrol ship. The dark green shores of the island were close aboard now, and he could make out details of the trees. There was a white streak of quartz in the rock at the island's end and a cluster of bedraggled pines.

Kohl called out suddenly. "She's on our tail, Cap! She's comin'!"

"Think they saw us?"

"I doubt it. If they didn't they'll have to look in those other inlets before they come up the Passage."

"Zinnovy knows I'm not the waiting type. He'll come on."

Out of sight of the pursuing ship, Jean conned the schooner around the kelp. Ahead of him was a strip of dark water and he pointed into it, muttering a wordless prayer that it was deep as it looked. The schooner slid through with yards to spare on either side, and then swung into the Tongass Narrows that divided Pennock Island from Gravina. Before them lay thirteen miles of clear water and Pennock was more than three hundred feet high and good cover for him. Even if Zinnovy had guessed right there was still a chance they could reach Behm Cannal before they were seen.

The black battalions of clouds lowered above storm-gored ridges, and the gray-furrowed sea licked at narrow beaches of sand and bare, black rocks. It was a strong land, a good land, unchanged through thousands of years. Off to the right the black, glistening arch of a rock showed momentarily above the water like the back of a porpoise and brown streamers of kelp trailed their mute warning into the gray of the sea.

The Narrows opened and the great bulk of Pennock fell behind. Kohl paused at the companionway rubbing the back of his neck. He hated to leave the deck, yet he knew fresh men would be sorely needed later. He stumbled down the ladder and fell into his bunk and was asleep as soon as he hit the mattress.

Duncan Pope, the sour-faced second mate, was on

watch. He was a slovenly-appearing man with a cast to one eye, yet long since Jean had learned he was a capable officer whose lean, almost scrawny body possessed an amazing resistance to hunger, cold, and long weary hours on watch. Pope was a man who kept his own counsel. He did not like Russians. He did not like the thugs of Sydney Town. He disliked most ship's masters on general principles, and he cared for few things aside from standing watch, reading his Bible, and fighting.

LaBarge was scarcely aware Pope had taken over. He was watching the Narrows open out before him, and soon he would make the turn around Revillagigedo where his information told him there was a passage. He was gambling everything on that, and hoping Zinnovy would continue the pursuit. If his luck held he would pass by within a short distance of where the patrol ship had originally waited and the *Lena* would be lost in the maze of islands, channels and inlets that lay behind.

An hour and a half later, with no evidence of pursuit, he rounded the corner and started north. Ahead of him was a wooded island with a yellow cliff, which would be Tatoosh. He kept close in so the ship would be invisible against the island if anyone was within sight.

He thought all at once of the Swamp, where as a child he had used the cover to hide from hostile eyes. And then he remembered Rob, and their dreams of adventure. "Rob," he said, half-aloud, "you should have been with me today. You would have liked this, I know you would."

19.

HELENA STOOD on the terrace outside the Castle. It was late evening. For two days there had been no news from the *Lena,* and a message from her meant news of the *Susquehanna.* Each day until then there had been a *bidarka* to bring news or lack of it. The last canoe had brought word the *Susquehanna* had been sighted and capture was imminent.

Reception of the news in Sitka had been mixed. Despite the fact that the Americans were foreigners they had brought wheat to Sitka, and their plight found sympathy among the people of the town. Baron Zinnovy was already unpopular, and the fact that he had impounded the wheat had won him no friends.

The wheat would have been lost to them but for an unexpected show of firmness by Count Rotcheff, who refused to permit the impounding and took the matter out of Zinnovy's hands. Rudakof, straddling the fence on most issues, met this one head on from necessity. Reluctantly, he backed up the Count, who was, after all, in authority.

Rotcheff's words were repeated all over the settlement. "I am afraid, Baron Zinnovy," he had said sternly, "you have exceeded your authority. Your mission is to protect Russian trade and traders, not to enforce your arbitrary decisions in matters of no concern to you. I must remind you, sir, to restrict yourself to your duties and cease interfering with the civilian authorities."

Helena, who had been present, was suddenly bursting with pride for her husband. The Baron had stood at attention, ramrod stiff, his eyes straight forward, his body fairly trembling with repressed fury. He saluted, made an abrupt about-face, and strode from the room, heels clicking on the hard floor. Yet all knew it was but one battle in a campaign and the decision was not yet.

Helena realized that there was more to the search for the American ship than the personal animosity Zinnovy bore for Jean LaBarge. If the *Susquehanna* could be captured with a cargo of furs—Zinnovy could claim she had been trading with the secret connivance of Rotcheff, and trading illegally. More than ever she appreciated the danger of their position, for had Rudakof failed to back up her husband, Zinnovy might have taken drastic action to free himself from interference, and orders were of no importance if they could not be enforced.

Scarcely more than a child when she had married Count Rotcheff, she had not been unhappy. He was thirty years older than she, but an intelligent, attractive man, respected for his genuine ability and his sometimes biting wit. She had grown up listening to talk of politics and intrigue, a game at which her husband was a master.

A door closed behind her and she turned to greet her husband. "I am glad you are out of that stuffy office."

"It is nice here." He inhaled deeply, then glanced at her. "Do you believe they will catch him?"

"No . . . no, I don't."

"Nor I." They walked a few steps together. "He is clever, this American of yours. Busch tells me he has friends all through the islands, and what Busch has learned of LaBarge's dealings convince him that LaBarge is extremely astute."

Somewhere out among those dark, mysterious islands he might even now be fighting, dying. The air was growing colder but she felt no desire to go in . . . this was the same air that he was breathing; even now he might be standing on his deck, watching the dark water slip past.

"I like it here," she said suddenly.

"Sitka?" He was surprised.

"I mean all of this, as it is now, young and free."

"And barbaric."

"Of course . . . and I like even that."

"There is something primitive in all women, I suspect. Women think in terms of the basic. Love, marriage, children."

"What better things to think of?"

"Of course. It is as it should be and lucky for us males, God knows. You are coming in?"

"Soon."

He paused near the door, watching the dark serrated edge of the pine forest against the night sky. Somewhere down in the town someone dropped a piece of iron and it rang loudly on the pavement. He glanced at Helena, feeling his age now in the growing chill of the evening. This bout with Zinnovy might be his last. He must move shrewdly . . . the man had influence, damn him! And he was vindictive, which Rotcheff was not. It was a pity, he reflected, that the men of good will are so poorly armed, for at times it was a handicap not to hate. It took a fanatic to win, a fanatic believer or one utterly ruthless. He, Rotcheff, thought too much of the other man's point of view, he could always see both sides of an argument. That would not do in a world where there were Zinnovys.

Yet Zinnovy was a Russian and they talked loudest when they faced weakness. We are basically, he thought, a race of tyrants and poets, and his own fault was in being too much the poet, too little the tyrant.

He looked again at Helena, standing by the stone parapet. In the world from which they had come it would be considered an absurd thing, but he loved his wife. He had not married for love. Helena was beautiful, she was wealthy, and her family was powerful in his world of intrigue and politics. Theirs had been a marriage of purpose. Yet he had been a lover once, and a successful one, with many conquests behind him. He knew all the little things that please a woman. He smiled thoughtfully. The best lovers were those who did not really love, for if one became too emotional there was in the place of eloquence a stumbling tongue, in the place of charm, awkwardness.

The surprise had been his. He found Helena, even though he was sure she did not love him, a thoughtful, attentive, and considerate wife. Had he met her twenty-five years before she might have loved him . . . but then he could not have afforded her!

Their life had been singularly happy, and if she did not love him she did respect and admire him. These last years had been his happiest. He was not sure when he fell in love with his wife; nonetheless, it had happened, and now for the first time he sensed her unrest, and he knew the cause.

Jean LaBarge was a handsome man, not in a pretty way as were some of the Czar's officers who had paid court to her, but in a tough, dangerous way. The Count, considered in his day a superb swordsman, and victor in four duels to the death, admitted to himself he would dislike to face LaBarge with a rapier in his hand.

The man had it in him to kill . . . not from malice, for there did not seem to be cruelty in him, but simply because he was, more than anyone in the Count's experience, a fighter.

"Helena"—he turned back to her—"have you ever been sorry you married me?"

Scarcely had he uttered the words than he was wishing they had not been said. Was he a boy to expect such a question to receive more than the obvious answer?

She turned to face him: "No, Alexander, I have not been sorry, and I shall never be sorry."

He welcomed the sincerity in her voice. "I'm afraid I have been a bad husband . . . too preoccupied." He waved an irritated hand. "Marriage in our lot is so much a matter of state. We scarcely know each other until it is too late."

"It has never been so with us," she protested. "You know it hasn't."

She was right, of course. There had always been a warm, friendly understanding between them, and in the past few years it had become even better. They had, really, been two of the lucky ones.

He remembered the first time he had seen her, when he was a young officer in the Imperial Army, and had come to her home to visit, accompanying her uncle. She had been a little girl with large, serious eyes who was always in a corner, reading. She had come running from the door to greet her uncle, followed by a huge wolfhound she called Tovarich. Suddenly seeing the strange young man, she had stopped, torn between eagerness and embarrassment.

He had seen her fear and had walked to her, bowing deeply. "Princess, I am your servant. And when was a mistress afraid of her servants?"

She laughed then. "You! You couldn't be a servant! With that nose?"

They had laughed together, and from that day on, they had been friends. . . .

The wind puffed through the pines and flurried her skirt. "It is cold," he said. "I shall go in."

"I'll follow . . . I want to be alone for a minute."

When the door closed behind him he went to the sideboard and poured a glass of brandy. He tasted it and the warmth went through his veins.

Zinnovy now: the man had friends in the high places but more than one road led to St. Petersburg. There was that boy, for instance, the boy Zinnovy had ordered flogged . . . did he not have an uncle who was a power in the iron industry? The uncle would be a man to be listened to. Yes, that was it, and they had met once in Kiev, a hardheaded man named Zarasky who had fiercely resented his nephew's flogging. It had nearly killed the boy.

That way it would not involve the Grand Duke or the Czar. There was no way of making someone tired of you faster than endless requests or complaints. It was the value of being a politician, that one knew other ways.

It occurred to him abruptly that being the kind of man Zinnovy was, and wanting what he wanted, Zinnovy dared not let him, Rotcheff, return to St. Petersburg.

Coolly, he considered the situation. There were ways of escape, of course, but he was no longer a young man, and all shipping out of the harbor could be controlled by Baron Zinnovy. Escape by the usual means would be barred to him, and any other means was closed by the danger to his health. That meant he must prepare a report now, with several copies, and see that at least two copies were smuggled out, for certainly Zinnovy would be checking all communications.

Busch . . . that was the man. Busch detested Zinnovy and was a patriot as well, shrewd enough to realize the danger Zinnovy meant to all legitimate business in Sitka. Moreover, and this was important, Busch had his own corps of tough and loyal *promyshleniki*. He was not a man to attack with impunity.

A long time later, while his pen still scratched, the clock chimed.

Eleven o'clock. It was very late. . . .

20.

SHORTLY AFTER NOON the wind fell away to nothing, and the *Susquehanna*, now barely making steerageway, held in toward the rocky shore. Jean was hoping to pick up vagrant breezes out of the numerous ravines that slashed the mountains. Twice during the afternoon there were brief squalls accompanied by heavy rain, and each time the schooner gained ground.

All hands that could be spared were catching sleep against the long watches ahead, and when they turned to, every one of them was given a jolt of hot rum. It was almost dusk when the wind picked up. Moving at a bare four knots they rounded into Gedney Pass.

Both shores sloped steeply back to three thousand feet, with the shore steep-to. Creeping along, the schooner made Shrimp Bay and dropped anchor until morning.

During the night it rained hard. The man on watch was relieved every hour; Jean wanted to take no chance because of a sleepy watch. All hands slept in their clothing, ready to turn to at a moment's notice, and LaBarge bedded down under the bottom-up whaleboat.

Tired as he was, he could not sleep. The cold wind made him grateful for his heavy blankets. Once while lying awake he heard something crash far up the mountainside and then a sliding of rocks and timber. There was a faint following rattle of stones, then silence. The schooner was ghostly in the night, but toward morning the air warmed a little and the fog lifted, shrouding her rigging in cobwebs of mist. His cargo was worth at least eighty thousand dollars and depending on how the market stood at the moment, might be worth at least half again that much.

Sometime after that he must have fallen asleep for he was awakened to find the sky turning pale yellow and the watch standing beside him with a steaming cup of black coffee. By the time the sun was halfway up the sky they had rounded Curlew Point and entered the Narrows along Bell Island. Here, for approximately eight miles, the channel varied from three-tenths of a mile in width to more than a mile. By report the water was deep and the shores steep-to, but as the fog held they had no idea if they were pursued or not.

Like a ghost ship on a ghost sea they slid along through the fog. He was coming up from below when Kohl called him. The schooner faced a continuing channel ahead, but to their right lay another opening, a little wider.

"What d' you think, Barney?"

Kohl rubbed his neck. "A man can only guess."

Together they walked to the bow and looked at the water. Just beyond the entrances both passages were blocked off by fog. One might be an escape, the other a trap, but which was which? A decision had to be made, yet Jean delayed, hoping for some indication, some evidence on which to base a choice.

"What's the book say?" Kohl had noticed the black book LaBarge occasionally referred to.

"It doesn't say. The man who told me about this channel hadn't navigated it, he'd only crossed it at the Narrows with some Tlingits after him. He did get a taste of the water and it was salt."

He stiffened suddenly, lifting a hand. "Listen! I heard something then! Something dropped on a deck!"

All ears strained into the silence and fog. Kohl grabbed his arm. "Cap'n . . . look!"

It was a piece of shelf ice such as forms along a shore, and it had drifted from the opening that lay ahead. It was moving upon some strong, unseen current.

"Put the helm over, Noble," Jean said. "We take the other opening."

Suddenly from out of the fog there was a cry, "Sail, ho! Dead ahead!" And the words were in Russian.

As one man the crew sprang into action, getting sail on the schooner. Putting the helm over sent them into thick, blanketing fog, and like a gray ghost the *Susquehanna* gathered speed, while behind them they heard excited talk in Russian.

"Gant, Boyar, Turk!" LaBarge grabbed the three men. "Lay aft with your rifles. Stand by to fire but not a shot until I give the word, understand?"

He turned on Kohl. "How did they see us before we saw them?"

"They must've had a man at the masthead."

Behind them a cannon boomed suddenly, and they heard the shell crash into the forest, some distance off.

"Shootin' up the other channel," Gant said. "They didn't see us duck out."

A half hour later, sliding more swiftly through thinning fog, they heard another shot, far behind them. The patrol ship had obviously taken the other, more obvious channel. Yet they themselves were sailing into the unknown and from brief glimpses of the shore nobody could guess the position.

Abruptly, they emerged from the fog and saw dead ahead of them a mighty shaft of rock towering over two hundred feet into the air!

Kohl whooped. "Cap'n!" He grabbed Jean's arm. "We're okay! That's Eddystone Rock an' we're not more than twenty miles above Revillagigedo Channel! I've been this far a dozen times!"

Far behind them the patrol ship *Lena* captained by Alexi Boncharof, with Baron Zinnovy aboard, felt its way slowly up the unknown channel. Boncharof, knowing the temper of his passenger and superior, was growing more and more worried. There was a current flowing against them and he was positive it was no tidal current.

"I think," he began hesitantly, "there is a river at the end of this inlet. I do not believe they went this way."

"I heard them, I tell you!" Zinnovy's voice was coldly furious.

They proceeded another mile, two miles. Boncharof was thoroughly unhappy. Experience had taught him it was foolhardly to pursue poachers; one had to wait until opportunity offered rather than venture into narrow channels filled with dangers of all sorts. But who was he to advise his superior, an officer of the Imperial Navy?

Yet when the fog broke they saw two rivers flowing into a dead-end inlet, and no sign of the *Susquehanna*.

Baron Paul Zinnovy stared wide-eyed with anger at the shore and the rivers, then he turned abruptly and went below, nor would he appear on deck again until they reached Sitka.

Below deck he poured a glass of cognac. The American had escaped him again, yet he dismissed his failure as he dismissed all failure. One thing he had decided. He dare not let Rotcheff return to St. Petersburg, nor his wife, either, for that matter. He turned the glass in his hand, knowing he must move soon and swiftly. He wished to return to St. Petersburg a wealthy man, to establish himself in the capital. There was no better place for a man to be who had wealth, but without it, one was nothing.

LaBarge now: the man must have taken a small fortune in furs! That schooner was well down in the water; it would take a lot of fur to bring her down so far. If he could have captured the schooner with that fur . . . !

Paul Zinnovy had come into the world as an only child in a country mansion remote from all others of his class, and on an estate where he ruled almost as a prince. His father's overseers had gotten work out of the peasants with the knout, and Paul had been taught to do likewise.

Zinnovy recalled his mother as an inconsequential woman in black who had lived for twenty years in fear of her husband, and as he grew up she came to live in equal fear of her son. At school he was the only child from the gentry and tyrannized over the others, yet he was intelligent and his grades were good. Later, at the university his grades were even better, yet there for the first time he felt discontent. He was no longer first. He found many who were richer, stronger, students who lived on vaster estates, and knew more important people.

A tall, handsome and somewhat cold young man, he repelled people rather than attracted them, and soon learned that his father, a tyrant on his estates, was only a provincial member of the petty nobility and of no consequence in St. Petersburg.

A fine navigator and an excellent officer, Zinnovy soon won promotion on his own merit. Several friends sponsored him in various ways, only to be promptly discarded when their usefulness was at an end. Paul Zinnovy had never heard of Machiavelli, but the Italian could have taught him nothing.

His reading had been limited to gunnery tables, charts, books and papers essential to his career. He was fiercely proud, without scruple or loyalty, and if it is given to any man to be so, he was without fear. His first duel at the university, where duels were usually concluded with the drawing of blood, ended in death. He easily ran his man through, and from that day he was feared. His second duel, with pistols, was with a drunken artillery officer and again he killed his man. Then had come the first of those "duels by request." A young journalist had written articles critical of the Navy, and a superior officer of Zinnovy's casually suggested that if Zinnovy were a loyal officer of the Navy he would resent the articles. He resented them, and killed a man who had known no weapon but the pen, until given a pistol for the duel.

There are always those who admire skill with weapons as there are women who are attracted by a reputation with no thought of what the reputation implies. Paul Zinnovy was valuable to the right people so he obtained promotion. He dressed with care and danced well.

There had been a riot at Kronstadt when Zinnovy was Officer of the Day. Although a mere outburst of rebellious fury on the part of seamen who had endured too much, Zinnovy treated it as the beginning of revolution. Acting with ruthless speed, efficiency and cruelty, he personally killed the ringleader with a pistol and summarily executed three others. He was commended publicly by his commanding officer, who commented in private, "Efficient, but too bloody."

During this period in Russia all books on logic and philosophy were forbidden, and although there was reform later it was so slight as to warrant no discussion. Censorship subjected all printed matter to rigid scrutiny. It was a period of stifling tyranny and obedience without discussion, an atmosphere suited to the development and rise of Paul Zinnovy.

Yet the new Czar, Alexander II, did not approve of undue violence, and his policy was somewhat more liberal than Russia was expecting. Baron Zinnovy had ordered the knout for a cadet, and he was about to be broken in rank for this offense when influence was brought to bear and he was sent to Sitka, instead. If he made good there he would be returned with honors. He was given other, strictly confidential orders.

Those orders concerned the mission of Count Rotcheff and future plans for a new company charter. The Count was to be rendered ineffectual at Sitka, and if this could not be done, he was to be destroyed, and in such a way that the Baron's hand would not be visible.

As for Jean LaBarge, Zinnovy thought, his time would come too. He was not important except that he was aiding and abetting Rotcheff, but Paul Zinnovy hated him.

He finished his cognac. LaBarge had gotten away, and nothing could be done about that, but there was much to be done in Sitka. He must make careful moves that would cut the ground from under Count Rotcheff's feet and leave him without authority.

Authority, to matter, must be enforced. If the means of enforcing it be taken away nothing but prestige is left, and little enough of that. Paul Zinnovy thought he knew a way. . . .

21.

THREE TIMES IN THE FOLLOWING YEAR Jean LaBarge took the *Susquehanna* to the northwest coast, and not until the third of these voyages did he encounter the patrol ship. Each voyage was carefully planned beforehand, and the route mapped out only after considerable study and an analysis of all reports from Alaska. On two of the voyages they held to the inside passage; on the third they remained far out to sea until in the latitude of the first trading point.

Contrary to usual practice among traders, they moved the ship only by night, in the first hours of the day or the very last before dark, and during the day they anchored in tiny, out-of-the-way inlets. Despite his precautions LaBarge was sure there had been spies in some of the villages and that Zinnovy was aware of his presence.

When each trip ended he paid his crew and gave each man a bonus depending on the size of the cargo and what the furs brought on the market. There was no news of either Rotcheff or Helena, though his crew circulated in port, listening to pick up information, and were given additional bonuses for this.

There was a rumor they were still in Sitka but he placed no faith in the story. Nor could he forget Helena.

His voyages had been highly successful, the profits enormous. On the last voyage he had bought gold from Skayeut.

He had written Rob Walker a long letter after returning from his first trip to Sitka, and had received some months later a very serious reply, which said in part:

> Your letter is here beside me, and if you were to see it you would find those passages concerning Russian America,

141

which you call Alaska, underlined in red ink. You would be even more surprised to find that you are very much quoted in the cloakrooms of both House and Senate. You have told me much of the wealth and size of Alaska, and of its proximity to Siberia. Nowhere else is the United States so close to the troubles of the old world as there, and, as long as Russia is on the continent of America, there is danger. I know . . . our two governments are now friendly, and I trust this may be ever so, but, should Russia and the United States ever have a falling out, it would be well that they have no foothold upon this continent. Jean, we must buy Alaska!

March of another year was drawing to a close when Jean, wearing a carefully tailored suit of dark gray, stopped by Winn's Branch for dinner. Part of the afternoon and most of the evening he had spent in the office of the rebuilt warehouse, planning a new trip to the northwest. The Branch was a large salon furnished in a manner both tasteful and elegant, standing at the corner of Washington and Montgomery Streets. It had become almost immediately after its opening a gathering place for the wealthy and successful of San Francisco. Seating four hundred and fifty, it was crowded most of the time.

Pausing in the entrance, Jean let his eyes move over the crowd, seeking familiar faces. His own table, reserved each evening at this hour, was empty. Captain Hutchins had not yet arrived.

At a table not for from his, Royle Weber sat with Charley Duane. Jean was quite sure Duane had at least protected the arsonists after the burning of the warehouse, and possibly had instigated the burning or served as a go-between.

He started for his table, but Royle Weber called out to him and motioned for him to join them. Hestitating, LaBarge remembered suddenly that Weber was agent for the Sitka people, and walked to the table. "You want something?"

Weber's face flushed at the tone. "Look, LaBarge, I have news for you."

"What news?"

"Sit down. We'll talk."

"I can stand, or you can come to my office. I won't sit down because I don't like the company you keep."

Duane's face went white and he started to rise but

142

Weber put a hand on his arm. "Forget it, Charley. LaBarge is joking."

Duane stared up at LaBarge, his hatred evident. "He's not joking," he said, "and I like neither the words nor the tone."

"With your associations, Duane, I shouldn't think you'd mind."

Duane wanted desperately to rise and smash LaBarge's face, but his memory of what had happened to Bart Freel and Yankee Sullivan was still ripe. He had himself seen the finish of the Sullivan fight, and knew he was in no such class.

He shrugged. "Have your fun."

LaBarge turned to Weber. "Whatever it is, I'll listen, but make it quick."

"You'll be interested to hear that Count Rotcheff has been ordered back to St. Petersburg immediately, and he has suggested a desire to be taken to Siberia in the *Susquehanna,* and by you."

"The order is signed by Rotcheff?"

"Yes. He wishes you to bring another cargo of wheat to Sitka, and you will be permitted to take a cargo of furs from there."

"I'll think about it."

"You don't understand. You must go at once."

Jean LaBarge crossed to his table and dropped into his chair facing the room. This could very well be a trap, a means of drawing him into Alaskan waters where he might be taken at will. On the other hand, the last thing Russia would want would be trouble in the Far East or Alaska. If the signature on the request from Count Rotcheff was genuine, he would go. Obviously, the Count did not trust himself on any ship under the command of Baron Zinnovy or subject to his supervision. . . . A cargo of wheat would bring a good price in Sitka, and with the furs he could make a substantial profit . . . and he would see Helena again.

Or would he? Weber had said nothing about the Princess. She might have already preceded Rotcheff to St. Petersburg. Jean chewed his lower lip, considering the situation . . . but there was no reason to consider . . . he was going.

Sitka lay warm in the morning sunshine when Jean LaBarge walked along the passage through the log warehouse. Much had changed. The equipment was worn, the clothing shabby, and it was apparent that few ships were arriving from the homeland.

Duncan Pope was in command of the schooner, and Kohl had accompanied Jean ashore. There were many men standing idle about the streets, most of them the hard-bitten *promyshleniki,* the same crowd who had brutalized the natives and fought the Tlingits. Many were former convicts, criminals shipped over from Siberia; others were renegades from various countries.

Leaving Kohl in the town, Jean started up the street alone. The booths of the merchants lined the way and the Tlingit women looked at him with interest. Two Tlingit men watched him approach, and one inclined his head as if to nod. LaBarge acknowledged the greeting, if greeting it was.

Baranof Castle was just before him. At the thought of seeing Helena his heart began to race. He was a fool to think of her, yet the fact remained that he could think of no one else. And as long as Rotcheff lived she would make no move nor allow him to make one.

The door opened as he crossed the porch and a servant bowed. "Captain LaBarge? Count Rotcheff is expecting you!"

Crossing the foyer, his heart pounding, he went through the door and saw Rotcheff rise from behind his desk, hand outstretched. He looked older, more tired.

"My friend! My very good friend!" His sincerity was obvious. "Captain, there have been times when I did not expect to see you again, but it is good! Believe me, it is good!"

The warmth of the greeting found him responding in kind, and he realized anew how much he liked this fine old man with his scholar's face and ready smile. "It is good to be here," he said simply.

"You brought the wheat?"

"Yes, and other things as well." He hesitated. "The Princess? She is well?"

"Waiting to see you. You will join us now?"

Helena turned quickly from the table where she was

arranging tea, and he saw the sudden way her breath caught, the quick lift of her breasts, then a glad, lovely smile.

"Jean! At last you've come to us!"

Over tea Rotcheff explained. Zinnovy was in charge, the director no more than a figurehead. Rotcheff's messages were intercepted, and although they were treated with bland respect, it was obvious they were prisoners. His demands for a passage to Russia were shunted aside with the excuse that there were no ships.

"I am sure the only reason we are alive is a fear of repercussions. But," he smiled, "please believe me, our greeting is for you, not your ship, relieved as we are to see it. We have missed you, and we have missed outsiders. Even the beauty of Sitka can become dull for lack of new faces." He went on to explain that after Zinnovy's failure to capture LaBarge, the Baron had returned and begun all at once to make changes. At first it seemed an effort to increase the efficiency of the operating force on the patrol ships, but soon it became apparent that one safe man after another had been taken from the Castle and replaced by someone obedient only to Zinnovy. Letters from St. Petersburg had convinced Rudakof that Zinnovy was in the driver's seat, and whatever Count Rotcheff might report would be discounted. Rotcheff and his wife were practically prisoners, and all ships coming to or leaving Sitka were checked by Zinnovy's men. At first none of this had been apparent. Zinnovy had either avoided them or been carefully respectful, but he had built carefully to the point where he would have the situation in hand.

"The people of Sitka?"

"Frightened, most of them, but they hate him. Right now the Baron is worried, I believe. When orders arrived recalling me to St. Petersburg he became very friendly and extremely polite."

"Does he know I'm here?"

"He was furious . . . but even he will be glad to see the wheat this time, and I've told him there was not a ship I'd trust myself in . . . not in Sitka harbor."

Later, Rotcheff returned to his desk and left them alone. When the door closed they stood for a long time looking into each other's eyes.

"Jean, Jean," Helena said, at last, "you've no idea how we've missed you!"

" 'We?' "

"Alexander, too. There have been times when we have thought of you as our only friend. You've no idea what it means to know there is someone, somewhere, who would come if called. Alexander has said as much several times.

"He is . . . he is not so young any more, and could never stand the rigors of a trip in an open boat. Had it not been for that we might have made the attempt."

"Has he mistreated you? Zinnovy, I mean."

"He wouldn't dare. At least, not yet. But wait until you see him. He has changed, too."

"Changed?"

"Perhaps it is just the veneer wearing off, but he has grown more brutal. He is not formal as he was, not so stiff or so neat. He drinks a lot, and goes to the village too often for his own good. Some night one of the Kolush will kill him. Last month he shot an Indian for nothing at all, and he has had several brutally whipped."

"How about you? Would he let you go?"

"Alexander believes he dares do nothing else, but I only wish I were as sure."

Shadows had grown long in the room and LaBarge became worried. His crew had been chosen for their fighting ability as much as for their seamanship; should they encounter any of Zinnovy's men there might be trouble.

"I can't stay," he said, but made no move to go. "When you return to Russia, what then?"

"We have no idea what will be planned for us in St. Petersburg. Alexander believes much could be done here, but it would take a certain sort of man to do it."

"And I'll never see you again."

She touched the teapot with idle fingers. "No . . . unless you come to St. Petersburg."

He chuckled. "And what would I do there? I'm not a courtier. Although," he smiled, "one American sailor did well enough—a man named Jones."

"John Paul Jones? I think he was a better hand with a ship than an empress." She turned around to face him.

"You've never told me about yourself. What was your mother like?"

"How can you answer a question like that? She was a little woman with big brown eyes and she used to take me into the swamp with her and show me the useful plants. I believe she came from a good family, wealthy at one time. She told me about the house they lived in: it had once been beautiful, but became very run-down, I guess."

He paused. "She wanted me to amount to something and was very sure I would, and she used to tell me it wasn't where a man started that mattered, but where he went. She believed the swamp was a good place for a man to begin. She may have been right."

"And you? What do you want, Jean?"

"You have a husband . . . a man I respect."

She brushed the suggestion aside. "I did not mean that. But there must be something you want, that you want very much."

"I suppose there is. It used to be wealth, but it isn't any more. When I first began to learn about Alaska I felt it was a new country, a rich country where a man could become rich in a hurry. But I've done a lot of thinking since then, and I have a friend, Rob Walker, who has given me a different slant. I want to be rich, I suppose, but I keep thinking of Jefferson. I'd like to see Alaska a part of the United States."

"Why?"

"I've heard men curse it. I've heard them talk about the cold, the wolves, the northern lights, but that's not important. I want it for my country because someday my country may need it very much."

The room was now dark and the town only a velvet blackness where a few lights shone like far-off stars. Down upon the bay the harbor lights shot arrows of gold into the black heart of the water.

"What of you, Jean?"

"What I want I can make with these—" He lifted his hands. "Where there's fur I'll have some of it, and where there's gold, I'll take my share. But that's not enough. More and more I want to do something of value, the way Rob Walker is doing."

147

"Tell me about him."

"He's a little man, the way my mother was a little woman. I doubt if he weighs more than one hundred pounds. But that's the only way he's small. I think he would do anything for his country, and he knows how to bring men together to work, how to use their ambition, their envy, greed, even their hatred. It's funny—I remember him mostly as a shy little boy, and now to think he's become a great man."

A servant entered and lighted the lamps. When he was gone she turned to him again. "You may get what you want, Jean. Strangely, perhaps, it is what Alexander also wants. We must talk to him of this."

"And what of us?"

She put her hand on his sleeve. "You must not ask that, and you must not think of it. There is nothing for us, nor can there be anything for us, except"—she looked up at him—"except to say, I love you."

The door opened and Rotcheff came into the room. "I am sorry, Captain, if I have kept you waiting. You will wish to return to your ship."

22.

HE WAS CROSSING THE FOYER when a door opened and in
the opening stood Paul Zinnovy. LaBarge needed only
a quick glance to see that what Helena had told him was
true. Zinnovy was a changed man. There was about him
now an air of sullen brutality. Little remained of the
immaculate perfection in uniform that he had once been.
His coat was unbuttoned and his shirt collar gaped wide.
He carried a bottle by the neck and in the other hand a
half-filled glass, but he was not drunk. He was heavier
than when Jean had last seen him. There were red veins
in his face and his features seemed somehow thicker.

"So? Our little merchant comes to pick crumbs from
the Russian table? Enjoy them while you can, Captain,
it will not be for long."

"Perhaps."

"So you will take our Rotcheff back to Russia, will
you? And that will be the end of Zinnovy, you think?"
He chuckled. "Think again, my friend. I have power
here. I have a warehouse filled with furs, I have wealth.
Do you think I would lose all that and what it could
mean to me in St. Petersburg for one man? Or a dozen
men?"

Jean was impatient to be away, but the man fascinated
him. It was a rare opportunity to see his enemy at first
hand. "Count Rotcheff is a good man," he replied
shortly, "and very close to the Czar."

Zinnovy smiled. "Is he now? How long does a man's
influence last when he is far away?" He held up two
fingers and rubbed them together. "See? I will have
this. Gold speaks an eloquent tongue, understood in
court or cottage. There are many men who stand between the Czar and any issued order. As for Rotcheff"
—he shrugged—"he might be dangerous if he gets back,
and as for that little bit—"

Jean swung toward Zinnovy. "I'd not say that if I were you."

Zinnovy's eyes danced with cynical amusement. "Ah? So that is how it is? Oh, do not worry, my American friend, I'll say nothing to offend either you or the lady, but it interests me that you would fight for her. Chivalrous, and all that." His eyes narrowed a little. "It interests me that you will fight at all. You have always seemed more ready to run."

Abruptly, Jean turned to the door. Nothing could be gained here and he had a ship to make ready for the sea. A long voyage lay before him and neither the Bering Sea nor the North Pacific was gentle. He walked out, drawing the door to behind him, conscious of Zinnovy's eyes.

Outside it was completely dark. Most of the lights in the town had been extinguished. Jean LaBarge paused at the head of the flight of wooden steps and looked down, not enjoying that descent into blackness. Hadn't there been a light there, at the foot of the steps? He started to step down when a low voice called to him.

"Captain! *Wait!*"

He drew back from the step and turned to find a girl, her head covered with a shawl. "It is I! Dounia! You must not go down the steps. There are Russian sailors waiting for you! They mean to kill you!"

"How many?"

"Nine, perhaps ten. I do not know."

"And my men?"

"They are with the boat."

"Is there another path? Where we can't be seen?"

She caught his sleeve. "Come!" Swiftly she led him through the darkness, past barracks and tannery, to the corner of a storehouse. There they crouched in the shadows, listening.

It was very dark and very still. The water was gray, with a fringe of white along the rocks. From where they stood he looked along the water's edge toward the landing stage. His ship's boat was clearly visible.

Now that they had come this far the girl waited, knowing he must decide the next move. The building loomed above them, and looking back he could see the Castle outlined darkly against the sky. A few of the Russians would be waiting at the bottom of the stair, growing restive now, and there would be others in the log warehouse, watching the boat. But they would not be watching closely for they would expect no movement there. It would be sounds from up the street they would be expecting.

As he watched he saw a man move in the boat; and taking a chance, he called softly. Ben Turk was at the boat, and so was Gant. Both men knew the call of the loon, and he made it now. The moving figure stood still, listening. Softly, he called again, and there was a stirring in the boat shadows. For an instant starlight glinted on an oar blade.

He realized suddenly he was holding Dounia by the arm. "What about you?" he whispered. "Will you be all right?"

"I know every path."

"You're sure?"

"I played here as a child."

"Your father should have sent someone else. You shouldn't be out at this hour."

"Nobody sent me. I . . . I just came."

He took her shoulders in his hands and squeezed them gently. "Thanks . . . thanks, Dounia. But you must never do this again, do you hear?"

"I won't."

Suddenly she stood on tiptoe and kissed him fiercely on the lips, then ducked under his arm and was gone in the darkness. He started after her, then realized how futile it would be to pursue someone in such dark and unfamiliar surroundings.

The boat was drawing close, drifting like a darker shadow on the gray water. The oars stopped and it glided through the water with only ripples to make a whisper of sound. "Captain?" It was Gant's voice.

"Here."

At that moment a shot sounded.

Jean LaBarge had stepped down to the water's edge, but now he stood still, listening, ears attuned to the slightest sound. Far away an unhappy coyote yammered his loneliness to the wide sky, the water rippled, water dripped from the suspended oars, and then a faint woman's cry, from the Castle.

151

"Wait here!" he called to Gant.

Spinning, he dashed into the darkness. How he found his way through the maze of buildings he never knew, but suddenly he was back on the Hill, and when he stepped through the door Count Rotcheff lay on the carpet, blood flowing from a wound in his side. Helena was kneeling beside him and two servants came running into the room.

Jean dropped to his knees. His familiarity with wounds had been bred of emergency, and he worked swiftly now. When he had stopped the flow of blood and sent one of the servants running for the doctor, he got to his feet.

The door to Zinnovy's quarters opened and the Baron came out, looking down at the wounded man. His face showed no expression, yet there was a faint flicker of amusement in his eyes. "It seems you've lost a passenger, Captain. He may recover, but it will take time . . . time." Zinnovy glanced at Helena and then at Jean. "In the meantime he must remain here."

"You shot him! You did!" Helena's face was white, her eyes enormous. "I will see you shot for this! You . . . you . . . !"

"Naturally, you're hysterical." Zinnovy drew himself up. "And of course, I ignore the accusation. It was some Kolush, no doubt, perhaps believing the Count was myself." He smiled again. "I forgive you, Princess, and assure you I shall see that everything is done, everything, I repeat, to speed his recovery. Of course"—he pursed his lips thoughtfully—"it may take months and months."

Turning to Jean he added, "And of course, LaBarge, there will be no need for your schooner. None at all. Your stay here is over at midnight tomorrow. If you are in Russian waters within four days I'll blow you out of the water."

When he was gone, Rotcheff opened his eyes. He glanced quickly after the Baron to make sure he was unheard, then he whispered, "Take her and go." His eyes were bright and quick. "Take her to the Czar, my friend. I cannot go . . . and he will listen to no one else. You must take her, Captain . . . and you must go at once . . . before they realize."

152

"But—!"

Helena's protest was brushed aside. The Count's voice was firmer and his eyes clear. "Your things are already aboard the schooner, as are mine. Go now, quickly."

"Leave you?" she protested. "Leave you wounded? Perhaps . . ."

"Perhaps dying? No, I shall not die, but unless you go now we may both be killed. We know now to what lengths he will go . . . for it was Paul. I cannot prove it . . . but it was he.

"If you escape, I shall be safe. If you remain here . . . he will try again and again. With you away, safe with the Czar . . . then he dare do nothing more for fear of repercussions. You are the only chance."

"He's right," Jean told her. "And if we go it must be now, before Zinnovy thinks of this."

He led her, still protesting, to the door. Suddenly she turned and fled to Rotcheff and fell on her knees beside him. For a moment she was there, then she arose and came swiftly to the door. As they stepped out to the terrace the doctor and a servant came in the Castle entrance. Wasting no time, Jean led her to the path he had twice covered that night.

Kohl helped her aboard and whispered to Jean, "Zinnovy went out to the *Lena*. What's that mean?"

"Is the cargo gone?"

"Gone. And we've loaded the furs. The last lighter cleared an hour ago."

"All right. As soon as we're aboard we clear for sea. As quietly as possible."

Ben Turk touched his sleeve. "We aren't the only ones, Cap. Look!"

The canvas of the *Lena* was white against the night as she caught for an instant the reflection of shore light. Phosphorus showed in her wake. Zinnovy was taking the patrol ship out and Jean needed no blueprints as to why she was going. Out upon the dark water the sea would swallow any evidence of what happened to the *Susquehanna;* here in the harbor there were too many witnesses. Without doubt he intended to sink the *Susquehanna* and end the problem presented by LaBarge, once and for all. Yet he could have no idea they in-

153

tended to sail this soon, nor could he guess that Helena was aboard.

A wind stirred along the face of the mountains, and clouds drifted in the wide sky. Lights from the town made golden daggers into the heart of the black, glistening water. The patrol ship had taken the Middle Channel between Turning and Kutken Islands, but it was only a little past midnight and the anchor of the schooner was catted and she was moving.

"He can sit out there and wait until we come out," Kohl said unhappily, "and when we're at sea and out of gunshot of the town, he can sink us at will."

Jean LaBarge was not thinking of Zinnovy; that would come in its own good time. Now he was thinking of a channel that led north past the Indian settlement and Channel Rock where the *Susquehanna* had lain at anchor on her first voyage. One of the clumsy Russian ships that lay in the harbor had moved across that opening. Zinnovy must have planned shrewdly, hours before; he seemed to have blocked every exit, leaving only the way the *Lena* had gone.

"Keep moving," he told Kohl. "Let her swing as if we were taking the opening past Aleutski Island, and then at the last minute, point her into that opening past the Russian ship."

The channel where the Russian was moored was not more than one hundred and fifty yards wide, and there were rocks along the shore of Japonski Island, but between those off-lying rocks and the Russian ship there was a space . . . very narrow.

"We can't do it," Kohl protested. "We'd be fools to try."

"You do what I tell you."

The wind off the mountains was picking up, the sails filled, and Kohl went aft and took the wheel from Noble. He watched the approach to the channel past Aleutski. A few Russians loitered along the bulwarks of the moored ship. As Kohl measured the distance sweat broke out on his forehead. It was narrow, far too narrow. He swore bitterly, then setting his jaw, he spun the spokes rapidly and pointed their bows at the Russian ship.

There was a long moment before comprehension dawned on the Russian sailors. Suddenly a man shouted

154

hoarsely at them and running aft began to wave his hands wildly at the schooner which was bearing down as if to ram.

"Steady on!" LaBarge walked away from the rail and stood, his big hands on his hips, watching the narrowing gap. Kohl stared at him. To have seen LaBarge at this moment no man would have guessed that he was gambling his ship, their lives, and at the very least a Russian prison. Kohl could not know that LaBarge's throat was so dry he could not swallow, and his heart was throbbing heavily. Had he kicked an ant's nest there could have been no greater burst of activity than there now was aboard the Russian. Men shouted and waved their arms to warn him off, but the *Susquehanna* plunged on.

"Gant! Boyar! Get forward and stand by with your rifles. If anybody lays a hand on the wheel, drop him where he stands!"

It was close. If anyone touched the wheel on the Russian bark it might be just enough to close off the channel and bring about the collision they feared.

The water gap narrowed. A hundred yards . . . seventy . . . fifty! A man standing at the bulwark suddenly ran to the bow and dove off into the black water, swimming wildly for shore. Lights appeared in doorways and people rushed out, shouting and staring seaward.

Kohl's eyes were riveted on the narrowing distance. "Cap'n!" he pleaded.

The moment seemed to stand still as the schooner closed that distance. Forty-five . . . forty . . .

"Hard aport!" LaBarge shouted. His mouth was so dry his voice sounded choked. "Hard over! *Hard!*"

Kohl swung the spokes and Turk jumped to lend a hand. Jean stood with his legs spread, watching the bow of the schooner swing. He had drawn the line very fine indeed, perhaps too fine. But he knew his ship, and the *Susquehanna* answered smartly to her wheel, answered as if she understood what her master wanted. The bow began to swing faster. Jean chewed on the stick of a match and watched the narrowing space.

Thirty yards . . . twenty-five . . . twenty . . . fifteen. The schooner was forging ahead now, but still swinging. She was . . . she was going to clear. Suddenly added wind filled her sails and she gathered speed, slipping past the stern of the moored ship with less than ten feet to spare.

Close off the port side were the off-lying rocks, but the *Susquehanna* slipped through and lifted her bows proudly to the seas.

"All sail!" LaBarge shouted the command and then walked forward alone so they could not see his hands trembling. He had, in that moment, risked everything. If the wind had fallen the least bit, if the schooner had yawed . . . but she had come through like a thoroughbred.

He turned, after a moment, and walked aft. They were not yet free. If Zinnovy knew they had started and had slipped out of the harbor he might sail north and round Japonski Island to cut them off. Only, it was dark, and while the night lasted there was still a chance.

"Barney." LaBarge stopped beside Kohl, who had turned the wheel over to Larsen. "You told me you once took a boat through Neva Strait."

Kohl was still sweating out the near collision. "But that was in broad daylight!" he protested.

Jean grinned at him. "Next time you see the crowd at the Merchant's Exchange," he told him, "you can tell them you're the only man alive who ever took a schooner through Neva Strait in the dark!"

23.

HELENA, WRAPPED IN A DARK CLOAK, returned to the deck. She had stood by during part of the escape operation, and now she listened to comments of the crew. This ship, she realized, was operated as though every man aboard had a real share in its success. Rolling along under a good head of sail with a following wind, the crew stood by, alert for whatever might come.

"Neva Strait," Kohl was explaining patiently, "is four miles of pure hell in the daytime. The Whitestone Narrows are maybe forty yards wide, possibly less. In the daylight the dangers are marked by kelp, and some of the rocks are awash. At night you can't see anything."

LaBarge knew that Kohl's first instinct when danger threatened the ship was to hesitate, to object to the risk. His second instinct was to weigh their chances and if the situation warranted it, to go along with the risk.

"And if we get through? What then?"

"Peril Strait around the end of the island, and once in the sound on the other side, we sail north."

"One thing I'll say," Kohl grumbled, "you've got guts."

"A good ship and a good crew," LaBarge added.

Together he and Helena walked to the waist, where a little spray was breaking over the gunwale, and it tasted salt on their lips. They were silent together, listening to the bow-wash about the hull, the whining of wind in the rigging, and the straining of the schooner against sea and wind. These were sounds of the sea, the sounds a man remembers when he lies awake at night on shore, and hears in his blood, feels deep in the convolutions of his brain, the sounds that have taken men back to the sea for these thousands of years. The winds that whispered in the rigging had blown long over the icy steppes and the cold Arctic plains, and over empty, lonely, unknown seas that lay gray under gray clouds.

Neither of them could avoid the realization that if all went well they would be together for months on end. Now, for the first time, they knew they were definitely committed to a long journey together. As their eyes grew accustomed to the darkness they could watch the whitecaps on the dark, glasslike waves, and see the darker, unknown shores that rose abruptly from the water's edge.

"You seemed very calm."

"I wasn't," Jean admitted, "I was scared."

"This story I must tell to my uncle. He will enjoy it." She changed the subject. "The Neva Strait . . . it is bad?"

"Did you ever walk down a dark hallway in a strange house, a hallway scattered at random with chairs? It will be like that."

"You leave it to the mate?"

"I'd better . . . he's twice the sailor I am. Don't be fooled by that business back there: I was gambling that they wouldn't think I'd take such a risk. Also, I've a good ship and a good crew, and I knew they would be ready for anything that might happen. For day-to-day sailing Kohl is much better than I am."

They were silent, watching the water. Helena knew that Zinnovy had gone so far now that withdrawal was impossible. Although the shooting of Rotcheff could not be proved, if she reached the Czar his position would be at least endangered and might be finished. It was always easier to explain a disappearance than to escape consequences of crime when confronted by a witness. Yet the longer Zinnovy pursued the schooner the better Rotcheff's chances of recovery without hindrance, and Rotcheff would be in touch with Busch. The merchant had as many fighting men as Zinnovy himself and would be no more reluctant to use them.

Long after Helena went below, Jean remained on deck. He walked forward to where Boyar stood lookout in the bow. "You have crossed Siberia, Boyar? How long would it require?"

"Who can say? Three months? Or three years? It is a long trip, nearly six thousand of miles, and the roads are bad, the *troikas* miserable, the people indifferent or criminal."

Three months . . . they could scarcely hope to make it faster even though she was a niece of the Czar. To secure an escort they must appeal to the very people they wished to avoid. The headquarters of the Russian American Company was in Siberia, and many of the officials were actually in the pay of the Company.

The shores slipped by in darkness. It gave him an eerie feeling to be sliding into these narrow channels, uncharted and largely unknown. How many men might already have lost their lives here, unrecorded by history? Captain Cook had been here, and the Spanish before that, and the Russian ships. The first Russians who had come to these islands had vanished. There was a story in the Tlingit villages that a chief covered with a bearskin had enticed them into the woods and into an ambush. A second boat sent ashore to find the first vanished in the same way. Their ship had waited and waited, then finally sailed away. But Chinese and Japanese fishing boats had been carried to this coast, and some of their crews might have survived. What strange lives they must then have led, with no hope of return to their homes.

"Neva Point ahead, Captain."

"Go aft and report to Mr. Kohl. I'll stand watch."

He tasted the smell of pines on the wind, heard the splash of something falling into water. Behind him the crew were moving about, taking in sail. The Point loomed suddenly on their left, well defined. On their right a breaking rock showed a ruffle of white foam where the angry lips of the sea bared its teeth against the shore.

Kohl came forward and spat across the rail. "Thank God, she's deep enough. There's four fathoms in the Narrows, and it's deeper beyond."

The Whitestone Narrows closed down on them like the jaws of a trap. It was cooler there, with the forest closer. They could hear the murmur of wind in the pines, but the schooner moved forward confidently. Ahead of them there was faint gray in the sky.

After what seemed a long time of creeping down the dark Narrows the schooner slid into the open water beyond. The Neva lay behind . . . how long had it been?

"Nearly two hours," Kohl said. "There aren't any fast passages of the Neva."

Pope came on deck to take over the watch. He glanced at the graying sky, a thin, silent man who seemed ever discontented with things as they were. He swore bitterly when he realized they had passed the Neva in his sleep, and swore again when he learned he must take her through Peril Strait.

Finally, more tired than he could have believed, Jean stumbled down the companionway and stood in the paneled cabin, watching the brass lamp sway to the ship's movement. Helena was at the table with a freshly brewed pot of tea. "Mr. Kohl took his to his bunk. Sit down. You looked exhausted."

Gratefully, he accepted the tea. The warmth went through him slowly, taking the chill from his muscles, the damp from his bones. He was the first to speak and it was of something he had considered for a long time.

"There's something you can do for me," he said. "You can do it if anyone can. I want to see the Czar."

She was startled. "The Czar! But why?"

"Maybe . . . I don't know . . . he might consider selling Alaska to the United States. If he should agree . . . well, Rob Walker could do the rest."

"I can promise nothing, but I can try."

She was silent, and he saw how white were her fingers that pressed the cup, and the shadows under her eyes, shadows he had not been able to see out on the deck under the clouds. "Jean, Jean," she whispered, "I wish I knew how he was."

"He'll be all right."

Rotcheff had made a tough decision but he had made it without hesitation, knowing exactly what must be done. It was another reason for admiring the husband of the woman he loved . . . and Rotcheff had a good chance. Familiar as he was with gunshot wounds, he knew that such a wound, low down on the left side, was more than likely only a severe flesh wound. With care and proper food he might make it.

"Where are we going, Jean? What is it we have to do?"

"The quickest way would be through Salisbury Strait

to the Pacific, but we might be cut off there, so we're going east up a passage called Peril Strait."

"Is it dangerous?"

"There are tide rips in all these passages, and unexpected currents. Water piles up in these narrow guts, then comes roaring through, and most of the rocks are uncharted. By this time Zinnovy undoubtedly has other ships out from Sitka to cut us off."

Above them the brass lantern swayed and in his bunk behind the small door Kohl snored in an easy rhythm. Jean's head lowered to his arms for a moment of rest and at once he was asleep. The night had been long . . . long.

Outside a small wave broke over the bow and the water ran along the deck rustling into the scuppers where it gurgled solemnly. Helena looked across the table at the black, wavy hair, glistening in the lantern's light, and put out her hand to touch it, then drew it quickly back, frightened by the impulse. After a moment she got to her feet and went into her little cubbyhole of a cabin and closed the door.

She stood then, her back to the door and her eyes closed, while the light from a crack moved slowly back and forth across her face. And then for a long time there was a silence made more silent by the sound of breathing and the lonely ship-sounds in the gray light of a breaking day at sea.

24.

FOR TWO DAYS the *Susquehanna* crept along through a dense fog that reduced visibility to zero, a cold penetrating fog that wrapped the schooner in a depressing cloud. With Zinnovy somewhere behind there was no chance to heave-to and wait it out, so they continued to creep along, using what little wind there was. With luck they could get into Icy Strait and so to the Pacific.

No sound reached them except that of breaking surf. Fog had come upon them in the vicinity of the Hoggat Reefs along Deadman Reach, and they had crept north to the point, rounded it and sailed southeastward toward Chatham. Every mile was a mile of danger for fog filled the Strait and tidal currents were strong.

During a brief interval when fog cleared they rounded another point and started north, ice becoming more frequent. Then the fog closed in again, thicker and colder than before. Several times, unable to see the floes in time, they were struck with brutal force.

Kohl, wrapped in sweaters and oilskins, joined Jean in the bow while the lookout went below for coffee. "We'd better heave-to, Cap'n. Not even the Russkies will try moving in this fog."

"If it gets colder we'll start icing up," LaBarge said. "Damn it, man, if we get caught in these narrow channels we're through!"

Kohl agreed gloomily. "If we could only get a couple of hours of sunshine and good wind."

"How far do you think we've come since turning into the Strait?"

"Your guess is as good as mine. We've been moving, but with the current against us part of the time, and there hasn't been a rock or a point to take a sight from."

"Do you know these waters?"

"No . . . but Icy Strait can't be far."

Men came and went like wraiths in the gray, clinging fog. Ghostly trailers of fog lay in the rigging and the great sails dripped water to the deck. Nowhere was there anything by which to gauge their progress, and much of the time they could not see beyond the bowsprit.

Yet they could not heave-to. Even now ships might be awaiting them off every passage to the sea, but if they could get through Icy Strait and Cross Sound the opening was wide enough for them to slip by . . . if they did not go past it in the fog and end up in one of the dead-end, ice-breeding inlets north of the Strait.

Jean held up a hand. "I thought I heard something, Barney. Listen. . . ."

At first there was only the ship sounds, the strain of rigging, the creaking of ship's timbers, a faint stir of unseen movement, and then they heard it dead ahead. The beat of surf against a rocky shore.

Unmoving, they listened for a clearer sound. Not far off was a shore upon which waves were breaking. "I wish I dared fire a shot." Jean was worried. "The echo might help us."

"Not in this fog. Besides, I think Point Augusta is a low shore."

Miraculously, the fog thinned and they glimpsed momentarily a low shore on which a light sea was breaking, a sea that hustled and whispered among the black rocks. Jean studied it, trying to remember what little information he had about the area. He seemed to recall that the point they must turn into Icy Strait was more abrupt, yet there was clear water ahead of them and as far as they could see on the starb'rd side. "All right," he said, "let's try it."

When he went below Helena was reading. She looked up quickly, and seeing his expression, said, "You're worried."

"Yes . . . we changed course and I'm not sure we should have."

"If we could only get some news!" She closed her book. "I've done all I can to keep from worrying, but I can't help it. Jean, I never should have left Alexander."

"You would have both been trapped. He was right to make you go, Helena."

163

He accepted a cup of tea. It was scalding hot and very strong. He had never appreciated tea until he started coming into northern waters, but there they all drank it.

Kohl stepped down the ladder. "Cap'n? It was a wrong turn. There's land off the starb'rd beam."

"Close?"

"It isn't the strait."

He went on deck and stood there, his fists balled in his pockets. "It's narrow," he said, "it would be a risk to attempt a turn with the tide running."

"It wouldn't be worth it."

Any decision was better than none. "Drop the hook and we'll wait it out. When the fog lifts we'll get the hell out of here."

"I've seen these fogs last two weeks."

"All right. Get a boat into the water and we'll explore a little. See? There's about four feet of clearance between the water and the fog."

They were taking a chance, he realized that. With the onset of darkness finding the ship again might be difficult. Still, there was no place it could go, and they had only to come back up the strait to find it. Strait? More likely an inlet. They shoved off and let the longboat drift along close to the shore.

Nearly a half hour had passed when Boyar, who was in the bow, lifted a warning hand. At the signal all rested on their oars, and then they all heard it. Somewhere not far off a man was whistling. Then something dropped on a deck and a man swore in Russian.

The boat still drifted, and then, plain to all of them, from beneath the fog they saw the gray hull of the patrol ship. She lay fair across the mouth of the inlet, blocking any escape.

A voice spoke in Russian. "I saw slops from a ship in the opening of the inlet. We've only to wait until the fog lifts and then go in after them. This is Tenakee Inlet and there is no other way out, I know the place well."

At a signal from Jean the oars dipped gently and turning the boat they started back the way they had come. His own ship was up the inlet and out of hearing of the Russian.

Tenakee Inlet . . . there was something he should remember about Tenakee. He scowled into the fog . . . it had been a half-breed who had come down the coast with old Joshua Flintwood, the Bedford whaler. Once on the schooner's deck he wasted no time. "We'll go to the head of the inlet. There may be a way out."

"If there is," Kohl said skeptically, "we'd best find it. Once the fog lifts the *Lena* is coming in, which leaves us like a duck in a shooting gallery."

"We've got that long." Duncan Pope spat over the rail. "He'd be a fool to come in here before the fog lifts."

All the long day through they crept up the inlet through fog like gray cotton, holding as close to shore as feasible, taking soundings as they proceeded. Twice they passed small openings but each proved to be a bay, and it was not until almost dusk that the fog thinned close to shore and they glimpsed the head of the inlet, fronting a mud flat. Wanting time, Jean had the hook dropped and the schooner swung to anchor.

"Any chance of slipping by?" Kohl wondered.

"No . . . not with his guns. He's just inside the opening of the inlet where he can cover the passage."

At the shore the fog was thinner. It drifted in ghostly wraiths among the dark sentinel pines. A break in the line of trees caught Jean's eye, and he had a sudden hunch. "Drop the boat over, Barney. Then pick four men and we'll go ashore."

Leaving the boat on the gravel beach, Jean LaBarge led the way toward the break in the trees. To the right and left the forest was a solid wall of virgin timber, dripping with damp from the fog, but before them the opening gaped wide and they stumbled into a narrow path that led into it.

It was very still. There was no movement of wind or animal. Only water dripping from the trees and the gray mystery of the fog. There had been a wider track here at one time, and only a few large trees in the opening, although some of the bordering pines were magnificent trees. When they had walked about fifty yards they found themselves looking out over another arm of the sea. Jean walked down to the edge and tasted the water. It was salt.

It was an arm of the sea of some size and it ran in a

northwesterly direction. Boyar shifted his rifle to his other arm, and got out his chewing tobacco. "That there," he said, "must open into Icy Strait."

The water was obviously quite deep only a few feet out from shore. He had an idea and it scared him. If a man could catch a spring tide . . . or even without it. But it was a fool idea.

He seated himself on a rock and stoked his pipe. The shore was flat and this was an old Indian portage where they had carried their canoes and *bidarkas* from one inlet to the other for many years. The water was deep off both sides, and at no place was the level of the portage more than six feet above the water level. There were indications that the sea had once been higher. No doubt the level of the water had fallen with years, but at present the distance was a bare sixty yards from inlet to inlet. Yet a schooner was not a canoe that one could pick up and carry across a neck of land.

Getting to his feet he strolled slowly back toward the *Susquehanna*, studying the ground with care. The big question was the fog. How long would it hold? How long would Zinnovy be content to wait him out? A slight change in the wind, or even a rise in wind strength, and the fog would be blown out to sea, leaving them naked and exposed. They had but one gun, although of very good range, and the patrol ship had ten guns and Zinnovy was a naval officer accustomed to handling ships under fire. If it came to a fight they would have absolutely no chance; the superior maneuverability of the schooner was useless in the narrow inlet.

The portage was wide enough, and they would have to fell some trees, anyway. Did he dare take the gamble? The Vikings used to take their ships over narrow necks of land, and there had been a pirate in the West Indies who had . . . Closer to home, Jean had himself seen the Missouri River steamboats "grasshoppered" over sand bars, an occurrence common to nearly every trip upriver.

"All right, Barney," he said finally, "break out that heavy tackle. Get twelve men ashore with axes and make it fast! We're going to take the *Susquehanna* over the portage!"

25.

THE FOREST RANG with the sound of axes and the torch-light cast weird, dancing shadows upon the backdrop of fog and forest. The first of the skids was in place and the two most expert axmen in the crew were beveling the edges, trimming them as smooth as if planed. The anchor trees had been selected and the brush cleared. The skids were run down into the water and as it was nearly high tide the bow of the schooner was being eased up to the skids.

Six men with poles on either side of the bow were helping to guide her into the troughlike opening of the skid. The smoothed-off sides of the skids were heavily coated with grease and a wire rope ran to the big tree well inland through two huge blocks with snatch blocks attached to trees along the portage to exert greater pull. The bow eased into the skid opening and the men dropped their poles and scrambled up the bow chains to the deck to join the others at the capstan. Setting their capstan bars in place they began to walk around and take up the slack. Twelve men leaned their strength into the bars and two more slapped grease on the skids. Slowly, the schooner began to inch up the skids.

"I've been thinking," Pope said suddenly, "—that other inlet over there. I think that's the same inlet where Hoonah village is. The directions line up right, and Hoonah is Chief Katlecht's village. He hates Russians."

LaBarge thought a minute. He knew of Katlecht; he was, in fact, one of the chiefs to whom he had sent presents, and from whose village had come some of the best furs he had been buying in the past years.

"I had an idea," Pope added, "one of us might go to

see him. We could use thirty or forty of those husky lads of his right now."

"Do you know him?"

"I should hope to smile." Pope chuckled. "Spent a couple of months in the village, even had me a Kolush wife. Maybe I should have stayed."

"Take Boyar and get on over there. Get what information you can, and if you can get some help, bring them on the jump."

The schooner was moving slowly, but it was moving. The rigging of the snatch block had increased the strength of the pull by several times and the schooner was inching up on the skids. The remainder of the crew were trimming felled trees for skids to be used further along.

Jean walked along the line of travel with a rifle under his arm, but from time to time he took an ax and spelled one of the crewmen. Kohl was himself taking a place at the capstan . . . day would soon be breaking. Would the fog lift?

With the schooner high and dry they would have no choice but to abandon it and take to the woods, and that would mean destruction of the schooner and their chance of escape as well.

Not far from the schooner was a promontory covered with forest and easily ascended from the shore side. Taking several men from the crew, Jean had their one gun lowered over the side and hauled to a position among the trees on that promontory. From its position it commanded the approach to the head of the inlet. A few shells might stand off the patrol ship for a short time at least.

By daybreak the schooner was completely clear of the water, holding its position with guy wires running to trees on either side of the portage. The hauling tackle was shifted then to a new set of trees and the men resumed their position at the capstan bars. Gant struck up a chantey and slowly and steadily they plodded around the capstan, and inch by slow inch the schooner began to move once more.

At midmorning there was a sudden shout from the woods, followed by a cheer from the crew. Led by Duncan Pope and Boyar a swarm of husky Tlingit Indians hustled toward the schooner. In the van was Katlecht himself, grinning broadly. He thrust out his hand as he had seen white men do, and with the fingers of the other plucked at the red flannel shirt LaBarge had sent him from San Francisco a year before. He also carried a bowie knife Jean had sent and displayed it proudly.

The exhausted sailors resigned their places at the capstan to the Tlingits, and twenty powerful Indians took over. Others hauled and pushed at the hull while still others cleared brush ahead of the moving schooner.

And the fog held, gray, drifting streamers of it lurking among the trees like lost ghosts. The air was damp and cold.

Helena had joined the cook in making tea and serving Tlingit and seaman alike, working from a fire beside the portage. By noon, with the fog showing no change, the schooner had advanced its full length out of the water.

Sweating and tired, Jean accepted a cup gratefully. Holding it in both hands he warmed his numbed fingers, his breath forming a little fog of its own. "You're all woman, Helena," he said. "I never thought I'd see a princess serving tea to my crew."

"Why should a princess not care for her"—she had started to say "man" but caught herself in time—"men as well as any other woman?"

She walked around the fire to him. "Jean, can we do it? How does it look now?"

"If the fog breaks we're in trouble. Otherwise . . . well, we're making progress. I think we can do it or I'd not have tried."

"Was there another choice?"

"No."

The schooner moved at a steadier pace. The Indians had brought grease from their camp, barrels of it that came in their *bidarkas*, and they were slapping it liberally on the skids. The *Susquehanna*, unnaturally tall now that she was out of her natural element, towered above them. Once a small gust of wind came through the pines and the fire guttered, and all waited, holding their breath, but the wind disappeared and the fog held.

Jean returned to the capstan and took his place, plodding steadily for an hour. When Kohl relieved him, he returned to superintending the shifting of the tackle and the guy wires. Also, with apprehension for what might happen, he had two tall poles cut to make a shears in the event they needed to grasshopper the schooner. He had never seen it attempted with a craft of this size but as a boy he had seen the heavy river schooners grasshoppered over sand bars on more than one occasion, and knew that at last resort this would be the method to use.

Yet once the schooner reached the far side of the portage they must skid it into the water. Mentally he calculated the times of the tides. They worked within narrow limits of time and their only hope lay in the fog. If the fog held they could do it, but if it did not. . . .

Small men trooped to the fires for tea and warmth. Twice Jean had rum broken out and laced their coffee when the switch was made to that beverage. During the late afternoon Katlecht sat by the fire sipping his coffee and rum when he suddenly looked up at LaBarge who had stumbled wearily to the fire. "Fog go," Katlecht said. "Fog go soon."

Jean glanced at Kohl, and their faces were grim. Indians were excellent judges of weather; if Katlecht was right their time was short. He sent a messenger to the men at the gun to stand by for trouble, then had guns brought from the ship's armory and passed around to the men to be kept close to hand in the event of attack.

Despite their weariness the men returned to their labors with a rush. The water ahead of them meant escape and freedom; to be caught here meant death or worse, a Siberian prison camp. The Tlingits, filled with their age-old hatred of Russians, fell to with a will and to the tune of chanteys they shoved and pushed on the capstan bars. It was slow, painstaking, backbreaking labor, but the schooner moved and the water lay ahead of them, only a short distance away now.

But the fog was thinning. . . .

Jean glanced up and saw a star . . . then other stars. "Pope," he said, "take the gunner, Gant and Turk, and go out and relieve the men at the gun. Don't take any unnecessary risks, but do what damage you can." He hesitated. "Wait until she's close, Pope, and for God's sake, hurt her."

Within the hour the fog was gone and darkness had come. Once more torches were lighted and the heavy blocks were shifted again, new anchor trees had been chosen and marked out. The shifting of the gear took less time now that the movements had become familiar. Once again the capstan was manned. The schooner was moving.

Taking his rifle, LaBarge started back toward the Tenakee side, Helena walking beside him. Bundled in furs against the penetrating chill of the night, she walked easily beside him, showing little of the exhaustion she must feel.

"Can we get into the water before daylight?"

"If the men hold out. They're weary now; how they keep going I can't guess, and Indians never work like this, anyway."

The skids had been torn up and taken to the opposite side to use again, and there was little evidence of what had been done except the cut brush and the trampled earth. Standing together they looked out upon the dark and silent water. There was no sound but the soft rustle of the water on the shore, and above them the vast sky, studded with stars. The sounds of working men, the creak of tackle, the groaning of the schooner's timbers and occasional cries of the men seemed farther away than they actually were. A coolness came off the water. Somewhere out on the inlet a fish splashed.

"Even if we make it here," Jean said, "we've far to go."

"I'll be in my own country, and I'll be safe."

"Siberia is not Russia," Jean replied bluntly. "You know that as well as I do. It's full of thieves and renegades with a corrupt administration to whom it won't matter at all that you're a niece of the Czar . . . if they believe you they'll be afraid of what you might report."

"There's still no reason for you to come."

"I'm coming, so don't bother your head about it."

They stood hand in hand watching the stars above the dark rim of the pines. There had been too few moments like this, and life without them was nothing. Their love was like no other love, for they could not speak of it, and each was on guard against desire. A word, a touch, it would take so little.

Nearing the lighted area, LaBarge suddenly quickened his step. "Something's wrong," he said.

The men stood about, muscles heavy with weariness, their faces showing their despair.

Kohl came toward them. "Captain," he said, "we're in trouble. Fifteen feet short of the downhill side and she won't budge an inch. We just don't have the power to take her over the hump. We're stuck!"

He led the way up through the cut-down brush and trampled ground to where the hulk loomed black against the night, the towering masts like leafless trees, stark and strong against the sky.

It was what Jean had feared. The power of the capstan and the arrangement of the blocks had enabled the men by their slow, steady push to move the schooner, inch by inch, out of the water and along the skids, heavily greased to aid them. The huge blocks and careful rigging had more than quadrupled the power they could exert; but now, near the highest point above the water, their combined strength was not enough to move the schooner farther.

"We can't budge her," Kohl said. "We broke a couple of capstan bars trying."

Glancing at the stars he could see they still had several hours of darkness remaining, but the men were exhausted. He believed he knew what to do, but he would need rested men to do the work that lay ahead. Despite the fact that the fog was gone, that the coming of the patrol ship was imminent, there was but one thing to do. "Barney," he said, after a moment, "have everybody turn in and get some rest. I'll stand by the gun myself. I'll want two men to stand watch here at the ship; the rest to sleep until four A.M."

"Lord knows they need the rest," Kohl said, "but what about the *Susquehanna*? The *Lena* will be along at daybreak."

"If she heaves her hook at daybreak it will take her all of three hours to get this far. I'll be standing by the gun. If you hear a shot, turn the men to and rig those shears as I told you. And send four men to me."

Kohl put his cap back on his head and started to turn away, then stopped. "Cap'n," he said slowly, "I figured I was a better man than you, that I should be master

172

of this ship, but believe me, I've learned better. You've pulled off things this trip that I'd never have tackled."

"Thanks, Barney."

LaBarge turned to Helena. "You'd better get some sleep. You'll need the rest."

"I'm coming with you."

"But, look—"

"I'm coming with you."

Together, they walked to the promontory where the gun had been placed, pointing its dark muzzle down the channel. The men arose as they approached. "Nothing yet, Cap'n."

"Turn in . . . you'll be turning to again at four A.M."

When they had gone he made a place for Helena between the trails of the gun, folding some blankets and placing them over a pile of evergreen boughs. When she was settled he lit his pipe and settled himself for the long hours of waiting. He was tired, but he forced himself to remain awake.

Somewhere out in the forest a pine cone fell, and upon the water a fish jumped, while far over the trees a night bird called. The rest was silence and the darkness.

The earth was soft beneath him with a deep carpet of pine needles and damp from the fog. A vagrant wind stirred in the pines and he could hear the far-off rushing of wind, a strange, lonely, wonderful sound that is a part of every evergreen forest. He listened, liking it, and listened to the water along the rocks below. These were old sounds, familiar sounds.

"It's a grand country," he said.

"I love it. I shall always love it."

"I've always lived close to the forest," he said. "I'm at home there. I like the wild lands."

Far-off in the forest a wind began. It had started somewhere in the pines along the rim of the world and it came down, awakening new ranks of trees to stirring life, moving the pine needles, brushing the arms of the spruce. It came down across Alaska and moved through the forests and then scattered itself among the coastal islands. It was a long, long wind and it was cold.

The wind rustled the pines above Tenakee Inlet and talked among the trees over the manless beds of Hoonah village, then felt its way along the bare flanks of the *Susquehanna,* so unnaturally naked without the shielding water.

Jean listened to the wind. "You'd better sleep," he told Helena, "we're going to have snow."

26.

JEAN CAME SHARPLY AWAKE, aware instantly that something had happened. Snow was falling gently and steadily through the pines, but it was not this that had disturbed him. Silently, so as not to awaken Helena, he got to his feet and rubbed his legs to restore the circulation.

When he could move quietly, he walked away from the gun and stood in a small opening in the forest, listening. There had been many such times when he waited in complete stillness, ears keyed to the slightest sound . . . and now he heard it.

It came from far off, but it was a noise not of the forest. The forest's sounds he had known since boyhood, and this was no murmur among the trees, this was the steady advance of a large number of men.

On still cold nights sound travels amazingly, and the men were several miles away. They were not Indians, for even a large body of Indians would not have been heard; these men were unaccustomed to travel at night in the forest.

LaBarge quickly realized what the movement implied: Zinnovy was sure of taking the *Susquehanna;* men had been put ashore to prevent the escape of himself or his crew. Undoubtedly the *Lena* was now moving upstream and had landed these men to take up posts on shore. The attack was to be both by sea and by land, and there were to be no survivors.

It was the one thing he had not anticipated, for which he had no plan, and he must move swiftly. An attack now, on the ground, could immobilize the *Susquehanna* and prevent further movement. From the trees his men could be picked off at will as they worked.

He went quickly to the gun and, stooping, touched Helena's shoulder. She opened her eyes at once, completely aware. He explained quickly. "We must go back now, and we must hurry!"

She was on her feet, straightening her clothing. "You go. I'll stay. The *Lena* may come in sight while you are gone and I could fire the cannon. It might stop her."

"You? Fire a cannon?"

She laughed at him. "You forget, Jean. I am a daughter of the Romanoffs, and Honorary Colonel of a regiment of artillery. Several times I have fired salutes with cannon. Is it loaded?"

"Yes."

"Then all I must do is get on the target and pull the lanyard."

He hesitated. "All right, but when the men arrive, you come back. Do you hear?"

She came to attention and saluted. "Yes, Commander! I return at once!"

Jean LaBarge plunged through the brush toward the now-dying fire. Quickly, he shook Kohl awake. The alerted guards awakened the crew and the Indians.

"They'll make a reconnaissance first. When they get close they'll hear the sounds of our work party and send men in to find out what is happening. My guess is that Zinnovy stayed aboard, in which case before they launch an attack they'll communicate with him."

Even with the Indians they would be outnumbered. If the patrol ship reached the head of the inlet before the *Susquehanna* could be launched it could blow the schooner to fragments. Nor did they have men enough to protect the gun from shore attack, although the gun was their only hope to slow the approach of the *Lena*.

How many men had been landed they could not guess, but it was likely that the number exceeded their own.

"We've one chance and one only," LaBarge told them after a moment. "We've got to get the schooner into the water and get the hell out of here. Kohl, take twelve men and get those poles sunk into the ground, make a shears of them, and get the rigging in place. If we can grasshopper her over the hump the rest will be easy."

LaBarge had previously explained the process to Kohl, who had never seen it done. Two long poles, as long as the masts of the ship and heavier, were hastily dragged from their resting places and holes were sunk just ahead of the schooner's bow and almost at the crest of the slight rise. The tackle was rigged and the men manned the capstan. Jean took six of the Tlingit warriors to the gun's position, and Katlecht took another twelve into the forest to intercept the landing party.

Leaving two men with the gun, Jean took the other four and moved up through the forest to aid Katlecht. The gun crew had already relieved Helena and she had returned to stand by the *Susquehanna*.

For a moment there was silence. At the crest of a small rise in the forest, a position that enabled them to look down various lanes between the trees, LaBarge and his Tlingits silently waited the approaching party. Only yards away was Katlecht with his group, scattering across the front and down the flank of the Russians. From behind him LaBarge could hear the hammer blows of the working men.

Suddenly men began to emerge from the trees into view. The first were *promyshleniki*, at least a dozen. Skilled woodsmen these, and dangerous fighting men. Quickly, Jean passed the word along to the Tlingits to select these targets first. In the forest they would be dangerous antagonists.

The *promyshleniki* were an advance party and now they waited the approach of the men from the *Lena's* crew. Then, quite suddenly there was a dull boom of a cannon, their own gun. The Tlingits took the signal as one to fire, and squeezed off as one man. His own shot was only an instant behind theirs. Four of the *promyshleniki* dropped and one seaman, but Katlecht's men were firing, too. The Russians dissolved into the woods but not before LaBarge wounded another man with a shot from his turret rifle. Instantly the Russians began a hot and determined return fire.

The Tlingits were eager to attack, but Jean ordered them to fall back on the gun's position. As they started to retreat, the cannon boomed again and then there was the tremendous crash of a broadside from the *Lena*. The shells were high, and whistled through the forest, cutting off limbs and sending down a shower of leaves.

A Tlingit near Jean, a man with a scarred face and a lean, hard body, was doing yeoman work with his rifle. As Jean watched he saw the Indian fire at what seemed to be a wall of brush and a *promyshleniki* fell face forward from the trees, hit the ground. He started to rise, but the scarred Tlingit nailed him to the earth with a shot through the top of the skull.

Then for a time there was silence. The Tlingits needed no advice when it came to woods fighting, and his own Indians scattered out and took good positions where they could cover every approach to the gun. Jean slipped back to lower ground and ran, crouching as he moved, to the gun position.

Lying flat he looked over the crest of a knoll to see the *Lena*, at least four hundred yards off, swung broadside across the inlet. From her position the portage was not visible; the disappearance of the schooner must have come as a tremendous surprise. One shell from his own cannon had struck her foretop and dropped a spar to the deck. Even as he sighted the patrol ship another shell struck it and sheered away a piece of the bulwark, scattering fragments in every direction. There was a scream of anguish from the ship's deck.

The landing party were, by the sound of the small-arms fire, falling back under the carefully aimed shooting of the Tlingits, who were skilled woodsmen to a man. Of the ten or twelve *promyshleniki* in the landing party at least five were out of action, and it had become obvious to the others that they were marked targets. To men who fought purely for money this was not an especially happy thought.

The *Lena* was shelling the woods now, but most of the fire was directed at the shore position of the gun with a view toward knocking it out of action. The gun's position, well behind the hummock with only her muzzle lifted over the top, was excellent.

Returning to the schooner Jean scrambled up the rope ladder that hung from her amidships bulwark and threw his weight behind a capstan bar. Slowly, under the pull of the huge blocks, the schooner's bow began to lift just as the bows of the river boats had lifted on the Missouri. As it lifted it moved forward, drawn toward the shears. Inch by inch, foot by foot it crept forward, then was dropped to the skid.

Holes had been dug for a new position and swiftly the big poles were transferred, and the men went to work to rig the grasshoppering at the new position. Glancing back down the portage, Jean knew their time was short. Sweat stood out on his brow despite the coolness of the day. If the *Lena* moved up to the head of the inlet she would have the *Susquehanna* at point-blank range and entirely without protection.

"Grease your skids, Barney. This hop should put it over the hump."

Moving swiftly, LaBarge gathered his crew and sent them to the schooner. He found Katlecht lying in the brush, his rifle tucked against his cheek. "You come with us? We must go now."

Katlecht shook his head. "We go mountains. All move now so they find nobody."

Jean gathered those of the crew who were not busy on deck and they moved down the portage ready to repel any attempted landing at that point. Under cover of brush near the end of the portage they watched the patrol ship and waited. Behind them they could hear the creak of the blocks and the complaining of the heavy lines as they took the strain.

The *Lena*, now that no more shells had been fired, was heading toward the head of the inlet. A man in uniform moved near the rail and Jean laid his rifle over a fallen log and took careful aim. He drew a long breath, then let it out easily, his finger tightening on the trigger. The rifle sprang in his hands, and the report laid a lash of sound across the suddenly silent morning. The man on the deck jerked, grabbed the rigging to hold himself erect, then slowly slid from sight.

Immediately, all the crew opened fire on the *Lena*. The man at the wheel, caught in the fire of several rifles, was knocked back and then he fell forward to the deck, the wheel spinning. Another man sprang to the wheel but the *Lena* yawed sharply just as she let go a broadside and the shells were wasted in empty forest.

Behind them there was a hail from Kohl, and Jean sprang to his feet. "On the double!" he yelled. "Move it!"

One man only lay still, and LaBarge ducked to his side. It was Larsen; the big Swede's shirt under his jacket was soaked with blood. He looked up at Jean. "It was a good fight."

Jean looked down into the usually florid features of the Swede. "You made every voyage with me, Lars. I'm taking you along on this one."

"You run . . . they soon come."

LaBarge looked up, hastily taking in the situation. He could hear the boatfalls on the *Lena*, which meant a landing party and immediate attack. He bent to lift the Swede and saw that he was dead.

An instant he stared at the dead sailor, and then at a shout from the schooner he was up and running. As he came abreast, the men working at the shears, lowering away, allowed the ropes to slip and the shears fell, the V astride of the skids. Even as it happened, the schooner groaned and creaked as she started to slide down the ways.

The men sprang away, frightened. An instant and all hung in the balance. If the schooner struck the shears it would be thrown on its side or the runway torn and the ship would slide off into the ground.

LaBarge glimpsed it all as he ran. Dropping his rifle he grabbed an ax from the nearest man and with a leap sprang astride the skid. Swinging the ax with all his great strength he struck the wire rope that bound the two poles of the shears together. As the ax struck he heard a shout of warning. The runway creaked as it took the schooner's weight, now only a few feet away and gaining momentum. He swung the ax again and again. Somewhere abaft the ship he heard shooting. The bow loomed above him. The ax fell for the last time and the wires parted. He fell rather than sprang aside and dropping the ax, stumbled to pick up his fallen rifle.

The last of the crew was running beside the dangling rope ladder. Scattered in a skirmish line, running toward them, were Zinnovy and his landing party. From the schooner's deck a sporadic fire began. The schooner eased forward, moving at a speed just faster than a walk. The log of the shears was pushed easily aside and fell off the skid to the ground. Jean took a shot at the advancing men, and sprang for the rope ladder. He caught it and started to climb, pausing halfway to lay his rifle across his forearm and fire. He gripped the ladder with his left hand more tightly, leveled the rifle again, felt a smashing blow in his side, then fired.

He felt suddenly weak. He grabbed a rung higher and pulled himself up. Hands that seemed desperately far away reached for him. Now the schooner was moving fast. He gathered his strength and pulled himself a rung higher. Somebody caught at his rifle, to which he had clung, held insecurely in front of his body. The hands grabbed at him, caught his sleeve and pulled.

Above him the sun was shining, and then it faded out and he heard rifle fire mingled with a sound as of rushing water. He felt himself lowered to the deck, and then he remembered nothing at all for a long time.

27.

Under a gray sky the gray water was ruffled by a wind raw with cold. The bare masts of the schooner and the bare roofs of the houses along a bare shore offered no comfort from the wind. On deck Jean LaBarge, still pale from blood lost by his wound, stood waiting for the gear to be lowered into the longboat.

"Take the furs to Canton," he advised Kohl. "You don't have a full cargo, but the furs are good and you should make a nice profit. Then return to San Francisco and report to Hutchins. You're in command."

"And you?"

"I'll make my plans as there's need for them. When I've escorted Princess de Gagarin to St. Petersburg there will be time to plan. I may return by this route, and may go across the Atlantic to the east coast."

Kohl did not like it, and said so. "Begging the lady's pardon, Cap'n, you can't trust them. These are a suspicious people, and Baron Zinnovy has friends ashore here. If he doesn't come after you himself he'll send a ship with orders for your arrest."

"I can take care of that eventuality," Helena said. "I believe we can also cope with Baron Zinnovy."

"I hope so." Kohl was gloomy. "You'd better take Boyar, Cap'n. He'd like to visit Poland, and he knows much of this country."

LaBarge glanced at Boyar. "Do you want to come?"

"If I can . . . yes."

"Get your gear on deck, and made it quick."

Snow lay in splotches on the gray slopes back of the town, and on the shaded sides of the buildings just back from the waterfront. Duncan Pope, suddenly gracious, helped Helena into the boat. His sour face anguished, he struggled to find words. "I . . . I never knew a princess before," he finally managed to say, "and . . . and you act like a princess."

She gave him a dazzling smile. "Thank you, Mr. Pope! Thank you very much!"

All the crew had gathered to say goodbye. One by one they bobbed their heads at her. Only Ben Turk was more formal, muttering something indistinguishable as he stepped back.

"Take care of the boys, Barney," LaBarge told Kohl, "and of the *Susquehanna*. And there's a letter on my desk for Robert Walker. Mail it, will you?"

The water was choppy but the men at the oars pulled strongly and the longboat headed for shore. Gant, who was in charge of the boat, glanced at Boyar. "Be careful, man. Remember you're a Pole."

"I'd do better here," Boyar said dryly, "to forget it."

Jean LaBarge looked back at the *Susquehanna*, experiencing once more the thrill he had felt when he first saw her lying on the waters of Frisco bay.

The shore offered nothing, just a gray slate shore with its patches of snow, and the weather-beaten buildings. This was Okhotsk, on the coast of Siberia, and the end of the world. Before them lay a journey of more than five thousand miles to St. Petersburg, and much of that distance was fraught with danger.

The boat grated on the gravel of the beach and a sailor jumped in and drew the boat higher. Jean sprang down to the gray sand and helped Helena from the boat.

He turned to the crew and shook hands all around. "Take her back, boys, and take care of the schooner for me."

Several people, bundled in shapeless clothing, had paused to watch the arrivals but they did not offer to approach. When the boat shoved off and left the three standing on the beach the observers walked away, apparently no longer interested. Taking Helena's arm, Jean started up the shelving beach toward the muddy street lined with its haggard buildings of logs or unpainted lumber, all equally dismal and unattractive. There was no evidence of warmth or welcome.

Helena had papers she often used when traveling incognito, which identified her as Helena Mirov, governess, of St. Petersburg. She had her own papers, but as she explained to Jean, "Nobody would believe a niece of the Czar could travel without entourage or luggage. They would certainly hold us for investigation, and that could take months and might lead to no end of trouble. And it would certainly alert all of Baron Zinnovy's allies here."

"Then you must use the other papers."

"Jean"—Helena looked up at him—"there is another thing. It would be better, I think, if it was believed I was your wife—recently married, to account for the names on the papers. There would be fewer questions."

"I agree with Madame," Boyar said. "And unless Madame intends to ask for an armed escort, I would suggest the sooner we start the better for us."

A square-built man in a heavy gray coat stopped across the street some distance away and watched them. Boyar glanced at him nervously, then picked up their bags and started hastily up the street. The man watched them without apparent change until they entered the office of the post.

Boyar paused in the door and watched the man cross the street and enter police headquarters. Boyar looked around the bare, uncomfortable room in which they stood. There was no one behind the counter and no one in sight. "Wait here," he said, and slipped out of the door and down the street.

The moments ticked slowly by. The fire in the pot-bellied stove gave off little heat. They looked at each other, saying nothing. For once, Jean felt out of his element. There was so much he did not understand. Shivering in the still cold of the post station, they waited for someone to come. A half hour passed before Boyar suddenly opened the door and motioned to them. "Come quickly!" he called. "We leave at once!"

Boyar caught up their bags and started out the door. He went down the street a few steps, then turned into a dismal alley to a low-roofed barn where a man was hitching three horses to an odd-looking vehicle.

"These are *volni*," Boyar explained, low-voiced. "They are 'free horses,' unattached to the post system. The driver is a peasant farmer willing to make some extra money."

The vehicle was a *tarantas,* a heavy, boat-shaped carriage mounted on four wheels with a heavy hood that could be closed in bad weather. The body of the carriage was mounted on two poles which connected the front and rear axles and served as rude springs to break the jolts on the always rough roads. The usual procedure was for the traveler to stow his luggage in the bottom, cover it with straw, and then to cover the straw with blankets and robes. On this he reclined, leaning against pillows. The driver sat on the front end of the carriage and drove the three horses hitched side by side with four reins.

Hastily, they stowed their luggage, and Boyar brought from the house some blankets and an odorous bearskin rug. Climbing in, they spread these out and then Boyar got to a seat beside the driver and the latter gathered the reins and shouted, *"Nu rodniya!"*

Eager to be off, the horses started with a rush. As they turned down the street the police official they had earlier seen glanced their way in an uninterested manner. He stepped to the door of the post station and entered. Instantly he was out on the street, shouting after the *tarantas.*

Boyar noticed but the driver did not, and Boyar lifted a finger to his lips. With the jangling harness, bumping of wheels over the rutted road and the ringing of bells over the horses' backs, the driver heard nothing.

Once on the road the man whipped up his horses. Their hoofs pounded smartly on the half-frozen road as they dashed off into the emptiness before them. Yet this emptiness would not remain with them for many miles. Beyond that lay the *taiga,* the world's greatest stand of virgin timber, a wild, lonely region of forest and swamp, inhabited by peasants and exiles, escaped convicts and outlaws.

This road was the famous *tracht,* leading from Siberia to Perm, at the edge of Russia proper. Travel by post road was easy, although subject to interference and questioning by the police. All that was needed for travel on the post road was the priceless *padarozhnaya*—the order for horses. The same carriage might be kept all the way through and only the horses changed. However, travel by *volni* was often best, for the farmers' horses were better fed and the travel faster.

It was cold. Not a piercing cold but the chill of late spring. The country over which they drove was a vast marshy plain scattered with clumps of alder and willow, stunted growths more like brush than trees. Helena moved closer to him and they leaned back against a duffel bag Jean had placed as a back rest, reclining rather than sitting.

Boyar turned his head to tell them they were headed, not for the post station, but for a farm where the driver knew free horses were also available. In this way, with luck, they might travel the entire distance without approaching a post station.

The curtains of the carriage were open and they could watch the country as it slipped behind them. Occasionally a cold blast of wind whipped the curtains and Helena snuggled deeper into the blankets and closer to Jean. From time to time they dozed, talked, watched the miles go by.

The farm at which they finally arrived had a high wooden gate, behind which were several log buildings, much less impressive than the gate that led to them. As they drove up two huge dogs ran out, barking wildly. The gate swung back and a man emerged, accompanied by a boy.

They were served a meal, hastily prepared, coarse black bread, pickled mushrooms, boiled salmon, wild strawberries and tea.

"He eats too well, this one." Boyar spoke in an undertone to Jean. "We must be careful."

Their host was a stocky, powerful man with a heavy beard. His smile was wide but the look in his eyes was hard and calculating. Those eyes took in their warm clothing, the bags in the vehicle, and several times his eyes returned to Helena, lively with curiosity. He spoke to Boyar in Russian, and Boyar commented, "He suggests we stay the night . . . I think it would be unwise."

"Thank him," Jean said, "and tell him we have no time."

When they rose from the table to return to their carriage, their host was talking to a stranger who must have come up after their arrival. He also said something to their driver. This was a new driver, a boy scarcely sixteen, with a sallow, vicious face and shifty eyes. His hair was uncut and his clothing was grimy and evil-smelling. Once, after the carriage was moving, he turned and glanced back at them with such an expression of malignancy that Helena shuddered. "I don't like it, Jean," she whispered. "I am afraid!"

Before them the narrow dirt road dipped into a forest of scattered pines that grew thicker and thicker as they rolled and rocked over the rutted road. The lowering clouds grew darker and a wind blew through the pines, skittering the dried leaves along the frozen ground. Off the road the forest was thick with an unrevealing gloom. Helena had fallen asleep against Jean's shoulder and slowly he himself relaxed and began to sleep fitfully, jolted awake again and again by the roughness of the road and the capacity of the *tarantas* to bounce around. . . .

He was awakened by a persistent shaking of his foot. He opened his eyes, aware that the vehicle was moving at a walk and something was pressing against him. Then he heard Boyar's whisper and realized that the weight against his side was the Polish hunter. "Captain, sir?"

"Yes?"

"We're in trouble. Our driver . . . I think he fixes to meet someone."

Wide awake, Jean eased himself into a sitting position. He whispered briefly into Boyar's ear, and the Pole moved back to his former seat. Outside a spatter of rain fell, then ceased. There was no sound but the creak of harness and of the carriage itself. Jean slid his his pistol from under his coat and waited, listening. Suddenly the *tarantas* stopped moving.

Boyar asked a question and the boy replied, his voice surly. Boyar ordered him to keep going but the boy became belligerent. In the vague light Jean caught a gleam on a pistol barrel and then the *tarantas* began moving again. In the moment before it started Jean heard a rush of hoofs, somewhere in the forest behind them. The carriage gathered speed. Helena stirred, awake now and listening.

As if on order there was a rift in the clouds and the moon shone through. Closing in around the carriage was a group of horsemen.

Jean held his fire. It would not do to fire into a troop of Cossacks or a party of innocent travelers. A voice shouted, the voice of the innkeeper at their last stop. Boyar spoke sharply and must have emphasized his command with a thrust of the gun barrel for the whip cracked and the horses began to run.

There was an angry shout from the riders. LaBarge lifted his pistol and took as careful aim as was possible with the *tarantas* bouncing from stone to rut to stone again. He aimed at a bulky rider somewhat to the right of the others, who might be the innkeeper. He aimed, hesitated, then fired. The rider jerked in the saddle, fell headlong into the road in front of the following horses. Promptly, LaBarge fired twice more into the dark mass of riders, bunched by the timber lining the road.

The pursuers fell back, astonished by the sudden burst of firing, and in drawing back they lost the race. LaBarge reloaded his pistol, taking his time. He carried another pistol and a two-barreled derringer as well, the latter in his sleeve holster.

The driver was frightened and sullen but he drove hard. Still it was well after midnight when the *tarantas* reached the wooden gate of their next stop. Jean got stiffly to the ground and Boyar closed in beside him.

Men with lanters gathered around and Boyar ordered them to change teams and be quick. He had neglected to holster his pistol, and the sight of it lent emphasis to his directions. From time to time the men stared at the boy who stood to one side watching LaBarge and Boyar. One of the men ventured a whisper but the boy snapped a one-syllable reply, his tone ugly.

Once inside the farmhouse Jean chose a seat against the wall that commanded the door, and drawing his pistol, placed it on the table beside his plate. The people outside were acquaintances or allies of those who had attempted the attack, and he wanted them to know he was ready for anything.

The room was long and low with a rough board floor and beamed ceiling. To one side there was a fireplace; the house might have been taken right from western

America. Food was brought to them, and hot tea. The man who served them was obviously much interested in the pistol: his eyes glistened with envy. "Such a gun!" he exclaimed. "I have not seen such a gun before!"

"I carry two," Jean replied, "and it was fortunate."

"Fortunate?" The man's thin face seemed to grow still. He looked at LaBarge. "There was trouble?"

"We were attacked by robbers."

There were three men in the room now, and the boy driver as well. Nothing more was said until Jean asked about horses.

The proprietor shrugged. "I am sorry. We will have no horses until morning, but it is better that you stay here. We—"

"We leave tonight." Jean looked across the table at the man and lifted his cup with his left hand. "And you had better harness the team at once, and with your best horses."

"It is impossible!" The proprietor was voluble with protest. "It is—!"

"If you believe those men who attacked us are following," LaBarge said coolly, "you're mistaken. Their leader is dead."

"Dead?" The proprietor looked with quick concern at the boy, whose face showed white under the dirt.

They stared at him, shocked to immobility. LaBarge put down his teacup and picked up the pistol. Immediately the room broke into movement. "You," La-Barge said to the proprietor, "come with us. The rest of you stay here. Think hard before you come outside. We don't care how many you bury here."

Boyar took the man to the stables and returned with three gray horses, in fine condition. Hastily they were harnessed and then Jean told the proprietor to call his driver. The last they saw was a small cluster of people standing in the road, staring after them.

Ahead the road wound over rough country but the gray horses galloped cheerfully on, their breath steaming in the chill air, their feet making a lively clatter on the hard ground. When they had been on the road about an hour, it began to snow.

28.

CROWDED TOGETHER AS THEY WERE, Helena and Jean bumped and jarred against each other as the *tarantas* jolted over roads made rough by traffic as well as by lumps of ice, frozen earth and ridges of snow. Their bodies twisted and jerked with the motion until every muscle ached. And all the while the driver kept up a din of shouts, yells, whipcracking and cursing which mingled with the jangling bells that hung from the bow over the shaft horse.

Occasionally they would emerge from the forest to race along between stubbled fields and clatter through peaceful villages where every dog within hearing rushed out baying and barking, only to be scattered helterskelter by the charging team. Inside the passengers were pitched, tossed, heaved and battered.

At last, in the cold gray of earliest dawn, they drove into the streets of still another village. The street was a mere alleyway of ruts a foot deep or more, lined on either side by buildings of logs or unpainted lumber, their gable ends turned to the road, each with a huge wooden gate beside it. Near the end of the street the horses turned of their own volition toward one of these gates.

Then began a period of shouts from the driver and faint replies from within, protesting argument, and finally after an interminable period, the gates swung back and they drove into a court flanked by a low-roofed stable covered with sod and an open-faced shed containing a bunch of decrepit carts, a weird and amazing assortment of vehicles, relics of some vanished era too remote to be guessed.

Jean fell rather than stepped down from the *tarantas* and straightened his bruised and aching muscles. Shin

Boyar's face was sullen with cold, showing its weariness, and when Jean helped Helena from the carriage she looked up at him with a glance of mingled despair and amusement at their situation. Painfully they walked toward the small door that offered little but a promise of warmth.

As the door opened under his hand a blast of odorous air struck them in the face. For a moment they hesitated, but the bitter cold left them no choice. They went inside.

Three small windows, their glass gray with dirt, looked out upon the road they had just left. Against the wall on the inner side was a long wooden bench, fastened to the wall. Before it was a heavy table and several stools lined the table's opposite side. In the corner opposite was a huge stove built of whitewashed brick, and from the top of the stove to the wall was a shelf some eight feet wide that was also built of the same whitewashed brick. On this *palati* the family slept at night, as well as any guests who might be present.

A buxom girl with two thick blond braids entered and began putting dishes on the table. On Boyar's advice they had brought their own tea and sugar, the custom of travelers in Russia, for the tea along the *tracht* was scarcely drinkable. The food on the table consisted of eggs, black bread, some thick green soup which was very hot, and butter.

"I think we should drive on," Boyar advised. "I am sure these are honest people here, but if Madame is not tired—?"

Helena looked up, smiling. "If you can ride farther, I can also!"

"How soon will you try to contact your friends?"

"At Perm . . . and that is a long way yet."

Outside the cold was bitter. The *tarantas* started with a rush, then settled down to a steady jog. The village fell behind and they entered upon a vast plain scattered with clumps of trees. The sky had turned gray and sullen, and as the miles went by the driver glanced again and again at the sky. Turning on his seat, he called back to them. *"Purga!"*

The clouds, a flat mass above the tops of the trees, seemed to press down upon them, and the cold increased.

191

Helena pressed close to him, her face against his arm. There were no buildings, anywhere, and the trees grew thicker, the country wilder and more desolate. Here the land was swept by great winds that had left the trees twisted into grotesque shapes. Snow began to fall, a few flakes at first, then increasing until all was shut out by a white, moving curtain. Boyar drew the leather curtains and the *tarantas* was black inside. It was like riding in a moving cave. The wind whipped under the curtains, however, and the cold could not be kept out. The driver sat hunched and silent, seemingly impervious to the temperature.

Jean leaned toward Boyar. "We've got to find shelter! This will get worse!"

The *tarantas* had slowed to a walk; the driver was having trouble staying on the road. LaBarge knew the *purga* was the dreaded black blizzard of Siberia which could uproot trees or blow the roof off a house. Travel in such a storm would be impossible. The temperature was already far below zero and growing colder. Yet the driver was apparently headed for some place of which he knew. Finally, just when the wind seemed to become a full gale, he swung the horses into a dark avenue of trees through which the storm roared in a mighty blast. Treetops bent, glimpsed through a momentary lifting of the curtain. Behind them a tree crashed, blown down by the wind. Occasionally a blast of wind would seem to lift the carriage off the ground, but the horses were running now, and then they were in the lee of a hill and drawing up before a window which showed a feeble glow of light.

There were two doors in a log wall built against the side of a rocky hill, one for people and a larger one for the carriage and animals. With Helena clinging to his arm, Jean LaBarge opened the smaller door and they stepped inside.

They found themselves standing in the mouth of a cave. Beyond a log partition they could hear Boyar and the driver stabling the horses. A small fire dying in a huge fireplace provided the only light. There was a table, a few stools, some broken harness and on one of several bunks, a man was lying.

Finding a stump of candle, Jean struck a match to

the wick. The flame leaped up, swaying like a dancer in the breeze from the chimney. The room was icy cold and there was no fuel. Crossing to the bunk, Jean lifted the candle and looked down at the man who lay there.

The man's face was white, the skin drawn tight against the skull, his eyes, wide open, were sunk deep within their sockets. For a moment he believed the man dead, and then he saw his lips move.

A door in the partition opened and Boyar came through with the driver. Boyar had his arms full of supplies, the tea, sugar, biscuits and some other articles with which they had provided themselves against emergency. "Get the tea on," LaBarge told Boyar. "We've a man here who's in a bad way."

"No!" The driver caught LaBarge's arm. He spoke in hoarse Russian. "The man is a convict! An escaped prisoner!"

For the first time Jean noticed the loop of chain descending from under the ragged blanket. Lifting the blanket, he saw that iron bands enclosed the man's legs around each ankle, each thigh, and just above each knee. The bands were joined by a heavy chain suspended from a belt.

Holding the candle close, LaBarge removed the blanket and examined the man. His dirty shirt was stained with blood; he had been shot twice. The first was only a graze along the ribs, although it had bled severely; the other was a wound through the chest. There had been a bad flow of blood from that wound but the blood had no bubbles in it and the lung did not appear to have been penetrated.

"You must do nothing!" the driver insisted. "If you are caught it is hard labor in the salt mines. Let him die."

"The hell with that." LaBarge turned. "Shin, how's the tea coming?"

"Soon . . . and there will be hot water enough for the wounds."

Gratefully, the escaped prisoner accepted the scalding tea. He tried it gingerly, then sipped again. With a clean cloth LaBarge bathed the wounds. Obviously, the second bullet had gone clear through, yet aside from lost blood no harm seemed to be done. Still, without care the man would bleed to death, and without fuel he would freeze.

Twice Boyar slipped into the night and each time returned with a huge armful of wood. Soon the fire was roaring. It was almost an hour before LaBarge completed his job of bathing, treating the wounds and bandaging them. By that time Boyar had prepared soup and Helena had broken bread into it. With a large spoon she fed the man, who scarcely took his eyes from her face, and then only to stare at LaBarge.

The driver sat hunched near the fire, his gaze averted, wanting no part in the crime. Yet from time to time he replenished the fire, and went with Boyar to gather more fuel. Finally, the driver went to a bunk and rolling up in his greatcoat, was asleep in a moment. Boyar gathered more fuel, ate a little, then followed him.

The prisoner dropped off to sleep and Helena joined LaBarge beside the crackling fire. Covering themselves with a blanket, his arm about her shoulders, they sat and watched the flames in silence. The cave room was warm now; the wind roared outside. Snow fell and hissed in the flames, and occasionally the wind guttered the fire, but there was no other sound but the snores of sleeping men.

Under the blanket Helena reached for and found Jean's hand, and so they sat, and so, propped against a chair turned on its side, they slept.

29.

THREE DAYS THE STORM BLEW without letup, but within the cave the fire kept them warm. There was fuel within a few steps of the door, yet each day found the driver, Liakov, more frightened. Obviously he wished to be far from the cave before a searching party would come for Marchenko, which, they discovered, was the prisoner's name. He had escaped, he told them, by ducking away from a column of prisoners in a blinding snowstorm, but not before he was struck by two bullets. With his last strength he had dragged himself to the cave.

"I knew of it as a boy," he told them. "It was a place where outlaws came." His eyes went to Helena. "That was before I served in the Army."

"With what regiment?" Helena asked.

"The Semyonovsky, Madame. I often stood guard at the Peterhof and the Winter Palace."

He knew her then, which explained the peculiar way he had looked at her when he had seen her that first night. He had probably recognized her at once.

"It is imperative," she told him quietly, "that I reach St. Petersburg." She kept her voice low so that the driver would not hear. "It is even more important that I reach there unknown to Siberian officials."

The pitifully thin lips smiled. "I am a poor convict, Madame. I have seen no one . . . only a wandering hunter who bandaged my wounds and went away . . . who knows where?"

By the evening of the third day the wind had died and LaBarge directed Liakov to make the *tarantas* ready for travel at daylight.

Liakov glanced at the convict. "What of him?" he asked. "We will turn him over to the police?"

"The safest thing for all concerned is to say nothing.

This is police business. The police will ask many questions. They will be pleased at no one for interfering."

The morning dawned gray and cold. While Boyar aided Liakov with the harness, LaBarge stood by the bunk. He handed Marchenko a fistful of rubles. "These will help. My advice to you is to get away from here, even if you have to lie in the snow. I've left some tea on the table, and a bit of cheese and bread."

Outside the cold was piercing. The carriage started stiffly, but the horses were eager to go after their confinement and soon they had broken into a run. Several times they were forced to stop and remove trees blown across the road, and fifteen miles from the cave they came to their first halt where they quickly changed horses and started off with a fresh team and driver. Glancing back as they pulled away, LaBarge saw Liakov staring after them.

"You are worried about Marchenko?"

"I hope he escapes, Helena. I hope he does."

"He is very weak."

"But his heart is strong."

With such a one there was always a chance. How about himself? Would he have the fortitude to stand what Marchenko had stood? Could he survive? Would he lose his will to escape? If Liakov went to the police . . .

As if to atone for the past, the clouds drifted away and the sun appeared. It was spring and here and there the hillsides showed a bit of green under the grays and browns. Twice they stopped to change horses, each time remaining with the *volni* system of free horses. The free drivers were known to the police, of course, but a man was harder to trace by that method than by the post system. Often the *volni* drivers were weeks in returning to their home villages, which meant weeks before they could be questioned.

The villages were as alike as peas, gray lumber and weather-beaten logs, a hint of decoration at the eaves. The few people who moved about were bundled to the eyes in odds and ends of clothing.

The steppe had changed to pale green with here and there the golden yellow of wild mustard or buttercups. The driver pulled off the muddy road to the prairie and drove more swiftly, crushing grass and flowers under the

196

spinning wheels. He was a younger man, this driver, and filled with good spirits. He sang as he drove, and seemed to know everyone along the road. He shouted at them and they shouted back. Several times they raced past trains of wagons whose drivers plodded beside them, and several times they raced for miles over plains that were blue with a carpet of forget-me-nots. Distant hillsides were thick with the slim white trunks of birch, and always the villages kept appearing, shutters hanging loose, gates sagging. They drove on and on with a succession of teams and drivers until all sense of time was lost and all was forgotten but their own spinning wheels, and the never-ending shouts of drivers who raged, cajoled, praised, petted and swore at their teams.

From Tiumen to Ekaterinburg the road was bordered on either side by a double row of splendid birches nearly eighty feet tall, set so closely their branches arched over the road and shut out the sun with their green canopy. This was known, Helena told him, as "Catherine's Alley," for the trees had been planted by the order of Catherine II, and now, almost a hundred years later, they offered shade to the traveler.

The peasants' huts were alike in their cheerlessness except for occasional flowers in the windows. Rarely was there a tree or blade of grass in any of the villages, but in the windows one saw geraniums, oleanders, tea roses, cinnamon pinks or fuchsias.

Then came the night when they slept in a two-story brick house near the river where the owner advertised "rooms for arrivers." LaBarge was awakened in the first gray of dawn to find a rough hand on his shoulder and bending above him the thin, cadaverous face of an utter stranger. He sat up quickly and the man stepped back. LaBarge glanced toward the connecting door to Helena's room.

"It's all right," the man said. "I tell you, mate, I've touched nothing, and as for the lady, I'd bother no lady, mate. Not I."

"What are you doing here? How did you get in?"

The fellow stood with his feet apart, grinning. His nose was a great beak, his red, wrinkled neck like that of a buzzard, and his eyes, small and blue, twinkled with a cynical humor. "How did I get in, you ask? Through the door, mate, through that very door. Locks, you know, I've no time for them, and I'd no wish to go knocking about on your door at this hour of the morning. Start folks looking, you know, and maybe start them thinking."

"What do you want?"

"Now that's more like it. I like a man who comes to the point. But it ain't so much what I want, mate, as what you need. It's the police, mate, and they're hunting you. You, the lady, and the sailorman who's with you."

"Sailor?"

"Aye . . . spotted him at once, I did. And you likewise, mate. I've seen a bit of the sea myself, seven year aboard a lime-juicer out of Liverpool. It's where I learned my English. But if I were you I'd be getting myself up."

Jean rolled out and dressed quickly. He had no idea who the man was, but a warning was a warning, and that the police were looking for him was more than likely.

"What is it?" LaBarge asked. "What makes you think the police are looking for me?"

"This is the way of it, mate. I've no love for the law, not to speak of, I ain't. Time to time they've given me a bit of trouble, so when I seen the man in the black coat, seen the wide jaws and bullethead of him, I says to myself, it's the law. So I listen. . . ."

"Inquiring, he is, for people of your description. Now I'd seen you arrive, knew where you'd gone and, thinks I, this man and his lady would like to know, so I've come."

"Where's the officer now?"

"Eating, he is. Eating better than I've eaten these many weeks, stuffing his fat jowls in the town, and when he's finished that, had a bit of tea and picked his teeth, then most like, he'll be after you."

"We'll need a team for our *tarantas*."

"They'll be ready for you, mate. Leave it be. A boat's better, and I've spoke to a man for you. He's owner of a barge, and he's made room for us."

"Us?"

"Look, mate. I've nothing here I can't leave behind,

198

and I'd best be leaving it, too. With a bit of cash I might make it, and if I come along with you, I might be helping you." He winked. "I'm one who says it will never go wrong with a man to help the gentry."

Coolly, Jean checked his pistols. To be taken now was not part of his plan. He slid the pistols into his waistband.

The man with the great nose and twinkling eyes glanced at the pistols and then looked up at Jean LaBarge. He had a sudden feeling that he would not like to face a pistol backed by those eyes and in those hands.

"Gentry, you said?"

"Did you think I'd not notice the lady? And a beauty too, if I may say so. . . ."

Helena came through the door, dressed for travel. She looked gay and excited. "Why, thank you! That was nicely said!"

The ruffian bowed, his eyes twinkling. "A lady, I said, and you, sir, anybody can see you're a gent." He canted his head at him. "And maybe a soldier, too, but a fighting man in any course. Take that from me, as one who knows."

When Boyar entered the room, LaBarge explained their situation hurriedly and the man led them out the back way, across the court and into one of the sheds that surrounded it. Here he lifted a board and they all emerged into an alleyway that ended in a field bordering the river. Walking along a path, half-concealed by a line of trees, they reached the stream and boarded the barge.

A man seated on a bollard got to his feet, knocked out his pipe and came aboard. He cast off while the red-faced man hauled in the plank that served as gangway.

"I'd go below," he told LaBarge. "You're dressed a bit well for barge folk."

The cabin was cramped but clean, and there was a samovar with a fire under it. When they were well into the stream, their guide came below and took cups from the cupboard and began to make tea.

"Murzin, they call me," he said. "It's a good name, short and handy-like." He was a long, bony man, slightly stooped in the shoulders and his body was so lean that every rib must show, but his thin hands were dexterous and swift. "A thief, they call me, and they are right. I steal from travelers."

"You have not stolen from us," Helena commented. Jean could see that she liked the man, and he did himself.

Murzin chuckled and grinned wickedly. "Because the police are after you. I'm not one to foul my own nest, to rob my own kind.

"Oh, I know! You two are gentry, although that one"—he pointed a finger at LaBarge—"would have made a fine thief. Maybe that's another reason I didn't steal from you. He would kill a man if he needed killing. He would kill a man very quickly, I think." He glanced sharply at LaBarge. "Is that why they want you?"

He decided to be frank. "Madame and I have enemies who would like to prevent us from reaching St. Petersburg. That could be it, although I think we lost them, but it may be another thing. Back there"—he jerked his head toward the Siberia that lay behind—"we helped an escaped convict. Our driver might have informed on us."

"That could be it . . . they don't like that, not one bit do they like it."

He gulped his tea. "St. Petersburg, is it? Aye, and I'm your man. I can help." He swallowed more tea. "We've ways of our own, you know. Ways of getting about that the police don't know."

"How much?"

"The bargeman will want fifty rubles, but you can give me what you like when we get there."

He looked slyly from one to the other. "And when you are there, where will you go?"

"We will have a place," Helena said.

"Where then? I say—"

Helena looked straight into Murzin's eyes. "There is a story that King Richard trusted a thief, and I shall. We go to the Peterhof."

Murzin's eyes were bright. "I know that story. Robin Hood, wasn't it? So you go to the Peterhof? Yes . . . yes, that would be it." His eyes lighted with savage, cynical amusement. "The Peterhof! What a place for a thief! What a place from which to steal!"

30.

Moonlight lay cold upon the Neva as their carriage rolled through the silent streets. Long ago they had left the barge behind, and since then had changed their means of travel several times. Now there was no sound but the *clop-clop-clop* of their horses' hoofs.

Sitting back against the cushions of the carriage in which they now rode, Jean LaBarge looked about him at the wide avenues and stately buildings, wondering that he, born in the swamps of the Susquehanna, grown to a fur trader among the northwest islands, should have come to this place. He rode now in the streets of the city of Peter the Great, riding beside a niece of the Czar, and within a few days, a few weeks at most, he would see the Czar himself.

At last they dismounted from their carriage before the palace of the Rotcheffs. A strange group: Shin Boyar, the Polish *promyshleniki* from Alaska, Murzin, the wandering thief, Jean LaBarge, merchant adventurer, and the Princess Gagarin, wife of Count Rotcheff and said by some to be the most beautiful woman in Russia.

It was her hand that rang the bell. They waited, saying nothing, and for a long time there was no sound within. Finally, after the third ring, the door opened slightly.

"Alexis! Open the door! It is I!"

The old man opened the door with fumbling haste, bowing and backing away, his face covered with a smile. Yet when he looked past her at the three men, he hesitated. "The Master? Is he all right?"

"He is in Sitka, Alexis, and wounded. He sent me home to see His Imperial Majesty, and these men have brought me safely here. We will want food, Alexis, and beds for these men. Quickly now, for we are cold."

The old man hurried away and somewhere in its vast depths the building began to stir and breathe as it came to life. When Boyar and Murzin had been shown to the servants' quarters, Helena led Jean to a sitting room where a fire was blazing. Food was brought to them there, and tea. Jean watched the firelight playing on her face, finding lights in her dark hair. "I suppose I'll see little of you now," he said unhappily.

"There will be time." He had walked to the fireplace with his brandy, and she followed, standing beside him. How tall he was! "Jean, we must work quickly. There is no telling what they will do, so I must arrange an audience with Uncle Alexander at once. Once that is done I shall try to arrange an interview for you. It will not be easy, Jean, for he is a busy man. I believe I can do it."

"I'll need some clothes. Tomorrow I'll hunt up a tailor."

She laughed. "You need not go to a tailor, Jean. We will have him come here. I will tell Alexis and the tailor will come at whatever hour you wish."

She left the room and he was alone with the portraits on the walls and the fire that crackled cheerfully on the wide hearth. The ceiling was high, and the flickering light played upon the faces of the pictured men. The food had been excellent, slices of cold beef, cheese, and a bottle of claret. It was all strange and very different here.

When she returned she joined him at the fireplace again. "So . . . at last we are here."

"Did you doubt we'd make it?"

"Not really. Yet sometimes. . . . Jean, I shall keep Murzin with me. I like him."

"He's a thief."

"Of course. But somehow I do not believe he will steal while he works for me. He has his own pride, I think."

"Yes, I've known men like that. They're rare though."

"Jean." Helena hesitated. "I shall never forget what you have done for me . . . for us. You have no idea how far Sitka seemed from here, even though it is part of Russia. It is like the end of the world. Without you we might both have failed, Alexander and I."

"That makes it harder . . . a man can't steal the wife of a friend. My kind of man can't."

"You couldn't steal me, Jean. He is my husband."

They were silent, watching the fire. "It's hard to believe that when I leave St. Petersburg I'll never see you again."

"I shall return to Sitka. I must go back to Alexander."

"Don't do it, Helena. You can't. Believe me, if you destroy Zinnovy, he'll end by destroying you. I know. The man I looked at that last night would stop at nothing. You can't put yourself in his hands again—you can't."

"I must . . . I must return to my husband."

"Someday," LaBarge said slowly, "someday I think I'll kill Zinnovy . . . or be killed by him."

"Then kill him. I do not want you to die."

"What use is it to live and not have the woman I love?" He spoke angrily. "I'm a fool, Helena. A double-dyed fool."

They stood together, staring down into the fire. The flames were smaller now, the bed of coals glowing and red, shimmering with changing color. They turned to face each other, looking into each other's eyes, then Jean drew her close and they stood for a long time, held in a tight embrace. Finally she stepped back, out of his arms. "Good night, darling," she spoke softly. "Good night, I—" She turned quickly and walked from the room.

A month passed. The Czar was in the Crimea and would soon return; until then there was nothing to do but wait. There were balls and parties and despite his restlessness Jean enjoyed St. Petersburg.

Helena had started the wheels moving to bring about the return of Paul Zinnovy. There had been no word from Count Rotcheff but his friends were also active. It was soon obvious, however, that Baron Zinnovy had powerful friends, at least one of them highly placed in the Ministry. Her statement that Baron Zinnovy had attempted to murder her husband met with polite disbelief, even among her intimate acquaintances. Officials were courteous, but whatever might be done seemed to die somewhere in the chains of bureaux and offices that lay between an order and its execution. The powerful influence of the Russian American Company blocked every move she could make.

No delays are more infuriating than the delays of officialdom. She knew that many officials regarded her as a pretty woman interfering in matters that did not concern her. The reports she brought back awaited the Czar's return; until then there was nothing to be done.

"They know who you are, Jean," she warned him, "and they will do all they can to prevent you from seeing the Czar. Be careful, for the Baron's friends are shrewd and powerful. They will stop at nothing."

Russia, under Czar Alexander II, was restless with impending change. The Czar was studying a plan to abolish corporal punishment in the armed services as well as in civilian life. He knew the time had come to institute social reforms and bring his country to the level of other western nations in that respect, yet it was necessary to move slowly. Many feared loss of prestige even more than income losses, others opposed change as they opposed anything that interfered with the *status quo*, with every stratagem at their command.

The Russian American Company's stockholders were among the elements he must win over, and they were well aware of the bargaining position they held. They used this position to avoid any change in the situation in Russian America, and indicated that faraway Sitka could wait until much was done at home.

Alexander II knew he must proceed with care. He had abolished many of the restrictions on the Jews, and had suggested the restoration of home rule for the Finns, but oddly enough, his greatest opposition came from the Liberals who demanded he do more and do it faster. Nothing would satisfy them but dramatic change and such a change was impossible under the circumstances.

Of these facts Jean LaBarge had been only dimly aware when he arrived in Russia, but Helena soon acquainted him with the situation. Then they received their first break.

Helena met him as he entered the palace one afternoon. "Jean! He's here! The Czar is back and he has permitted an audience!"

"When?"

"The night after tomorrow. It will be very late, and

he will see us at the Peterhof, in a private audience."

It was, he knew, a rare privilege, and without the help of Helena it could never have been managed. Now they could do something for Rotcheff and there was a chance he might have time to talk of Alaska itself.

A half mile away a slim, erect man with iron-gray hair and cold eyes shielded by square-cut glasses sat behind a desk. He was tall; even seated he seemed tall. His desk was bare of all but one sheet of paper and from time to time he glanced at it. There was a knock at the door.

"Come in!"

A young man in a naval officer's uniform stepped into the room and closed the door carefully behind him, walked to a position before the desk, clicked his heels and saluted.

"Lieutenant Kovalski"—the man behind the desk studied the officer as he spoke—"I am informed that you have killed three men in duels with a pistol, two with the saber."

"Yes, sir."

"Lieutenant, there is a man in this city who is very dangerous to Russia. He interferes in Russian affairs and he endangers the position of a naval officer who is very important to Russia. The man I refer to has arranged to have a private audience with the Czar. It is not wise that such an audience take place, yet the Czar has given his word. You understand?"

Lieutenant Kovalski understood perfectly, just as he had understood when a superior officer had suggested his coming to this address. There were enemies of the state who must be destroyed and it was often inconvenient to bring them to trial. He was also aware that the man before him controlled many avenues to power and prestige, and that a word from him . . .

"The man to whom I refer is called Jean LaBarge. He is an American and at present resides at the Rotcheff palace."

Kovalski's eyes flickered. He knew the man in question by sight. A tall, dark man with a scar . . . there was something about him . . . for the first time he felt uneasy at the prospect of a duel, yet it was foolish to be disturbed. He was one of the finest pistol shots in all Russia. Before coming here he had been informed that he would be transferred to the Army and given the temporary rank of Colonel, and that might be only the beginning.

"It must be done at once, you understand? The audience is for the night after tomorrow."

"Thank you, sir. Is that all?"

"Only this." The man behind the desk took a long envelope from a drawer and handed it to Kovalski. "Examine this in private when you are gone from here."

The man removed his glasses and placed them on the sheet of paper, taking the bridge of his nose between his thumb and forefinger for an instant.

"One thing, Lieutenant. You must not fail. Do you understand?"

"Of course." Kovalski snapped to attention, did an about-face and walked from the room. When he reached the street he paused briefly opposite a lighted window and drew the papers from the envelope. The first was a deed for a small estate in Poland, a place he knew well. He glanced at the date and saw it was for several days in advance, and below was a note to the effect that to be valid the deed must be presented at the estate by Colonel Kovalski, in person.

He smiled wryly. "And if I'm dead . . . ?" The answer was obvious.

He shrugged. No matter. He would not be dead. It would not be the first time he killed a man on instructions.

31.

THE PLACE CHOSEN FOR THE DUEL was near a small castle outside of St. Petersburg. Jean stepped down from the carriage and strolled casually across the grass under the trees into the small open park that lay beyond. Beside him was Count Felix Novikoff, who had consented to act as his second.

The challenge had been an obviously arranged affair. In company with Novikoff, who was a friend of Helena and the Rotcheff family, he had gone to a fashionable café. Several Russians in uniform had entered, and in passing, one of them deliberately bumped him. Then, turning, the officer looked LaBarge right in the eye and said, "Swine!"

Novikoff started to speak, but LaBarge was smiling. "Swine?" he questioned. "How do you do, Mr. Swine? My name is LaBarge."

For an instant the Russian stood very still, blood rushing to his face. Then someone laughed and the Russian's face stiffened with anger. He raised his hand to slap LaBarge, but Jean was in no mood to be slapped, so he struck first and hard, knocking Kovalski to the floor, half stunned.

There was silence in the café. The officers who had entered with Kovalski were shocked. Novikoff caught Jean's sleeve. "Come!" he whispered. "We must go . . . now!"

He had recognized Kovalski at once, knew the man's reputation, and what the sequel must be. Novikoff realized the quarrel had been deliberately provoked and was intended to result in a legal assassination.

Jean turned to go when Kovalski staggered to his feet. "Wait!" he shouted hoarsely. "Wait, damn you!"

LaBarge turned to face him. Kovalski drew himself

up. He was wearing the uniform of a colonel in the Russian Army. "My seconds—"

"Send them. Send them, Colonel, and I'll tell them what I tell you now. If you challenge me the choice of weapons is mine, and I choose revolvers, at thirty paces. We walk toward each other at the command and cease firing only when one or both of us is unable to continue."

Kovalski opened his mouth to speak, then closed it. This was all wrong. LaBarge, he had been informed, was an American businessman, not accustomed to duels. He . . . with a shock the terms of the duel came home to him. They were to walk toward each other, firing! He had never fired a pistol while walking in his life.

"Will you act as my second, Felix?" LaBarge asked.

"Gladly, Jean! Gladly!"

Appalled by Kovalski's challenge, Novikoff had seen the shock of LaBarge's terms, and realized at once that Kovalski was disturbed. It had, perhaps, been LaBarge's sudden acceptance, his immediate dictation of terms, and his coolness. Also, it had been as obvious to Kovalski as to Novikoff that if the two men went toward each other shooting, one of them was sure to die. Many a man who is a fine marksman in firing at a fixed target is helpless in firing at a moving target while moving himself. And to know at each step that his own danger would be greater. . . . Many a duelist who is master of his weapon can act with complete composure as long as he is sure he is master, but at close quarters even a novice would have a chance.

Later, leaving the café, Novikoff, who was twenty-five, watched LaBarge with unstinted admiration. "Have you used a pistol? In a duel, I mean?"

"In western America every boy begins to carry a pistol as soon as he becomes a man, usually at fifteen or sixteen. I've had duels, but on the spur of the moment, without warning, and always with men used to the pistol."

Count Felix Novikoff was excited. From Shin Boyar he learned more about Jean LaBarge, learned about his life in the west as Boyar had heard it, and about the fur poaching in Alaskan waters. LaBarge overheard

Novikoff repeating the stories to friends, and did not mind. He knew that before long the stories would reach Kovalski.

When they had walked through the trees to the open park in the middle, Jean paused a moment, his eyes glancing over the area across which they must walk. He did not wish to step into an unexpected hole or trip over some unforeseen obstacle. The grass was smooth and well trimmed. He figured that if Kovalski was accustomed to firing from a stance he would without doubt attempt to score with his first shot from the original position.

Kovalski was jumpy and irritable. LaBarge looked to him almost like a professional duelist, although the terms he had proposed were ones no professional in his right mind would suggest. For the first time since he could remember, Kovalski had not slept well.

The distance was paced off and the two men took their positions, some thirty yards apart.

Colonel Balacheff stood at attention midway between the two and well out of the line of fire. "Does either gentleman wish to extend an apology?"

"No." LaBarge's voice was calm. "I do not."

He stood very still, waiting. His stomach felt hollow, his mouth dry. This was the worst part, this waiting. But he knew exactly what he was going to do.

"No." Kovalski's voice was steady.

"I will count." Balacheff spoke clearly. "I will count to three. At the count of three you will commence firing and will move toward each other firing at will. You will not cease to fire until one of you is unable to continue. Am I understood?"

Both men nodded.

The sun was not yet above the trees; there was still dew on the grass. Somewhere a bird rustled in the leaves and off across the fields a raven cawed hoarsely into the still, clear morning.

"One!"

Jean felt a trickle of sweat start down the back of his neck. Kovalski stood sidewise to him, his pistol raised in the orthodox position. He would shoot as the pistol came level, and Jean would be stepping out with that shot. If he led off with his right foot and Kovalski fired, his step would carry him a bit out of line with the bullet . . . he hoped.

"Two!"

The raven called suddenly, and Jean saw Kovalski twitch, almost as if he had started to fire, then caught himself. Jean could feel the sweat on his brow; he hoped it would not trickle into his eyes. A muscle in his leg started to jerk.

"Three!"

Jean LaBarge stepped off with his right foot and felt the whip of the bullet. Kovalski could shoot, but he had missed.

Holding his own gun slightly above belt height, Jean walked swiftly toward the Russian. The morning was very still and he could feel the grass against his shoes. A bead of sweat was trickling down his cheek and the stillness of the morning was slashed by a second shot. Only a split second had passed, yet he was moving. He felt the second shot go by him, then realized it must have been the third shot because he had already heard the report of the second.

He was walking fast but he was counting his steps and when he had taken seven steps he was going to fire. He felt the shock of the bullet as it struck him and the air lash of two more as they missed, and then his foot came down on the seventh step and he fired.

He fired his shot from hip level, the gun thrust out with his elbow close to the hip to steady it, the trigger squeezed off gently. He felt the gun leap in his fist and thumbed back the hammer for the second shot.

Kovalski wavered, then buckled at the knees and began to fall. As he fell the pistol dropped from his hand and when his body hit the turf his feet rebounded, fell hard, and he was dead.

LaBarge looked at the man who had been sent to kill him. He lowered the hammer on his pistol and from habit thrust it into his waistband. Novikoff rushed to him, hand outstretched. "Wonderful! Wonderful!" Novikoff was excited. "I never saw anything like it! He kept firing, and you—!"

Balacheff had picked up Kovalski's pistol. He glanced at the cylinder. "Empty!" He looked at LaBarge with

210

unbelieving eyes. "Sir, let me congratulate you! I have never seen a braver thing! *Never*, sir!"

"Thank you."

Jean held himself stiffly against the beginning pain. There was a dampness of blood within his shirt.

When they were seated in the carriage, Jean said, "Right home, and don't stop!"

Novikoff stared at him, arrested by something in his tone, then abruptly, he felt alarm. "You're hurt! You've been shot!"

"Just get me home."

When the carriage drew up at the curb, Jean descended and walked stiffly to the door. He heard Novikoff paying the driver and then the door opened and he stepped blindly into the great hall. Then his legs buckled under him and he felt himself falling. From the stair there was a scream. The last thing he remembered was Helena rushing to him.

Lying in a canopied bed he looked up into the vague darkness above him. When he turned his head Helena was sitting across the room under a shaded light, reading. For a long time he lay watching her, tracing the way her lips were shaped and the proud lines of her face, softened now by shadows as they were sometimes softened by sunlight. He did not speak, nor feel like speaking, but lay still, thinking of her and of all that had transpired since their first meeting on the rain-wet dock in San Francisco. All that seemed far away now, all the distant Pacific, the wastes of Siberia, all of it. It had been months since they had left Alexander Rotcheff wounded in Baranof Castle, and now he himself was wounded, and for the same reasons.

"How bad was I hit?"

Helena dropped her book and rushed to him. "Jean! Oh, Jean! You're awake!"

"Seems that way. I wasn't hard hit, was I?"

"No . . . the bullet went through you and nobody knew, nobody even guessed you were hit. The doctor says it is only a flesh wound, but you lost a lot of blood, your clothing was soaked with it, underneath. But nobody knew."

"And they must not know. What day is today?"

"The same . . . it is almost midnight. I was waiting until you became conscious before I sent word to the Czar."

"There's no need to send word. We'll go."

"But you're hurt! You can't possibly go!"

"Want to bet?" He grinned at her. "And if you think I'm not capable, just try sitting down beside me."

She drew back quickly. "Jean! You mustn't talk like that." She looked down at him with excited, happy eyes. "You frightened me so! When you fell I thought you were dying."

"May I have some brandy? I could use it."

"Of course! What have I been thinking of! But then you must rest."

Nowhere in the world were there so many fountains, nor fountains of so many varieties, and when turned on simultaneously, as they were now, all the splendid parks were filled with a wondrous and mysterious splashing of water, making a strange music all its own. From the front of the old palace, where Helena and Jean paused on the wide terrace, a broad avenue of fountains and cascades led all the way to the seashore. And everywhere the scent of lilacs.

As they mounted the steps a Beethoven German dance was being played on the terrace by the Court orchestra. From the terrace where they had paused the view was magnificent, gilded statues mingling with the sparkling silver of the fountains. Pausing by the balustrade, neither wished to speak, they stood absorbed in the beauty of the moment. Behind them the Peterhof was ablaze with lights. They turned from the display of fountains, to watch the arrivals. Tall old men in mutton-chop whiskers, resplendent in uniforms, younger men with handsome mustaches, officers of the armed services and members of the nobility.

The audience arranged with the Czar was to take place privately, but during the grand ball. Standing beside the balustrade, Jean watched the colorful sight before him and was glad it had happened this way. He would never again see such a sight. He listened to the low-voiced comments and greetings, and was introduced to people whose names he never managed to distinguish but who were alike in extraordinary titles. All of them were anxious to talk to the Princess Gagarin of her experiences in Alaska, all curious about Count Rotcheff, and equally curious, he realized, as to his presence there.

Conscious of the beautiful girl beside him, more than ever conscious of her position, conscious of the music, the fountains and the scent of the lilacs, he could not help but draw a comparison between this place and the deck of the *Susquehanna* as she had been, gliding through the dark waters of Peril Strait. Nor could he forget the old man who lay wounded in Baranof Castle, and whose future as well as his life might rest on the interview that lay before them.

"Do you feel all right, Jean?" Helena looked at him anxiously. "Maybe we should not have come."

"Nonsense. I've never felt better." And he did not lie. True, the bullet had gone through him, and there was a stiffness in his chest muscles and his side. But he had suffered much more from slighter wounds, and weak though he might be, his enormous vitality and the strength built into him by years of outdoor living made the wound of little moment. He smiled a little, thinking of Hugh Glass crawling his miles upon miles across the plains of Nebraska after being clawed by a grizzly, and of a trapper he knew who had survived two weeks in the wilds when unable to walk from wounds and a broken leg he had set himself.

Count Novikoff crossed the terrace to them, clad in a blue and gold uniform, accompanied by a tall young Hussar in white and gold with a scarlet dolman flung over his shoulder.

"Captain LaBarge? I should like to present my friend, Prince Wolkonski."

A remarkably handsome young man, the Prince was scarcely more than a boy, with smooth blond hair and the face of a Greek god, and he was excited. "I am honored, sir! All St. Petersburg is talking of your duel with Colonel Kovalski, and how you allowed him to empty his pistol before you fired a shot! And while walking toward him! Remarkable, sir! Remarkable!"

"Thank you." Embarrassed, Jean took Helena and

slipped away as quickly as possible. When alone for a moment, he turned to her.

"They believe I did it because of honor," he said dryly, "that I deliberately gave him every chance. I don't like to appear under false banners. I took my time because I wanted to fire one shot and kill him when I fired."

"Nevertheless, you gave him every chance."

"Helena," he smiled gently, "I don't want you to misunderstand me. I didn't give him any chance I could withhold. These boys, they make a hero of me because they believe I acted the way I did as a matter of honor. Actually, from the minute of the challenge every move I made was calculated to put him at a psychological disadvantage. His trouble was that his marksmanship was better than his strategy."

Even among the two thousand guests present, eyes turned again and again to Jean LaBarge. His height, the great breadth of his shoulders, the dark, piratical face with its scar, all were calculated to draw attention to the man who had killed the noted duelist.

The Emperor and the Empress opened the ball with a formal polonaise, and soon, despite his wound, Jean was dancing also. He felt good . . . shaky in the legs, but good. Yet soon at a tug from Helena's fingers, he followed her from the floor and into the great park.

The shaded walks were silent except for the distant music and the play of the waters in the fountains. They walked, arm in arm, under the dark trees.

"Jean, we shall be seeing His Majesty in just a few minutes. When we were changing partners during the last dance I was told to be ready. We are to meet him in a little pavilion built by Peter the Great."

The park was empty of people. Jean moved carefully, not liking the shadows, suspecting danger everywhere.

As they walked up the path to the pavilion a man came down the steps to greet them. He was tall, bearded, and in uniform. He glanced quickly, sharply, at LaBarge. "Follow me, please."

They followed him through a small door and Jean found himself in a long room with a large fireplace and several pictures at which he merely glanced. Before him stood Alexander II, Czar of all the Russias.

"So, Captain LaBarge, you celebrate your arrival in my capital by killing one of my officers!"

Jean LaBarge bowed slightly. "Only, Your Majesty, because he would have prevented my audience with you!"

32.

ALEXANDER'S TONE WAS IRONIC as he said to Helena, "We must keep this gentleman with us, Princess. He talks as well as he shoots."

The Czar, a tall man with keen gray eyes, studied Jean thoughtfully for a moment, then said, "You have visited our Pacific colonies, sir. What do you think of them?"

"I think they are too far from St. Petersburg, Your Majesty."

"In other words, you agree with the report forwarded to me by Count Rotcheff?"

"I haven't seen the report, Your Majesty, only Russian America. And I believe that when a private company runs a territory for its exclusive profit it will give more thought to the profit than to the welfare of the territory."

Alexander seated himself abruptly. "Sit down, Captain." He gestured to a chair, "Helena?" When they were seated, he said, "Now, sir, tell us of your experiences in Alaska."

LaBarge thought quickly. He could lie, and paint Alaska as a territory no one would want; he knew this was the opinion of many of those in important positions in Russia as well as in the United States. Or he could tell the truth, relying upon the Czar's own intelligence to realize that a rich colony in an exposed position invited seizure. He decided that frankness was the best policy. It was likely, anyway, that the Czar knew a great deal about Alaska.

He began with his first awareness of Alaska, led his listeners quickly through the buying of furs, his first information in regard to fisheries, lumber and coal. He also mentioned the costs of exploitation, the distance

216

from markets, and his own ventures into the area. The only thing he did not mention was gold.

"You traded in Russia against the orders of the Russian American Company?" demanded the Czar. His features were cold, revealing nothing.

"Yes, Sire."

Alexander raised an eyebrow and glanced at Helena, who restrained a smile. "You fired on a Russian warship? You evaded her demands to heave-to?"

"I did, Your Majesty, in the belief that the warship was acting upon Company orders rather than your own. Also," he added it without more than the merest trace of a smile, "because I believed I could outsail him."

Alexander laughed. "You are frank, sir."

"What's to be gained by lying? I trust to your judgment, Your Majesty, and also to your realization that the captain of a ship is often in the same position as the head of a state. He has to accept the risks of his position, and sometimes he has to act boldly."

Alexander tapped his fingers on the table. Jean had a feeling that the Czar agreed with him in principle, and might be reasoned with. He decided to speak out.

"Your Majesty, it's said in the United States that you are Europe's most enlightened monarch; it's said you plan to free your serfs. Did you know that the Indians in Alaska, who were free from the beginning of time until the Russian American Company came to Alaska, are greater slaves than your own serfs?"

He paused momentarily. "I deal in furs. I know the income from those furs. I know that on every trip to Alaska I have made a very substantial profit. Still I understand that the Alaska company has to ask appropriations from the government of Russia to keep operating."

Alexander's face hardened. "Are you suggesting that the stockholders are being cheated? That the government is being robbed?"

"I'm only saying that each of my trips was successful. The trips of dozens of other traders whose furs I bought were successful. But the Russian American Company, which is on the ground, is losing money."

Alexander got to his feet and walked slowly across the room and back. Then he stopped and asked LaBarge

217

about the matter of the wheat. Jean explained in as few words as possible, told of the burning of the wheat but without any suggestions or accusations. Then his own ride north and the delivery of wheat that resulted. The Czar asked many questions about the ride, the terrain crossed, and dangers.

"Obviously, Captain LaBarge," he said finally, "you honored your agreement with Count Rotcheff at great personal risk to yourself." He hesitated. "You are staying long in St. Petersburg, Captain?"

"No, Your Majesty, I'll return now. My only wish was to see the Princess safely returned to her home, and if possible to speak to you."

"I see . . . and what did you hope to gain by speaking to me?"

"I hoped to suggest, Your Majesty, that Russia sell Alaska to the United States."

If the Czar was surprised, he gave no evidence of it. Perhaps Helena had mentioned it, perhaps he had seen it coming, or there might have been some such suggestion in the report forwarded by Count Rotcheff.

"And you, a private citizen, are in a position to negotiate?"

"No, Your Majesty. But," Jean added, "I have a friend in Washington who might be. His name is Robert J. Walker, and he is former Secretary to the Treasury of the United States, and former Senator from Mississippi. I know he favors such a plan, and is in touch daily with others who do."

Alexander changed the subject and they talked quietly for nearly an hour on conditions in Alaska, the rapid westward expansion of the United States, and of the building of railways.

He arose suddenly. "Captain, I have taken much of your time. I thank you for coming to see me, and especially for assuring the safe return of the Princess, my niece."

"Thank you, Your Majesty."

"As for your suggestion, I shall give it much thought. It remains a possibility."

Outside in the park it was cool and pleasant. They stood for a long time watching the play of light among the sparkling waters of the fountains, and listening to the cascades as they ran down to the sea. From the palace came the sound of music. The dance continued still, although it seemed forever that they had been gone.

"And now?"

"San Francisco. But I believe this time I'll cross the Atlantic and see Rob Walker."

"I shall return to Sitka."

He turned sharply around. "Helena, you . . ."

"You think I am a fool? But Alexander is there, and my first duty is to him. Would you think more of me if I remained here?"

"Less, maybe, of your loyalty, more of your judgment. It isn't safe, Helena."

"No matter, I must go back."

33.

Jean LaBarge picked his way across the rutted, muddy street. He had arrived in Washington scarcely an hour before and was shocked by the appearance of the capital. Heavy army wagons had furrowed the streets and plowed the avenues into rivers of mud. Here and there Negroes walked about with planks and for a consideration aided passengers alighting from vehicles to reach the sidewalks, or pedestrians to cross the streets. Hacks were few and hard to find, and often became stalled in the street where their passengers must remain marooned or wade through mud to the sidewalks.

Without waiting for a cab he picked his way through the streets and at last reached the impressive mansion on the tree-bordered square where Robert Walker made his temporary home. He walked up the steps and scraped the mud from his feet on the door scraper, then pulled the bell.

The Negro who answered the door was a short, stocky man who recognized the name at once. "Mistuh LaBarge, suh? Mr. Robert, he's sho' gonna be pleased! He sho'ly is."

The man who sat behind the desk in the high-ceilinged room was short and slender. He looked up from his desk as the door opened, then came suddenly to his feet. "Jean!" he said. "Jean LaBarge!"

"Hello, Rob."

They gripped hands for an instant, smiling at each other. It had been a long time.

"When did you get in?"

"Less than an hour ago. I took a room at the Willard."

"You needn't have done that."

They walked on into the room and Jean handed his hat and cloak to the Negro. Rob glanced at LaBarge's wide shoulders and the perfectly tailored suit.

"Whiskey?"

"Please. . . ."

Rob poured the drinks. "To the Honey Tree!"

Jean grinned at him. "The Honey Tree!"

He downed half his drink, then put his glass down. "I've often wondered about it, wondered if anyone ever got all that honey."

"I have no idea, Jean, but I do know there has been some talk of draining the swamp and logging it off."

"Then I don't want to go back."

For a half hour they talked of various topics, then Rob lit a cigar. "All right, Jean, tell me about it. Tell me about Russia. . . ."

It was growing light when Rob suddenly got to his feet. "Jean, you're tired. Can you come for dinner tomorrow night?" He glanced at his watch. "I mean, tonight? I want you to meet some friends of mine."

"Sure."

"You should have told me you were coming. The Willard is all right, but—"

"It's best for me. I'm lunching with a friend tomorrow. You may know him. Senator Bill Stewart."

"Of Nevada? I know of him, and a very able man."

"He was a cattle drover for a while as a boy, drove them right along Mill Creek Road once, he told me."

"How does he stand?"

"On Alaska? He's for it, I'm sure. He came early to California and is in favor of opening up new country."

"Sumner is the man you must meet. He's been against us, but I believe he is wavering a little. Jean, I want you to talk to him, I want you to tell him about Alaska.

"There's been no question about Seward. He's been for it from the beginning, perhaps even before I was, and he has been taking the brunt of the ridicule while I've been gathering the support. The papers refer to it as Seward's Folly, Seward's Icebox, but he found many of the arguments offered against Alaska were the same as those offered against the Louisiana Purchase. Seward dug up all those old arguments and has published the lot."

"Will it go through, Rob? Will they buy Alaska?"

He shrugged. "Who knows? I believe we will. I believe, in spite of the opposition, that the treaty will be

221

ratified, but we've got a fight on our hands. Sumner is lukewarm, unconvinced but willing to listen, but I will tell you something about him, Jean. He likes facts. He likes to *know*, and when he speaks, he likes to deliver facts. Given the proper ammunition, I think he'll be with us."

The streets were dark and silent. When the door closed behind him Jean LaBarge walked slowly up the street. Several times he paused in his walking, feeling the mistlike rain on his face, looking up a broad avenue. The mud was obscured by darkness, and the tree-lined streets were softly beautiful.

Robert Walker did not go to bed. The excitement of seeing his old friend was joined with another realization: it was Jean LaBarge, if anyone, who could swing the balance toward ratification. His actual presence here, the chance to talk to a man who knew the country. LaBarge's own dramatic personality was sure to do much to convince a few laggards. He spoke easily and well, and above all, he seemed to know everything there was to know about Alaska.

Seated at his desk, Robert Walker considered the situation that faced him. Pleased as he was to see his old friend, he knew at once he must utilize his presence, and he knew that LaBarge would have been the first to agree. A less colorful person would have been less valuable, but the dark, handsome LaBarge with his romantic scar, his stories of the fur trade and the islands, his recent visit to the Czar's court and the duel that preceded it, these were sure to make their impression.

From the beginning of his political career Robert J. Walker had devoted himself to his country. He was an American who was filled with the ideas that filled many Americans at the time. He wanted to see the United States possess the entire continent, and the subjugation of a continent seemed a small task for men who had crossed the plains in covered wagons, who scouted the first trails and built towns where none before existed.

Walker had not made the westward trek, yet he had lived much of it with Jean LaBarge. He had not helped organize a mining village into a law-abiding community but he knew how it had been done, and to the little man from the banks of the Susquehanna it was vastly exhilarating.

The United States was bound to grow, as Muraviev had foreseen. In Walker's files there was a letter Muraviev had written to the Emperor:

... It was impossible not to foresee the swift expansion of the United States power in North America; it was impossible not to foresee that these States, having secured a foothold on the Pacific, would soon surpass all other powers, and acquire the whole northwest coast of America. ... We need have no regrets that we did not establish ourselves in California twenty years ago. Sooner or later we should have lost it ... it is foolish not to realize that we should, sooner or later, have to surrender our North American possessions. It is also inevitable for Russia to hold sway over the whole of eastern Asia.

Walker looked thoughtfully at his dead cigar. It was strange that a man like LaBarge, with no apparent interest in politics, had yet become a key figure. This man, sure to be forgotten in the march of history, at this important moment possessed the information that might swing the vote, and a personality dramatic enough to convince.

He, Walker, had been called a genius of party management. To many outside the understanding of world affairs, the term might seem less than flattering, yet Walker preferred it to any other. He knew how to line up the votes, knew what the states and territories needed, and he knew that statecraft consists of a reconciling of viewpoints, and to be a superior statesman one must also be a superior politician. It was not enough to have vision, to have a program. It was not enough to be strong, sincere, honest. In a democracy one also needed votes, and to put over a program one must find a way to win the votes of those with less vision and possibly even less loyalty to country.

The United States must have Alaska, not only as a possession, but as a state. To win a land is not to possess it; the land must be populated and held.

The first person Jean saw when he entered the room was Seward. From descriptions he recognized him at once, standing near the fireplace chewing an unlighted cigar. His limp gray hair was rumpled and untidy, and some cigar ash had scattered itself over his satin-faced waistcoat.

Seward acknowledged the introduction with a brief, limp handshake and a glance from his shrewd, appraising eyes. "You are much spoken of these days, Mr. La-Barge." He rolled the cigar in his teeth. "You have the advantage of us, sir. You have seen Alaska."

"And I have talked to the Czar."

"You have assumed a lot, Mr. LaBarge. By whose authority did you speak?"

Despite the words, his voice held no animosity. Jean replied quickly, smiling as he spoke. "By yours, of course, sir. Mr. Walker tells me that in a speech at St. Paul a few years ago you said, speaking to the Russians, 'Go on and build your outposts all along the coast to the Arctic Ocean, they will yet become the outposts of my own country.' "

Seward's eyes flickered for an instant with humor. "Mr. Walker's memory is very convenient for you, Mr. LaBarge."

Jean sensed rather than saw that other men had joined them. One of these he was sure was Charles Sumner, for Seward then said, "Tell us about Alaska, La-Barge. Tell us what you saw."

Robert Walker glanced quickly around the room. Here, in this room, were a dozen of the key men in the Senate, men who might make or break ratification of the treaty. So much depended on the next few minutes. Suddenly he found himself wishing that Fessenden were here. One of the ablest speakers in the Senate, Fessenden was a bitter opponent of the purchase of Alaska.

LaBarge had turned, almost casually, with his back to the fire. What he was to say now need not convince Seward, for Seward had been a consistent fighter for Alaska from the beginning; it was the others he must win. Charles Sumner was a man who dearly loved to present facts, to speak with authority, and he was a man whose words carried weight.

"What can any man say of a land the size of Alaska
224

in a few minutes? I've seen its furs, its miles upon miles of forest, its gold, its iron, its fish. I have hunted in woods teeming with wild game, and seen valleys as fertile as any upon earth."

From his vest pocket Jean took a small lump wrapped in skin. It was the nugget he had bought, long ago, from the trapper. "See this? Gold . . . and there is more of it there. But believe me, Gentlemen, gold is the least of Alaska's riches."

For an hour LaBarge talked, replied to questions, and told stories of his experiences in Russian America. He told of the cruelties of the *promyshleniki*, and gave figures on the fur shipments. In forty years the Russian American Company had shipped over 51,000 sea otter skins, 291,000 fox pelts, 319,000 beaver and 831,000 fur seal hides.

"And that, Gentlemen, says nothing of what our own ships took out, nor the British. My own ship has taken out more than 100,000 skins, much whalebone, walrus, ivory, Tlingit blankets and some gold."

It was late before the party broke up and at last Walker and LaBarge sat down together.

"I think," Walker said, "you've won some allies for us, and certainly you've given our backers some ammunition. What are your plans?"

"I'll leave for the coast at once. I have the *Susquehanna* to think of." He glanced up at Walker. "When do you think this can be done?"

"The purchase?" Walker shrugged. "Congress rarely does anything swiftly, Jean, and there are enemies to the plan. Some think it a waste of money, and General Ben Butler is bringing up the old matter of the Perkins claims. He says he will use their claim against Russia to stall ratification of the treaty. It may take months yet, even years."

"I see." Jean got up. "Rob, I'll write from San Francisco. I'm anxious to get back."

"The Princess de Gagarin has returned to Sitka, you said?"

"I'm worried, Rob. I must get back there. If Zinnovy was willing to risk shooting Rotcheff, he won't hesitate to rid himself of them both. As you say, politics isn't always a fast business, and although the Princess turned her husband's reports over to the Czar, it may be months before anything can be done. There will be delays, hesitations, arguments . . . you know more about that than I . . . and in the meantime, they are there."

For a moment the two men stood together, and then Walker put his hand on the younger man's arm. "Jean . . . take care of yourself."

"You do the same."

It was snowing when he reached the street, a light, unseasonal snow that melted as it hit the pavement. Jean LaBarge walked quickly away into the darkness.

Robert Walker returned to his study. Now he could move, now he had ammunition, facts, figures, arguments. And Sumner, he thought, was won. And Sumner would dearly love a debate with Fessenden.

So tomorrow. . . .

34.

Baron Edouard Stoeckl had arrived in New York from St. Petersburg on February 15th, 1867. As he was recovering from a severe injury to his leg he remained in New York for two weeks, but during this time he was in touch with Robert Walker. His purpose in returning was to negotiate the sale of Alaska.

A draft of the treaty was before the cabinet by March 15th, and on March 29th, Stoeckl received word from the Czar that the treaty was approved. Although it was very late when the news came to him, he at once joined Robert Walker and together they went to see William Seward, Secretary of State. All night they worked.

As the *Susquehanna* prepared for sea, Jean LaBarge read in the *Alta Californian* that the treaty "will hardly be considered at this session, but will go over to next winter."

Seward increased his campaign of education. The papers rarely came out now without some information on Alaska, and by letter, Jean continued to supply information on various parts of the Russian-held area. On April 4th it was reported that there was no chance of the treaty being ratified. But a letter from Rob was optimistic, and with that final word, the *Susquehanna* sailed.

For several days a fast-sailing sloop had been lying alongside a wharf near Clark's Point, and during none of those days had a man been ashore. Within the hour after the *Susquehanna* cleared the Golden Gate, Royle Weber dropped into Denny O'Brien's bar.

Much had changed. Yankee Sullivan, under threat of lynching by the Vigilantes, had committed suicide. Charley Duane had been escorted to a ship and sent off to New York, and O'Brien had much to worry about.

But his memory was long, and the night when he had stood at his own bar with his pants around his heels with the click of his vest buttons on the floor in his ears was not easy to forget.

Crossing the room he dropped into a chair opposite Weber. Weber shifted his weight on the chair seat and smiled. "Well, Denny, we've waited a long time!"

"It's now?"

"The *Susquehanna* cleared port this afternoon."

Denny turned and motioned to a dark-skinned man who loitered at the bar, and when the man leaned over, spoke to him. Instantly, the man was out of the door and running. Less than an hour later the sailing sloop slid away from the dock and pointed herself north for Sitka.

"I'd like to be there," Denny O'Brien said. "I'd like to see his face."

The *Susquehanna's* second port of call was at Kootznahoo Inlet. The information LaBarge had received was clear. No ship had called at Kootznahoo since his own last trip, and there were many furs. It would be a rich cargo to pick up. When the *Susquehanna* dropped the hook off Kootznahoo head the *bidarkas* were swift to come.

A few days before the fast-sailing sloop had put into Sitka harbor, but had not gone near the dock. Rather, it had gone at once to the *Lena* and tied up alongside. Within an hour both the *Lena* and the *Kronstadt* slipped out of Sitka harbor, the *Lena* sailing north and around the island through Peril Strait, while the *Kronstadt* sailed south, rounded Point Ommaney and started north. The sloop, taking water and provisions from the *Lena,* never even docked at Sitka for fear the grapevine would carry word across the islands, but sailed immediately back to the United States.

The weather was good. Ben Turk, Gant and Boyar had gone ashore to hunt in the hills back of the inlet. Kohl was also ashore. Trading had been brisk that morning, but now it had begun to lag. Jean LaBarge went below and stretched out in his bunk.

He was half-asleep when from the deck there was a sudden wild yell, then a tremendous explosion. Leaping from his bunk he was thrown off balance by a second concussion. Lunging for the companionway he heard screams of agony from the deck, then a concussion from aft. He sprang out into a cloud of smoke and flame. Something forward was burning. The forem'st lay in a welter of tangled ropes and splintered wood. After, Duncan Pope and Ben Noble were working the gun, and near them, sprawled in the wreck of the helm, lay one of the Indians in a pool of blood.

Across the mouth of the bay lay the *Lena*. At a glance, LaBarge knew the situation was hopeless. There was no other way out of the inlet, and inside, the water was not deep enough to take the schooner. She would be shot to wreckage before they could get moving.

"Cut loose the anchor" he yelled. "Get a jib on her!"

A shell screamed overhead and lost itself somewhere in the woods. The schooner was moving slowly now. If they could get around Turn Point. . . . He had no hopes of saving the ship, what he wanted now was a chance for the crew to take to the hills. Once there, with the friendly Indians, they could hide out for weeks until they might reach the mainland.

Pope fired their own gun again, and LaBarge had the satisfaction of seeing the shell burst amidships, smashing the whaleboat to splinters and ripping sails and rigging. Now the *Lena* moved closer, getting into position to rip the *Susquehanna* with another broadside.

Enough of the wheel remained to swing the schooner and LaBarge started to put it over when a shell struck forward and he felt the ship stagger under a wicked blow in the hull. Then the shelling stopped. Their own gun had ceased to fire and turning he saw Duncan Pope sprawled on the deck, his skull blown half away. Noble caught his arm.

"We'd better run for it, sir!" he shouted. "They'll be alongside in a few minutes!"

Two boats were in the water, pulling strongly toward the wreck of the *Susquehanna*.

Dazed, he glanced around. Pope was dead, and another man lay sprawled amidships. The schooner was drifting helplessly, but the current, slight as it was, was taking them deeper into the inlet. The tidal currents there, he recalled, were fearfully strong.

The way was blocked. The *Lena* lay fairly across the

only entrance and her boats were drawing near. There was nothing else for it.

"Abandon ship," he said. "Get for shore, all of you."

"What about you?" Noble protested.

"I'll come," he said. "Get going!"

He turned to the companionway and went swiftly down the ladder. For the first time he realized how badly hulled they were: water stood on the deck of the saloon. He slipped a pistol behind his belt, caught up a coat. Alongside he heard splashes and yells as the crew jumped over the side. The shore here was nowhere over fifty yards away.

He went swiftly up the ladder and reaching the rail, turned back for a last long look. The forem'st was gone, trailing over the side in a mass of wreckage. The stern was a wreck and the deck was literally a shambles. Pope and Sykes were definitely gone, both killed in those few minutes of shelling. Luckily, most of the crew had been ashore. Yet . . . the *Susquehanna* . . . it was like deserting an old friend. He sprang to the rail.

Below him and not twenty yards away was the Russian longboat, and in it were a dozen men, six of whom covered him with rifles. In the stern sat Baron Paul Zinnovy, smiling.

To jump was to die, and he was not ready to die.

The boat came alongside and the Russians swarmed aboard. Two men seized him and bound his hands behind him, stripping him of his pistol.

Zinnovy scarcely glanced at him, walking about the ship, looking her over curiously. Other men had gone below to inspect the cargo.

As he was seated in the boat one of the men spoke to the other and indicating LaBarge, said, "*Katorzhniki.*"

It was a word that stood for a living death, it was the term applied to hard-labor convicts in Siberia.

May had come and gone before the news reached Robert Walker, and he acted with speed. The purchase of Alaska hung in the balance and the Baron Edouard Stoeckl was worried. He wanted to be back in Russia, or to have an assignment in Paris or Vienna, and everything depended on this mission. Now this LaBarge affair had to come up, and the man involved had to be a personal friend, a very close friend of Walker himself, known moreover to Seward, Sumner, all of them.

Ratification of the treaty was not enough. The appropriation must be made. He had watched Congress in action long enough to know that the whole sale of Alaska might fail right there. And if any man could get out the necessary vote, it was Walker. Why couldn't that confounded Zinnovy have kept his ships in Sitka?

He sat now, in Walker's home, and the little man with the wheezy voice glanced over at him. "Is there any news of LaBarge?"

The Baron's face shadowed a little. He had hoped the subject would not arise. "We have done our best, but—"

"Could it be possible," Walker suggested, "to arrange for the transfer of such a prisoner? Supposing he is in Siberia?"

"There is no record of such a prisoner," Stoeckl protested, "nor of any such capture. I am sure the whole affair is the figment of someone's imagination."

"Sir," Walker's voice was stiff, "the man whose letter lies on my desk is a man of honor, LaBarge's partner and my friend. Not only was an American vessel shelled but its cargo was taken. This, sir, savors of piracy."

Baron Stoeckl had friends in the Russian American Company, but Baron Zinnovy was not one of these. However, he had a very good idea as to Zinnovy's duties in Sitka, and it would not do to have such news reach the ears of the Czar. Stoeckl knew that following the return of Princess Helena there had been a great fuss, which had been calmed down only after some time. At this moment orders for a complete shake-up at Sitka were carefully pigeonholed in the Ministry of the Interior. A *revisor* was to be appointed to investigate, but so far this had not been done.

"I cannot see what good it would do to have the prisoner transferred if he remained a prisoner."

Walker brushed the question aside. "I have heard, correct me if I am wrong, that some convict labor is used in Sitka?"

Baron Stoeckl almost smiled. So that was what the fox was thinking! Maybe this man was married to Benjamin Franklin's granddaughter with some reason . . . a prisoner transferred to Alaska on the evening of the sale would most certainly be freed when the Americans took over.

It was a very sensible idea . . . and this he, Baron Stoeckl, might arrange. There were people, the superiors of Zinnovy, in the Ministry of the Interior who wanted LaBarge to remain a prisoner. Yet a prisoner might be transferred without incurring the displeasure of these people. It was something that might be done without endangering his own future prospects.

There was one thing Walker did not know and which Stoeckl had no intention of telling him. There was every prospect that Zinnovy himself would be appointed *revisor* at Sitka.

"It is, as you suggest, a possibility that another shipment of convicts might be sent to Sitka. . . . How do the votes stand, Mr. Walker, for the appropriation?"

They talked far into the night, weighing the pros and cons and Stoeckl nursed his injured leg and cursed under his breath.

It was bad luck that Zinnovy had gone to Siberia without putting in at Sitka, and the prisoners had been landed there and turned over to the police. Probably not even he knew what had become of LaBarge by now. It was several days before he saw Walker again. They met briefly, over a glass of sherry.

"By the way"—Stoeckl was on his feet ready to go—"I understand a shipment of twenty prisoners will leave Okhotsk on the last of the month."

"I shall hope for further news. Are any prisoners I know involved?"

"At least one," Stoeckl replied, "that I am sure of."

They parted and the Baron walked away. There was no reason why he should feel guilty. It was too bad for LaBarge, and the Baron felt real regret for Robert Walker. A good man, this Walker, a genius at managing things like this treaty. Seward might be the key figure, but it was Walker who lined up the vote, did the lobbying, the entertaining, and the leg work to arrange the purchase.

Walker must be content with that. For the rest of it, there was no hope. Prisoner Jean LaBarge was going out of the Siberian frying pan into the Sitka fire.

35.

FROM THE WINDOW OF HER ROOM in Baranof Castle, Helena looked out over the city and harbor where sunlight lay bright upon the water, and gleamed from the serene loveliness of Mount Edgecumbe. The Castle was no longer the gloomy place it had been. In the capable hands of Prince Maksoutof and his wife it had become warm, comfortable, even gay.

The same eighty cannon looked grimly over the city from the parapet below. But there was more shipping in the bay, and several of them were American ships.

She had been a fool to come, yet if Rob Walker's hint in his letter to her had been founded upon fact, Jean LaBarge might soon be arriving here. If she could not free him she could at least, through Prince Maksoutof, relieve his imprisonment a little.

So few words had actually passed between them, yet she knew how he had felt, and she also knew, only too well, her own feelings. But what would prison have done to him? She had seen men who returned from Siberia, some of them scarcely human after the hard labor and punishments. Yet there was something about Jean that seemed indestructible.

There had been so little. The warmth in his eyes, the pressure of his hand, their bodies close together in the bouncing, jouncing *tarantas*.

She had loved a man for the first time, and she had lost him. Her husband had always been more like a kind father, tender, thoughtful, and considerate, and she had loved him for this. But it was nothing like her feeling for the tall, dark, dangerous-looking man with the scar whom she had loved with a love that bridged the bitter months and made them seem an age.

If this was being a fool, then she was a fool, and she

233

had come across Siberia again, and across the ocean, merely on the hope that he would be here, and that he would still care.

Prince Maksoutof was questioning himself as to why she was here. Both the Prince and Princess had tried to find some clue from her conversation or her guarded replies to questions.

The Russian American Company still operated in Sitka although its charter had not been renewed. Something was impending, some change of which she could find out nothing. So far as she had been able to discover, the plan to sell Alaska had failed at the last minute. There were rumors of negotiations and rumors of the collapse of negotiations.

From the beginning of Jean's disappearance she had corresponded with Robert Walker. In his last letter he had hinted that Jean, as a convict, might be transferred to Sitka. She knew from here an escape might be arranged and she was perfectly prepared to do her part in making the arrangements.

A schooner that had come in only last night had brought news that a Russian ship was due in today, and Murzin was down in town even now making friends. If anyone could help Jean escape it was the former thief, that wiry, narrow-faced man who had never left her service since that meeting on the trip across Siberia with Jean.

At breakfast she had been gay, chatting cheerfully of St. Petersburg, the court, that handsome Count Novikoff, and the last ball at the Peterhof. She had told them of San Francisco and its warm green hills, sometimes misted with rain. She had talked of everything but the ship that hour after hour, minute after minute, was drawing nearer to Sitka. Even now it might be coming up the bay through those beautiful islands that resembled so much the islands of the Adriatic. A warmer sea, but never a more lovely one than this.

She went down the steps slowly, not wishing to reveal her excitement. If Jean was aboard she must help him escape, and that before the *revisor* came on his inspection trip. Maksoutof had told her the man was coming, but nobody knew when.

"Helena," Princess Maksoutof suggested, "why don't

we go to the teahouse and watch the people land from the ship? They will come up the street and if we get in the right position we can see them leave the dock."

She got up, almost too quickly. "I'd like a walk," she said. "I'd like it very much."

Although from the teahouse they could see little, Helena forced herself to wait quietly, knowing whatever news there was would first be known here, long before it was heard on the Hill.

The waitress was excited. "They are bringing convicts ashore! They are to work here!"

"Irina"—Helena could wait no longer—"let's go down and watch them come in!"

They came, preceded by soldiers, in a column of twos, the gray-clad prisoners marching in slow, even steps, swaying as though to a soundless rhythm.

The first two were a red-bearded giant and a slender man with a twisted face. They blinked their eyes against the light after standing for some time in the shadowed warehouse. There was one man, tall, whose head was bowed. It could be Jean.

"Helena!" Irina caught her arm. "Look! Isn't he magnificent!"

He stood straight and tall, and he wore his chains in this town where he was remembered as another man might have worn a badge of honor. His face was shaggy with beard and his hair was long . . . he was much, much thinner! But he stood tall and he walked tall. He carried his head up and his eyes were clear. How could she ever have imagined they could break or tame him? He was one of the untamed, and so he would ever be.

He walked beside a shorter man who was also bearded, but Helena had eyes only for Jean. She moved to the edge of the walk, hoping he would see her, hoping he would know she was here to help.

"Jean!" She must have whispered it, for Irina turned suddenly to look at her.

"Do you know him?" Irina's eyes were bright with excitement and curosity.

"Yes . . . yes, I know him. I know him well. I love him."

"You needn't have told me that. I can see." Irina looked at Jean again. "Yes, without so much beard, and

235

if his hair was cut—" She glanced around at Helena. "Is that why you came? Did you know about this?"

"I came on hope," she said.

Jean hunched his shoulders inside the thin coat. His eyes swung to the crowd, and suddenly he saw Helena.

An instant, a step only, he paused. Their eyes met across the heads of the people and suddenly there was a great smile on his face and Helena started forward. Irina caught her arm. "No! No, Helena! You mustn't! I'll arrange—"

"Whatever you arrange"—the voice was cool, amused—"do it quickly. He goes on trial tomorrow."

Baron Paul Zinnovy was heavier, his thick neck had grown still thicker. There was in his eyes more cynicism and cruelty than Helena remembered.

"What are you doing here?" she demanded. He had been ordered back to Siberia, to Yakutsk. She remembered that. It could have been only a few months after Jean was captured.

"Why, I am the *revisor,*" he said, "here to rectify mistakes, conduct trials and discharge incompetent officials, but most particularly, to conduct trials."

"Haven't you done enough to him? And to me?"

"To you?" His eyebrow lifted. "To you, Princess?"

"You murdered my husband." She spoke deliberately, coldly, and heard Irina's startled gasp. "I shall not be able to prove it, but you murdered him, and we both know it."

"It is a weakness of women to be overly imaginative, but if you wish to see reality, you may come as my guests to the trial of Jean LaBarge for theft, for smuggling, and for murder."

36.

THE ROOM was packed with spectators. As Sitka had little entertainment, the prospect of a trial conducted by Baron Zinnovy as *revisor* held an unusual interest. And the man on trial was as well known to them, by name at least, as the Baron himself.

LaBarge was seated, still in chains, inside a small enclosure. He had been allowed to shave, and his clothing had been carefully brushed. Here and there in the crowd he saw familiar faces, but there was no welcome on those faces, no expression of sympathy. He was alone here.

Yet he had seen Helena. Did that mean that Count Rotcheff had never left Sitka? Or had he too returned again as Zinnovy had?

He had seen American ships in the harbor but there was no activity around them, and he had seen no Americans ashore in the town.

His thoughts returned to Rotcheff. If he was here he could do nothing, for LaBarge had been long enough in Siberia to know the power of the *revisor*. Appeal from his judgments could be made only to the Minister of the Interior or the Czar himself, and all such appeals were reviewed by the Ministry.

Siberia had made him suffer, but it had been a few months only, and this recall to Sitka had given him hope. If he could do nothing else, he could kill Zinnovy. He needed no weapon but his hands, and once those hands were on Zinnovy's throat nothing, nothing at all would stop him. He would kill Paul Zinnovy.

It would be absurdly easy. He could see where Zinnovy must sit, and he, LaBarge, must rise to receive sentence. His guards would be behind him, but the distance he must travel was short and they would not dare shoot at first for fear of hitting Zinnovy. Afterwards they would shoot him, but it would be better than Siberia again. Or the knout. He kept thinking of that.

Yet somewhere Rob Walker would be trying. By now he would know what had happened and Rob would move swiftly. No doubt he was working even now, and had been working, but it was too late. It was up to him, LaBarge, to do what he could.

He saw Prince Maksoutof and the Princess take their places, and Helena with them. Her face was pale, the circles under her eyes testifying to a sleepless night. Maksoutof had been pointed out to Jean by one of the guards. He was now the company director here, and governor of the colony. But even he could be removed by a *revisor*. The prison grapevine had a rumor that the Company had sent Zinnovy as *revisor*, appointed by somebody in the Ministry of the Interior who was a stockholder, to wipe out all evidence of the graft, cruelty and outright theft the Company officials had been perpetrating here.

Jean's mouth was dry. He was tired and the room was warm. His clothing stank of prisons and of unbathed bodies. This was an end of it then, the end of all his dreams, hopes, and ambitions. Rotcheff, the only friend he might have expected here, was not present. Helena could not help him, and Busch was not present: the merchant must have returned to Siberia. He was alone . . . alone.

What could be done? Being familiar with Russian courts, he knew that a trial was actually no trial at all but merely a hearing to air the crimes of the accused and pronounce sentence. The very fact that a trial was called meant the prisoner had been convicted.

The voices in the large room stilled, the clerk stood, then the spectators. Baron Zinnovy, resplendent in a magnificent uniform, entered and seated himself behind the desk. "Proceed with the trial," he said.

The clerk stood, then cleared his throat. The crowd leaned forward, the better to hear.

"The prisoner will stand!"

Jean LaBarge got to his feet, the chains clanking in the silent room.

"You, Jean LaBarge, are accused: you are accused of illegal trading with Tlingit people in Russian territory;

238

"You are accused of refusing to obey a command to heave-to given by a patrol ship of His Imperial Majesty;

"You are accused of evading capture;

"You are accused of firing on the patrol ship *Lena* while it was in the service of His Imperial Majesty;

"You are accused of firing upon and killing three members of the crew of His Imperial Majesty's ship, *Lena;*

"You are accused of the theft of furs belonging to the Russian American Company;

"You are accused of resisting capture. . . ."

The clerk's monotonous voice rolled on with the long list of accusations, some carrying at least a grain of truth, most completely false, yet the voice droned on and on.

Behind the judge's desk Baron Zinnovy filled his pipe and considered the clerk a dull stick and a fool, but it was something that must be done. Zinnovy stifled a yawn. It was warm in the overcrowded room. He had expected this to be a triumph, but LaBarge showed no weakening, no fear as yet. The whole affair was a confounded bore. He should have shot the man when captured, then he could have saved himself this.

Helena listened, her eyes half-closed against the sight she dreaded, against the heaviness of the room and the heat of the crowded bodies. From such an array of charges there could be no appeal, no hope of escape. The droning voice ended. There was silence in the room.

From the back of the crowd a voice said, "It's a pack o' lies!"

Baron Zinnovy did not lift his voice. "Arrest that man," he said, then turned his heavy-lidded eyes on LaBarge.

"Has the prisoner any statement to make before sentence is passed?"

There had been a knothole, long ago, through which came the first gray light of morning. It had been a long, long night but he had never doubted that help would come because his friend Rob Walker had gone for help, and Rob would not fail him. There was a knothole here, high near the eaves of the building, and a ray of light fell through it, too. He stared at it, remembering that morning so long ago. He began to smile.

Behind his desk Zinnovy's eyes tightened a little and a line appeared between them. Why was the fool smiling? Had he gone insane? Could he not realize what sentence would mean? That there was no appeal? La-Barge got slowly to his feet.

"You ask for a statement." He spoke in a dull heavy voice that gained in strength as he spoke. "Whatever I might say in denial of your false accusations would be ignored. To some of the charges I admit my guilt." He smiled broadly. "I admit to buying furs from the Tlingit and paying honest prices; I admit to evading the patrol ship because it was absurdly easy to do; but—" His eyes strayed to the beam of light from the knothole near the eaves. . . .

Puzzled by LaBarge's expression, Zinnovy followed the line of his gaze to the knothole, puzzled even more when he realized at what LaBarge was staring.

Suddenly, Jean knew he was going to take a chance, a daring chance, but one through which he could lose nothing.

"I admit the truth of some of the statements," he repeated, "but I deny they are crimes, Baron Zinnovy, I deny your right, as a Russian official, to conduct a trial *on the territory of the United States!*"

"*What?*" Zinnovy came half out of his chair. "What nonsense is this?"

"People of Sitka!" LaBarge turned suddenly to face the crowd. "You stand now on the free soil of the United States of America! The treaty of purchase has been ratified and signed by the Czar, and this territory now belongs to the United States of America, and the Czar has proclaimed an amnesty, freeing all prisoners at present held in Sitka!"

The audience rose to their feet, cheering. Zinnovy was shouting, his face swollen with anger. Soldiers ran along the aisles, threatening the crowd. Slowly they subsided. Jean LaBarge remained on his feet, his heart pounding heavily. He had attempted a colossal bluff and now he must carry it through.

There were American ships in the outer harbor, and those ships had given him the idea. He knew that ship-

240

ping men have a nose for developments, and that coupled with his great faith in his friend inspired him to the gamble.

The room was quiet and Zinnovy straightened in his chair. "Prisoner, I sentence—"

"You are without jurisdiction, Baron Zinnovy." Jean's voice was calm, but it carried to every corner of the room. "Sitka is now a territory of the United States and if sentence is carried out on me, you will yourself be liable to prosecution under the laws of the United States."

Zinnovy hesitated. He was trembling with fury, but he was never an incautious man, and now a beam of cool sanity penetrated his rage. LaBarge was too positive, too sure. If the sale *had* gone through, and especially if the money was not yet paid, and he passed sentence on an American citizen, he was buying himself a ticket to Siberia from which even his friends could not save him. And the Princess Helena was right here to report every detail, so he could never deny he did not know.

The room was filled with excited whispering; he was enraged to see with what excitement the news had been greeted. Here and there was a solemn face, but all too many had been made happy. Some of the smiles were from loyal Russians who were pleased to see him thwarted. This was nonsense . . . merely an attempt by LaBarge to delay sentence . . . yet, suppose it were true?

The thought was an unpleasant one; he knew even his powerful friends would sacrifice him if it became necessary . . . but how would a prisoner know if such a treaty had been ratified?

Even as he denied the possibility he answered the question himself. It was with prisoners as with the army: many times they knew things in the rank and file before the colonels of regiments knew. It was the grapevine, that word of mouth telegraph that could not be shut off or stopped. Perhaps –

"Sentence will be passed tomorrow afternoon," he commanded abruptly, rising to his feet. "Return the prisoner to his cell."

37.

WHEN HE AWAKENED it was night. Returned to his cell he had fallen across his bunk and slept like a man drugged, but he now lay wide awake, listening to the night sounds, for his was the hunter's brain, always tuned to the little sounds, the creeping sounds. He got up and walked to the narrow window.

Out there were the stars, the same he had watched long ago from the Great Swamp. Was he a fool to trust in a man so far away? Outside a night bird called, and a wind talked gently among the pines and whispered of far-off mountains, a wind that came from distant glaciers, caressed the restless waters and blew into his small window.

There was a rustle in the corridor, a rustle of movement. He turned quickly, knowing that sound. A key grated in the lock and the door opened, and in the instant before it swung wide he caught a whiff of perfume.

"Jean? . . . *Jean!*"

She was in his arms then and they clung to each other, clung with a strength that hurt. "Jean! Oh, Jean! I've been so frightened!"

Helena drew back suddenly, the guard was still in the door, but he had politely turned his back. "Jean, is it true? Has the United States bought Sitka?"

"Helena"—he spoke softly so the guard would not hear—"I don't know anything more than you. It was a bluff.

"Of course," he added, "I know Rob. I know he has made this thing go through if anyone could, and when I saw those American ships out there, just lying there waiting . . . well, what could I lose?"

She hesitated, fearing to tell him. "Jean, Rob Walker

has been writing to me, and they have tried everything to find you and free you. It was because of that that I am here, but at the last minute it all came to nothing. The treaty was not ratified."

He shook his head stubbornly. "I can't believe that. If the treaty was written, if a price was agreed upon, then Walker would get out the vote. No, Helena, if that treaty was written and submitted to the Senate it was ratified."

"But it wasn't, Jean! You mustn't depend on that! You must escape!"

"No. I think Zinnovy wants me to attempt an escape . . . if I do I'll be shot and his problem is solved. Don't you realize he would expect you to see me? That he might deliberately make it easy believing you would bring me something, a weapon? No, I'll stay. If Count Rotcheff can help, then—"

"Jean?" Her throat found difficulty with the words. "Jean, Alexander has been dead for nearly a year. He died before I returned to Sitka."

"Dead?" The word did not make sense. If he was dead then she was free . . . free.

Free . . . they could be together. They could belong to each other. Nothing would stand between them. Only tomorrow he would be returned to Siberia . . . or hanged.

The improvised courtroom was jammed. The clerk took his place. Opposite Jean, Helena sat where her eyes could see his, and beside her were Prince and Princess Maksoutof. The crowd was large, and contained many familiar faces. His eyes stopped a full second.

Barney Kohl . . . his face was solemn, but there was an obvious bulge at his waistband. Beside him was the square, tough face of Gant.

Suddenly, Jean was filled with excitement. They had escaped then . . . none of them were known to Zinnovy, and they were here. That meant they had been able to hide out after the attack on the *Susquehanna*.

His eyes searched the crowd . . . Ben Turk . . . beside him was Shin Boyar. There were several other men he did not know but he was sure they were Americans; they looked like Frisco seamen, right off the waterfront. And they were scattered, scattered in a perimeter around the

243

room. Kohl was seated right behind a guard. Boyar was beside another. That meant they intended to break him out, which meant shooting unless they had a plan, a good plan.

Baron Paul Zinnovy came into the room. He walked to the desk and seated himself. He was cool, composed, sure. If he noticed the strange faces in the crowd he gave no evidence of it.

The clerk got to his feet. "Jean LaBarge, stand and receive sentence!"

Jean LaBarge got to his feet, and Baron Zinnovy looked over the papers he held in his hand. He smiled at LaBarge, finding pleasure in the moment.

Suddenly there was a rustle of movement at the door, a shoving, a whisper, a shout, and then the door pushed open and a man in civilian clothes entered followed by a line of American bluejackets.

The man passed LaBarge by without speaking and stopped before Zinnovy, whose face had turned ashen. "Baron Zinnovy? I am Brigadier General Lovell H. Rousseau, United States Commissioner to accept the Territory of Alaska from the government of Russia."

A Russian officer walked from the door to a place beside the general. He stood at attention and bobbed his head. "Captain Alexei Petchouroff," he said. "Special Emissary of His Imperial Majesty the Czar of all the Russias!"

Baron Paul Zinnovy leaned back in his chair, his face without expression.

Captain Petchouroff extended an envelope to Zinnovy. "My orders, sir, and yours. You are to return to Okhotsk to await His Imperial Majesty's pleasure."

Zinnovy got to his feet. "Of course, but we have a trial here, and—"

Petchouroff waved a gesture of dismissal. "In honor of this great day, His Imperial Majesty has declared a general amnesty. A pardon for all on trial and all awaiting trial in Russian America. They are free, and you are freed of this disagreeable duty!"

Jean LaBarge turned to meet Helena as she ran to him from across the room, and then the crew of the *Susquehanna* moved in around him.

244

The morning was bright and clear. Brigadier General Rousseau and General Jefferson C. Davis, backed by a solid square of two hundred American sailors, soldiers and marines, stood at attention. Across from them stood one hundred Russian soldiers in their gray, red-trimmed uniforms. The music began, and officers on both sides mounted the steps of the Castle where Prince Maksoutof awaited them. They turned and faced the square, Captain Petchouroff descending to a place beside General Rousseau.

As the Russian flag was lowered, Princess Maksoutof sobbed gently. Among the Russian civilians several were openly crying.

The American flag climbed the staff and out on the bay the guns of the U.S.S. *Ossipee* boomed a salute.

Behind the gathered civilians Jean LaBarge stood beside Helena, and as the flag climbed the staff, Jean whispered, "Do you know what I'm thinking of now? I'm remembering a boy who grew up back on the Susquehanna, a boy who was smaller than any of us, but bigger in a lot of ways than any of us would ever be. In the future they may forget, or they may say cruel things about him. But what he did was not small, and there will always be a few who will not forget."

Helena squeezed his hand. "What about the other boy?"

"He now has"—he took her arm gently—"all he could ever want."

They stood together, watching the flag flutter at the masthead, and listened to the dull boom of the guns out on the bay, and heard the echoes thrown back by the mountains, while on the ageless slopes of Mount Edgecumbe the sun made a moment of glory.

ABOUT THE AUTHOR

LOUIS L AMOUR, born Louis Dearborn L'Amour of French-Irish stock, is a descendant of François René, Vicompte de Chateaubriand, noted French writer, statesman, and epicure. Although Mr. L'Amour claims his writing began as a "spur-of-the-moment thing," prompted by friends who relished his verbal tales of the West, he comes by his talent honestly. A frontiersman by heritage (his grandfather was scalped by the Sioux), and a universal man by experience, Louis L'Amour lives the life of his fictional heroes. Since leaving his native Jamestown, North Dakota, at the age of fifteen, he's been a longshoreman, lumberjack, elephant handler, hay shocker, flume builder, fruit picker, and an officer on tank destroyers during World War II. And he's written four hundred short stories and over fifty books (including a volume of poetry).

Mr. L'Amour has lectured widely, traveled the West thoroughly, studied archaeology, compiled biographies of over one thousand Western gunfighters, and read prodigiously (his library holds more than two thousand volumes). And he's watched thirty-one of his westerns as movies. He's circled the world on a freighter, mined in the West, sailed a dhow on the Red Sea, been shipwrecked in the West Indies, stranded in the Mojave Desert. He's won fifty-one of fifty-nine fights as a professional boxer and pinch-hit for Dorothy Kilgallen when she was on vacation from her column. Since 1816, thirty-three members of his family have been writers. And, he says, "I could sit in the middle of Sunset Boulevard and write with my typewriter on my knees; temperamental I am not."

Mr. L'Amour is re-creating an 1865 Western town, christened Shalako, where the borders of Utah, Arizona, New Mexico, and Colorado meet. Historically authentic from whistle to well, it will be a live, operating town, as well as a movie location and tourist attraction.

Mr. L'Amour now lives in Los Angeles with his wife Kathy, who helps with the enormous amount of research he does for his books. Soon, Mr. L'Amour hopes, the children (Beau and Angelique) will be helping too.

LOUIS L'AMOUR 1

BANTAM'S #1
ALL-TIME BESTSELLING AUTHOR
AMERICA'S FAVORITE WESTERN WRITER

☐	13601	HIGH LONESOME	$1.95
☐	13704	BORDEN CHANTRY	$1.95
☐	13606	BRIONNE	$1.95
☐	14328	THE FERGUSON RIFLE	$1.95
☐	13622	KILLOE	$1.95
☐	13602	CONAGHER	$1.95
☐	14829	NORTH TO THE RAILS	$2.25
☐	13879	THE MAN FROM SKIBBEREEN	$1.95
☐	14763	SILVER CANYON	$2.25
☐	13857	CATLOW	$1.95
☐	13611	GUNS OF THE TIMBERLANDS	$1.95
☐	13605	HANGING WOMAN CREEK	$1.95
☐	13717	FALLON	$1.95
☐	13779	UNDER THE SWEETWATER RIM	$1.95
☐	14234	MATAGORDA	$1.95
☐	14119	DARK CANYON	$1.95
☐	13684	THE CALIFORNIOS	$1.95
☐	13969	FLINT	$1.95

Buy them at your local bookstore or use this
handy coupon for ordering:

Bantam Books, Inc., Dept. LL1, 414 East Golf Road, Des Plaines, Ill. 60016

Please send me the books I have checked above. I am enclosing $_____
(please add $1.00 to cover postage and handling). Send check or money order
—no cash or C.O.D.'s please.

Mr/ Mrs/ Miss_____

Address_____

City_____ State/Zip_____

LL1—1/81
Please allow four to six weeks for delivery. This offer expires 7/81.

BANTAM'S #1
ALL-TIME BESTSELLING AUTHOR
AMERICA'S FAVORITE WESTERN WRITER

☐	13561	THE STRONG SHALL LIVE	$1.95
☐	12354	BENDIGO SHAFTER	$2.25
☐	13881	THE KEY-LOCK MAN	$1.95
☐	13719	RADIGAN	$1.95
☐	13609	WAR PARTY	$1.95
☐	13882	KIOWA TRAIL	$1.95
☐	13683	THE BURNING HILLS	$1.95
☐	14013	SHALAKO	$1.95
☐	13680	KILRONE	$1.95
☐	13794	THE RIDER OF LOST CREEK	$1.95
☐	13798	CALLAGHEN	$1.95
☐	14114	THE QUICK AND THE DEAD	$1.95
☐	14219	OVER ON THE DRY SIDE	$1.95
☐	13722	DOWN THE LONG HILLS	$1.95
☐	14316	WESTWARD THE TIDE	$1.95
☐	14227	KID RODELO	$1.95
☐	14104	BROKEN GUN	$1.95
☐	13898	WHERE THE LONG GRASS BLOWS	$1.95
☐	14411	HOW THE WEST WAS WON	$1.95

Buy them at your local bookstore or use this
handy coupon for ordering: